THE VAULT OF POSEIDON

(Joe Hawke #1)

Rob Jones

ISBN-13 978-1517421007
ISBN-10 1517421004

Other Books by Rob Jones

The Joe Hawke Series

The Vault of Poseidon (Joe Hawke #1)
Thunder God (Joe Hawke #2)
The Tomb of Eternity (Joe Hawke #3)
The Curse of Medusa (Joe Hawke #4)
Valhalla Gold (Joe Hawke #5)
The Aztec Prophecy (Joe Hawke #6)
The Secret of Atlantis (Joe Hawke #7)
The Lost City (Joe Hawke #8)

This novel is an action-adventure thriller and includes archaeological, military and mystery themes. I welcome constructive comments and I'm always happy to get your feedback.

Website: www.robjonesnovels.com

Facebook: https://www.facebook.com/RobJonesNovels/

Email: robjonesnovels@gmail.com

Twitter: @AuthorRobJones

DEDICATION

To the first step

THE VAULT OF POSEIDON

PROLOGUE

The Ionian Sea, Greece, September 1943

Gottardo Ricci scrambled along the crumbling shaft of the island's largest marble mine. The bright Mediterranean sunlight spilled in at the entrance and stung the eyes of the elderly Italian archaeologist as he clawed himself forward through the filthy grit and sand. Checking that the bag was still over his shoulder, he made one final attempt to free himself from the terror behind him.

Then his worst fear came true – a second gunshot thundered through the cavern almost deafening him and sending a burning, searing pain racing through his leg. He had been shot a second time, and now both legs were wounded and bleeding heavily.

He heard the man's voice once again.

"You have something that belongs to the Reich, Dr Ricci."

The voice was cold, emotionless.

Ricci twisted in agony to see the man approaching him from behind. He thought he had gotten further away from him than this. He was wrong.

Now, just a few yards away, walking calmly along the

dimly lit mineshaft was SS-Sturmbannführer Otto Zaugg of the 4th Schutzstaffel Polizei Panzergrenadier Division. He was tall and powerfully-built, with blonde hair and ashen white skin.

The Nazi officer raised his pistol to Ricci's head and smiled grimly. "You hand the document over to me now, and perhaps I will let you live. I have studied you for many months, Herr Doktor, and I know you have a beautiful wife and two sons. You do not want to die, and yet now both your legs are wounded. You will never walk again, but if the bleeding is stopped, you never know… perhaps you will live to see your children."

"You are just a Nazi," screamed Ricci, the sweat running off his forehead and into his eyes. "All you know is murder!"

The archaeologist glanced forward – the end of the tunnel was so close. He thought about screaming for help, but the entrance to the mine was on an isolated stretch of the coast. There was no one out there to hear his screams.

"Give me what I want, Herr Doktor!"

"Never. You can take this back to Himmler and tell him I hope it kills him!"

Zaugg laughed. "Who says I am going to give anything to Himmler? Perhaps I want it just for me."

"You're insane."

"And you're bleeding to death. Don't make me kill you for it – just hand it over and you will live. I can have army medics in here in minutes."

"You can take this document from me, Zaugg, but you can never have what's here." Ricci tapped the side of his head.

"And is that really worth dying for?" Zaugg said.

"You really have to ask if stopping the Nazis from annihilating the entire planet is worth the life of one fading archaeologist? Of course it is, you fool! You are a

Nazi. You will always be ignorant, with or without my discovery! Without my knowledge the clue trail will be lost to history."

"You give us less credit than we deserve, Herr Ricci. Now you have proved the existence of the Ionian Texts, all that remains is to start the search for the greatest treasure in history."

"You have no idea what you're fooling with," Ricci said, a look of concern now appearing on his thin face. "We're talking about the greatest discovery in human history. Older than time itself."

"We're talking about *gold*," Otto Zaugg replied, laughing. "We're talking about wealth and power."

Ricci tried to laugh, but the pain stopped him. "Gold? You mean the Ahnenerbe didn't tell you? Perhaps they thought a simple Panzer officer wasn't capable of understanding. This is about more than simple gold, Major. This is about the greatest secret in the world, and without my knowledge and research you and your army of ignorant, racist apes will never uncover the truth. Your Ahnenerbe will never find what they seek so desperately."

"You lie!" screamed Zaugg. He aimed the pistol once again at Ricci's head, his hand trembling with renewed rage. "You're simply playing for time. Trying to save your own wretched skin."

This time, Ricci managed to laugh through the searing pain in his ruined legs, but once again he was sobered by the sight of the dark blood pouring out of his thighs into the dirt of the mine. It slowly congealed in grisly pools around him.

"I'm too old for games, Major."

"In all the months we've had you under surveillance, Dr Ricci, I never took you for a fool, but now I begin to wonder."

"*You* are the fool if you think you can control this power."

The pistol thundered in the silence of the shaft, and Ricci felt the third bullet tear into his stomach. He doubled over in agony. The pain rose like a burning tide of fire which enveloped him until it was all there was in his life.

He closed his eyes for a moment and tried to stifle his screams. He saw his children playing on the beach, his wife opening a bottle of wine. Memories of long ago flashed before his eyes.

Then his mind raced with the unfolding horror of the moment. After all these years of research, it had all been for nothing. All these years of hunting for the evidence he so desperately wanted and finding it buried deep in the mines, just as he always knew it would be. But now it was going to end like this – with his death and the Nazis getting their hands on such unbridled power.

And worst of all was the knowledge that it was all his fault. It was his years of diligent research, of trawling through the artifacts, poring over the texts, believing in the legends when all those around him mocked and ridiculed him, that had led to this discovery. And it was his own foolishness that had allowed the Nazis to follow him and take his discovery away.

It pained him even to think about it.

The SS officer walked over to Ricci and put his boot on the dying man's shoulder to hold down his body while he wrenched the sack away from him. He jerked at it, pulling with such force he snapped the strap.

Ricci looked up at the Nazi once again, perhaps for the final time. Outside, he now heard the familiar cry of the kestrel he had watched just that morning, gliding in the thermals above the cliffs in the sunrise. He thought about what would happen if the Nazis found what they were looking for – what they had used Major Zaugg to find.

Zaugg opened the sack and looked at the piece of ancient, crumbling text inside and his smile faded. Ricci saw the Nazi's face change expression instantly.

The archaeologist spoke through dry, cracked lips. "Now the truth dawns! The Ahnernerbe lied to you. What you are looking at is evidence of something a thousand times more powerful than mere gold. What you are looking at would give you the ultimate power over mankind – but only I can find it!"

Zaugg looked down at Ricci, a greedy smile crossing his lean, unshaven face.

"I think not, Dr Ricci. You overestimate yourself and you underestimate the Reich. If this is what you claim it is then you are no longer necessary. Whatever this leads to, we do not need you."

Ricci realized his blood pressure was dropping. He felt suddenly cold and clammy in the hot dry air of the mine. Dizziness overtook him.

Suddenly now, Zaugg aimed the Mauser squarely at the elderly archaeologist's head and offered one final, narcissistic smirk.

"Before you die," Zaugg said coolly, "I want you to know that I will find this, and the Reich will rule the world – all thanks to your brilliant discovery, but now I must bid you farewell."

He squeezed the trigger.

A roar of gunfire.

Ricci's world went black.

CHAPTER ONE

London, Present Day

Joe Hawke sprinted to the edge of the high-rise with all his might and leaped off the building with as much velocity as he could muster. He sailed into the air and started to wonder if he could make the gap and land on the roof of the adjacent building a few meters lower. Below was a ninety meter drop to a concrete staircase, but Hawke never looked down.

He landed smoothly, using the classic parachute landing fall he was trained to do by the Special Forces, and seconds later was on his feet and sprinting across the roof of the second building.

It was night, and the air was cold. Below in the streets he heard the sound of traffic and was aware of the faint orange glow of the streetlights. Above his head he heard the growl of a Boeing 747's engines, lost somewhere above the thick clouds of London as it lumbered towards Heathrow Airport.

Hawke had gotten into parkour as a way of keeping fit after leaving the military, and it worked well, except he had learned the hard way to practice it at night when he couldn't be seen. For some reason, the authorities didn't take too kindly to people leaping from public buildings and doing handstands on the edges of high-rises, but that didn't stop him from freerunning.

He would have preferred to keep fit by running on a beach, but for now he lived in the city and this was the only option. He wasn't about to run on a treadmill in a gym like a hamster on a wheel.

Sprinting forward to a low pebble-dashed wall which ran along the side of the second building, Hawke reached out, grabbed the ledge with his hands and performed a smooth two-handed vault, swinging his legs over the wall and landing like a cat on the far side.

He was now on a narrow path leading to the elevator shaft at the end of the car park. He made a fast speed-vault over a low wall just in front of the elevators, keeping his hips level and flying over it as if it weren't even there. He landed with no loss of power or speed inside the covered elevator housing and sprinted forward to the doors.

Hawke stepped inside and looked at his watch: nearly midnight. The elevator doors opened and he was at street level. He ran through a grimy underpass, his breath visible in the flickering greasy yellow of a faulty strip light, and emerged into a courtyard at the bottom of the tower block.

He saw some teenagers huddling together in the gloom of a distant stairwell, probably a drug deal, he thought, or maybe guns. They looked at him for a second, judging the threat. Not his problem, lucky for them. Not tonight. Jogging out of the courtyard he was now on a main road. A night bus trundled lonely into a gathering mist as Hawke jogged home. With a simple wall-run he launched himself over the top of a three meter wall and cut ten minutes off his journey.

Almost home now, he jogged home through the dark. A light drizzle swept over the streets and his mind turned to thoughts of a warm shower and a cold beer. Tomorrow his brand new life began.

*

The doors of the British Museum burst open.

"Here they come." Hawke stood against the far wall in the standard security guard pose – hands crossed in front of his body, sunglasses on and covert earpiece headset concealed in his right ear. His first day of work in Civvy Street had arrived at last. Time to settle down, he thought.

"Just keep your eye on everyone," he said. He was talking to Farrell, one of his employees, hired just two days ago as part of his expanding new business.

Moments later the room filled with the best of London's high society, or at least those who thought they were the best. Like a servant, a security officer was there to be seen and not heard, and Hawke understood what this meant better than anyone. Spending so many years as a Royal Marines Commando in the notoriously tough Mountain and Arctic Warfare Cadre and then serving in the elite Special Boat Service meant he knew how to take orders and blend into the background.

Now he was watching the room slowly fill up with honored guests. He was at a special exhibition, providing security for the museum because of a visit by the enigmatic Sir Richard Eden MP, here in his capacity as head of a new fundraising committee for the Council of British Archaeology.

Archaeology was Eden's first and only love, but his day job was as a Member of Parliament who was particularly concerned with national security. There were rumors that he was soon to make an announcement concerning a discovery on a Greek Island that could change the world. Public interest in Eden was consequently running at an all-time high, so the museum had put on extra security in the form of Joe Hawke.

Hawke hadn't decided how this new civilian life as a security guard measured up to his former existence, but he was making a go of it. For former Special Forces soldiers it wasn't bad work – especially if you owned the company like he did. Many of the lads ended up doing door duty on pubs. Compared to them, Joe Hawke had it easy, even if it meant he had to stay in his old hometown London and put his dreams of escape on hold.

"They're all here tonight, boss!" said Farrell's voice in Hawke's earpiece.

Hawke watched as the celebrity guests slowly trickled into the plush exhibition room of the museum. It was a different world to anything he knew. Growing up had been tough, and the military tougher. Hawke didn't know much about Champagne cocktails and ancient artifacts, but he was willing to learn.

He was at heart a soldier who had loved his work. After leaving the SBS everything seemed like a let-down, except when his sister told his girlfriends they were dating a cross between James Bond and Indiana Jones. Hawke winced whenever she said it, but it didn't do any harm.

"Is that Princess Eugenie?" said Farrell.

"Pack it in, Farrell," Hawke said. "Focus on the job."

"Yes, boss."

Hawke monitored the large room for any anomalies. His job was to protect the museum and its guests. Sir Richard Eden had his own security detail headed up by a woman he had not been properly introduced to, who was now standing a few yards behind the MP, silently surveying the room.

She was startlingly good-looking, and he guessed in her mid-twenties. For some reason he was surprised that she looked so young, but everyone was starting to look young to Hawke these days.

He refocused his attention on the gathering. A far-cry from the muddy ditches of commando life, he was now surrounded by dukes, duchesses and a princess, as well as various charity CEOs, the King of Tonga, the Beckhams, and Sir Alan Sugar, who was laughing with Sir Richard's eldest daughter Harriet. Hawke watched the high and mighty as they mingled and worked the crowd, sharing in-jokes and investor tips and sipping from cut-glass flutes twinkling in the chandelier light.

Carefully concealed behind his sunglasses, he rolled his eyes. *And some people actually have to work for a living...* He thought about his mates still serving in the commandos and the SBS on active duty. That was a different world, and now he had to adapt to this one. Maybe one day his company would be big enough for him to sell up, and then he could retire somewhere exotic, just like he always dreamed of, but until then, it was this. There were worse fates.

"Check out the woman over there," Farrell said.

"I told you to focus, Farrell."

"No, I mean watch what she's doing – she looks like she's high or something."

"Can't see her yet – where is she?" Hawke scanned the room and saw that Eden's private security had also seen the woman. She stepped forward and whispered something in Sir Richard's ear. He turned to look at the woman.

Farrell spoke next: "I've got her, boss. I think Victoria Beckham's blocking your view."

"No – got her now. Tall, pale with blonde hair."

"You've got her right side, yeah?"

"Correct."

"Well I've got her left side, boss. Her best side, I like to think."

"Farrell..."

"She's talking to herself, boss, and approaching Sir Richard."

Hawke focused on the woman across the room. She was beautiful, but something wasn't right – she was mumbling something to herself. The room was now full of dignitaries and those serving them drinks. Hawke watched the woman weave in and out of the crowd, almost falling over in places. Whoever she was, she had no place here. He stepped forward to apprehend her.

Suddenly everything changed.

Hawke saw the fear on the woman's face two seconds before he saw the blood on her wrists. Sir Richard's security officer moved forward to protect her boss.

"No!" said Sir Richard. "I know this woman. Let her through."

The woman was clearly confused and staggered closer to Sir Richard before falling on her knees. She crawled towards him, terrorized by some unseen thing over her shoulder. She looked into Sir Richard's face with bewildered, delirious eyes. Hawke knew immediately that she had been drugged – he recognized the symptoms easily enough. The crowd turned to see what was happening and fell silent.

"Richard, please! Help me!" Her words were slurred.

"What is it, professor?" said Sir Richard.

"How do you know this woman?" Hawke asked, surveying the room for other threats.

Eden said: "She's..."

Then the first shot rang out and everyone dived for cover. The assassin's bullet plowed through the woman's shoulder and knocked her violently to the ground.

Hawke searched the mezzanine for a glimpse of the shooter but saw no one. Eden's security officer turned herself into a human shield to protect the senior politician.

Despite the terrible wound to her body, the woman heaved herself back to her knees and turned to Sir Richard who was now staring at the unfolding situation in wild disbelief. The crowd broke into chaos and began to scatter.

"I made the trans... the translation, Sir Richard." She coughed up blood and struggled to breathe. "*Those who seek the ultimate power must look within his kingdom...*" More coughing.

Eden crouched down and tried to help the woman. "Lucy, what's happened? Who did this to you?"

"No time... He put them inside the amphorae! All this time and it's been right in front of our faces... Poseidon and the Nereid, Richard – they are the keepers of the legend..."

"Someone call an ambulance!" Eden screamed, his hands shaking with adrenalin.

"You have to... stop them, Richard. They beat it out of me and now they're going to New York. You have to stop them before..."

The final gunshot was lethal in its accuracy, blasting a high velocity round straight through the woman's heart and spraying a jet of blood across Eden's face and body. She collapsed in a lifeless heap on the polished parquet floor of the exhibition room.

Another series of shots from the mezzanine, and this time Hawke saw the shooter. Eden's private security officer and Farrell saw him at the same time but it was a second too late for Farrell who was killed with the next shot.

Hawke had no time to think about the loss. Any doubt that the woman was the only target was removed when the assassin fired another series of shots at Sir Richard, his security officer and then finally Hawke himself. Chaos reigned.

A horrified Sir Richard Eden pointed at the assassin, who was now visible on the balcony at the top of the stairs and shouted at his security officer to get after him.

And so she did.

And so did Hawke.

CHAPTER TWO

Hawke and the security officer sprinted down the steps of the British Museum's south exit and saw the sniper running towards a black BMW X5. It was parked on the sidewalk beyond the wrought-iron gates at the entrance to the museum.

The driver was waiting for the shooter with the rear door open and the engine revving hard. The man leaped into the back seats and with a squeal of burned rubber the X5 raced down Great Russell Street.

By the time they reached the gates, the X5 was already several hundred yards away, and Hawke had no time to think. A few yards to his right, a tour bus was idling in a parking bay waiting to collect a group of tourists who were ambling out of the museum.

Some of them had already got back on the bus and were sitting on the open top deck eating ice creams and taking pictures from their elevated position of the museum's impressive façade. Hawke knew what he had to do.

"Get out," he said to the driver.

"Who the hell are you?"

Hawke didn't reply. He grabbed the man by the scruff of his neck, dragged him out of the driver's seat and shoved him from the bus. "Don't worry," Hawke shouted as he cranked the six cylinder engine up. "There'll be another one along in a minute."

"You're a real charmer," the security officer said. Irish. He placed her accent in the south – Dublin maybe.

"Nice to meet you," he replied, offering her his hand. "Joe Hawke. I had a contract to work as security for the British Museum until about three minutes ago."

"I'm Lea Donovan," she said coolly. She refused his hand and instead used the moment to pull a Glock 17 casually from an inside pocket.

Hawke glanced at the gun. "You're armed! That's not exactly legal."

"Hush now. I'm security for Sir Richard Eden and he's the one who gave it to me."

"Fair enough." Hawke shrugged his shoulders. "Do you know how it works? The end with the little hole in it is the dangerous bit."

He swerved the bus violently around a line of parked cars and screeched to a halt behind a black cab.

"And if you knew how to drive properly I could probably get a shot off and take out those bastards' back tires, but as it is, it looks like we'll have to wait until they pull up for a coffee."

Hawke ignored this, and slammed his foot down on the throttle, steering out from behind the taxi. The tour bus jolted forward sluggishly at first, but then gathering speed as he went up through the gears. "Let's see what this little baby can do."

Up ahead, the X5 was already trapped in more of the London gridlock, trying to negotiate its way out by mounting the sidewalk. A cacophony of angry car-horns was raised in response, as well as lots of fist-waving from pedestrians and a few people even kicked the side of the assassin's car. They dispersed in a hurry when the window came down and several warning shots were fired into the air.

"Those guys are insane!" Hawke said to himself as he drew closer to the gridlock.

Now the X5 was weaving through the traffic and

turning right into another street. Hawke slammed his foot down and drove the bus down the middle of the road, furiously hammering on the bassy horn to make the cars pull away to the sides of the road.

Progress was slow, but thankfully the same went for the X5, which was once again stuck in even more gridlock around the corner. Not unusual for this part of town, Hawke considered.

He swung the bus around into the next street so fast it almost went up onto two wheels. The sound of the tires squealing on the ludicrously tight turn was rivalled only by the noise of the terrified passengers screaming for their lives on the top deck.

"Hold on, folks!" Hawke shouted as he pounded the throttle and raced towards the next block of traffic.

Moments later the sound of sirens filled the air somewhere behind him – police. The inevitable consequence, Hawke considered, of stealing a tour bus full of foreign tourists and driving it like a maniac in pursuit of an assassin in a BMW X5. At any rate, he considered, it would certainly brighten up the police's morning, if nothing else.

Now, the X5 was through the gridlock and racing against the traffic outside the museum's archive on Bloomsbury Square Gardens. The way they turned the next corner and deftly weaved in between a couple of Routemaster buses made Hawke realize this was no rushed getaway but a planned escape route.

As he watched them slip away from him, bright sunlight reflected off the rear windows of the cars in front and made him squint for a few seconds, almost losing sight of the X5.

They jumped the lights and swung right, smoke billowing out from the rear tire arches as the powerful German SUV accelerated away from the bus.

Moments later another wave of traffic had ensured Hawke caught them up by the time they hit Kingsway. By now there were at least three police cars behind the tour bus, and somewhere above him Hawke heard what he presumed was a police helicopter.

Lea reached for her mobile and made a call.

"Richard, it's me, Lea. Slight problem – there seems to be a growing interest in our activities by the local constabulary."

Hawke weaved the bus neatly in between a Vespa and an ice cream van.

There was a pause while Lea listened to Eden's reply before responding to him. "At least three cars and a chopper. I'd be grateful if you could let them know they're chasing the guys in front and not us."

They were now rapidly closing on the end of Kingsway where the road turned into a horseshoe shape leading to the east and west before both joined up with the Strand. The X5 was running out of options.

Lea put the phone in her pocket and turned to Hawke.

"He says he'll make a call."

The X5 mounted the sidewalk before swinging left and burning past the Australian High Commission. Hawke pursued as best he could in the Arriva, only to see the men abandon the X5 in Temple Place and vault over the steel railing near the Underground Station.

Hawke dumped the bus and sprinted after them, reliving his parkour training from the night before. Behind him the sound of sirens closing in on them filled the air, and the chopper was now circling ahead of him and hovering over the Thames.

"You twats aren't getting away from me!" he shouted.

Lea was sprinting behind him, and almost keeping up. *Impressive*, he thought.

Hawke saw the two men jump into a red motorboat

moored on the north bank of the Thames. A second later it was speeding away across the river.

He ran up to a boat moored behind the one they had just taken. Inside a man was whistling and polishing the windshield. He wore a jaunty sailing cap and yachting daps.

Hawke stepped up to him. “Get out.”

Lea rolled her eyes. “Oh God, not again.”

“I'm sorry?” said the man.

“Seriously, it’s step out of the boat or go for a swim in that.” Hawke pointed at the cold, brown water that not even the bright sunshine could make the least welcoming.

“Now, look here, I’m a member of the Rotary Club!”

Hawke raised his fist, and the man reversed course and stepped backwards out of the boat.

“Good man,” Hawke said. “We’ll bring her back unharmed. Probably.”

Hawke revved the engine and the boat shot forward into the river faster than he expected. Back on the riverbank an indignant amateur sailor pulled out his phone.

“What’s he doing?” Hawke asked Lea as he navigated the boat into the busy river.

“Looks like he’s furiously dialling every emergency services number he can think of.”

Hawke laughed. “And maybe even the Rotary Club.”

They looked ahead and saw the motorboat getting away at a serious rate of knots.

“Floor it!” Lea shouted, while taking aim at them. She fired two shots and the sound of them crackled incongruously on both sides of the Thames in the otherwise normal morning. Both shots were slightly high of the target.

“Excellent work, Donovan, but if I were you I’d ask

the Girl Guides for my money back."

"Zip it, Mr Hawke, and try and keep this damned thing steady while I take a shot."

"It's a motorboat, Lea, it doesn't do steady. Next time we chase someone I'll make sure to steal us a pedalo."

"Oh, you are *so* not as funny as you think you are."

Hawke looked ahead and saw the red motorboat weaving with ease in between various tourist boats and even a few industrial vessels. They passed beneath London Bridge and zoomed alongside HMS Belfast spraying the cold, brown wash up its sides.

"Can't you get us any closer?" Lea said, annoyed.

A short volley of machine-gun fire crackled from the back of the red motorboat, instantaneously matched by the shattering of their windshield into a dozen spider web fractures. "Shit!" Hawke shouted, ducking as much as he could while retaining visibility of the river.

"Not fair!" Lea shook her head. "They have Uzis."

Now they were passing under Tower Bridge, and Hawke saw something that made his heart sink. "Look!"

One of the men was shouldering a rocket-propelled grenade launcher.

Lea looked at him. "That is *so* not good."

Seconds later, he fired it. Hawke and Lea ducked instinctively and Hawke swung the boat hard to the left. He watched the missile climb into the air above their heads.

"They're aiming at the police helicopter!" he shouted.

The missile struck the chopper dead-center and it exploded in the air in a giant fireball, showering the Thames with pieces of twisted airframe and burning aviation fuel. What was left of the wrecked cabin plummeted like a rock into the murky water.

"Lea, shoot the man with the RPG please, and quickly."

The man was reloading and now aiming the RPG at their boat.

Lea raised her Glock and squinted carefully through the sights.

Pop. A puff of smoke from the chamber.

Hawke watched the man fly backwards with the RPG launcher still in his hands and crash dead into the Thames.

"Not too shabby," he said, smiling. "And now we're gaining on them!"

The motorboat sliced through the icy water, the gutteral roar of its engine ricocheting off the buildings on either side of the river. People peered over the walls and bridges to see what was happening.

In fast pursuit of the red speedboat, they were now steering a hard right to follow the river as it twisted south into the Docklands, the glittering skyscrapers of Canary Wharf looming to their left.

"Just where the hell do these absolute tools think they're going?" Lea asked, shaking her head.

"Quicker to escape on the river in this town."

They raced onwards, slowly gaining on the boat in front, now swinging north around the Isle of Dogs and passing the O2 Center. Another volley of machine-gun fire ripped great chunks out of the fibre-glass nose of their boat and showered them with the tiny fragments.

Hawke finished rounding the next bend in the river and violently rammed the throttles forward, making the boat zoom up almost above the surface of the water, a thick white wake spilled out for hundreds of yards behind them.

Lea was thrown back into the rear of the boat and landed in a puddle of the Thames that had collected there during the last sharp turn in the river. "Oh, now that is just *disgusting*."

"Sorry! At least you won't need a bath tonight though – look at it that way."

Lea gave him the bird as she climbed back up and this time grabbed on to the rail at the front.

"So what rank were you?" Hawke asked casually.

"Lieutenant, in intelligence."

"Oh no, not a bloody *officer*."

"Afraid so. What about you?"

"Sergeant."

"I think you should call me ma'am in that case," she said with a smirk.

"Yeah, I don't think so. You should know I can't stand officers."

"That's not very nice. They're not all bad."

Hawke scoffed. "They're a bunch of incompetent idiots, and I'll tell you something else as well, I... uh-oh."

"What?"

"I have some bad news," Hawke shouted to her, changing the subject.

"You are bad news, Joe Hawke."

"Seriously – look."

Hawke pointed to the boat in front which was pulling away to the north bank. The men inside clambered out and after emptying their magazines into Hawke's motorboat they ran through the Royal Wharf.

"Where are they going?" Lea asked.

Hawke frowned. "I have a pretty good idea."

They pulled the boat up just ahead of the Thames Barrier and followed the path the men had taken, only to see them entering London City Airport.

"Come on – maybe we can still catch them."

Inside they saw the men enter a private departure lounge. Through the smoked glass they watched them present passports and then they were taken immediately to a smart blue Eurocopter.

Airport security stopped Hawke and Lea in their tracks.

"No one goes airside without passports and a security check."

They watched helplessly as the chopper lifted into the air moments later, heading eastwards out over the water.

CHAPTER THREE

Sion

The snows of winter were early in Switzerland this year, and roared through the valley below. Hugo Zaugg wondered pensively back and forth on the thick white carpet of his study. Ever since he was alerted to this latest discovery his mind had touched upon nothing else. It was amazing what tracking keywords on certain email accounts could yield.

Most alarming to him was how to keep such a thing secret from the world. His father had done it for forty years, and he had diligently continued in his footsteps. That was the business he was in, after all.

His father had done it in Greece during the war, and it was thanks to Major Otto Zaugg's archaeological work in the Ionian Sea that his son Hugo had known the legend was real. Now it looked like he was about to finish what his father had started, and it was all thanks to Richard Eden's hard work.

Far below in the valley, the town lights came on one by one as darkness approached and the storm built in power. With Christmas on the horizon the streets were festooned with fairy lights and bunting.

Sion was an expensive place to live – one of the most expensive in Switzerland, but its appeal was minimal to the elderly billionaire as he went about his life's work. The closest he had come to the streets below was the occasional time when his private helicopter flew over it en route to his mansion's helipad.

He swivelled his telescope and watched a young couple struggling against the wind to get back to their apartment from a car which was parked in the snowy street outside. Zaugg studied their progress as he might watch a line of ants marching along a garden path. Sometimes life bored him.

But not tonight.

Zaugg turned to face his team. He was a short man, in an expensive gray suit with a navy blue tie and silk polka dot pocket square emerging somewhat flamboyantly from his breast pocket. He had a smooth, shaved head and a salt and pepper goatee beard trimmed to perfection. He smiled at them coldly.

His team of personal assistants and business associates watched him in silence for a long time before one of them spoke, fearful of Zaugg's response.

"It was a mistake letting that woman get away," the man said in French. "Who knows how much she told Eden before she was silenced? If this ever gets out the world as we know it will be over. Yet perhaps Eden doesn't know what he has."

"You think Sir Richard Eden doesn't realize what was almost in his grasp?" Zaugg said, still looking through the window. He was speaking in French. "He spent two years and five million dollars funding that excavation. He knows what he has."

"But we have the only translation," said another man in German, excitedly. It was Dietmar Grobel, Zaugg's number two. "How it will enlighten us! It is so precious."

"*Indeed*," Zaugg purred, this time in German. Yes, the original Ionian Texts and their translation were precious, but nowhere near as precious as what they would lead him to, he thought.

He considered Professor Fleetwood's full translation in the context of the documents handed to him by his father. They whispered to him from the deep past: *Those Who Seek His Power, Will Find It Buried In His Kingdom.* He smiled and rolled the words over his tongue: *Only Then Shall Divine Illumination Be Granted...*

Zaugg closed his eyes. Poseidon and Amphitrite would lead him to their ultimate power, and Sir Richard Eden and his ragtag army of nobodies could not stop him.

"Their power will be mine," he said. "It is merely a case of locating the vase in question and then we shall be given the next step in our long quest."

"A glorious moment in history, sir," Grobel said.

"But we must neutralize the Eden Group," said the woman.

"Leave that to me," Zaugg said in a whisper.

"But we must do it now..."

"I said leave it to me," Zaugg repeated, his tone indicating that was the end of the matter.

"Are you sure you can keep something of this magnitude quiet?" said a thin man, swallowing anxiously at the end of his sentence. "Surely not even someone as powerful as you could keep something like this secret. What if Eden leaks it? If we hand everything over to the United Nations, perhaps..."

"What you say is madness!" said the woman.

Zaugg stopped his pacing and began to study the pattern of the snowfall as it raced past his enormous window wall. More snowflakes than stars in the universe, he thought. "The world is not ready for this and neither is Eden. Only I have what it takes to control such a power."

"I concur," said Grobel. "And we have invested too

much for this to become public. We will lose everything. Eden will not reveal anything to the public. He understands its significance."

"Herr Grobel is right," continued the woman. "If this becomes public knowledge everything we aspire to will be in grave jeopardy."

Zaugg walked to the leather swivel chair behind his expansive mahogany desk and gently sat down. He turned slowly once again to face his team.

They were a good lineup – the best that money could buy – archaeologists, geologists, historians, and experts in folklore and mythology. They knew what they were talking about, and they also knew the value of keeping him happy. Zaugg happened to agree with the majority opinion in the room – the world was not ready for such a find, the import of which would be truly earth-shattering if he got his way.

But it was not without precedent.

It was true that he already had one piece of the puzzle – discovered by his father in Greece during the war which he then smuggled into Switzerland under a false identity when the Allies occupied Germany.

Without that evidence he would never have believed the legend. But without the Ionian Texts it revealed nothing. The texts, recently found by Sir Richard Eden, his great rival, had proven without a doubt that the legend was real and that the vault was true and could be located.

Zaugg had never doubted. And others were equally keen to find the truth. There were people in the world beside him who dedicated their lives to finding the truth. There had even been attempts to steal the document handed down to him by his father, but the punishment he meted out to the thieves was not in exact alignment with the Swiss judicial code.

But now the Ionian Texts were found and translated, he would be able to locate the vault of Poseidon and take control of the ultimate power on earth.

"So what shall we do, Herr Zaugg?" asked the woman. "Are you prepared to take responsibility for what this discovery will do to the world, or are you going to guard it for more enlightened generations?"

"I am confident Richard Eden will not release the details of his discovery to the press and the matter will not be spoken of again. I trust you know me well enough by now to know how reckless it would be to defy me. The world will know of this soon enough and at a time of my choosing."

A murmur of concern rippled around the warm room, but another withering look from Zaugg brought about an immediate change of heart.

"This is the right choice," said the historian.

"I concur," said the geologist.

"I still think the world should be told now," said the archaeologist. "This changes everything! If the legends turn out to be true – and in the light of this discovery I see no further reason to doubt them – we're talking about something very dangerous indeed – the whole of human history will be rewritten. We are playing with fire."

"You think I have made the wrong decision?" Zaugg said, suddenly darkly serious.

The archaeologist fell silent for a moment. He looked at the carpet, and then spoke up. "Of course not, sir. It's just that..."

"Excellent," snapped Zaugg. "Then we are all agreed. A discovery like this is too explosive for the average man or woman on the street. They are occupied with the mundane, with the humdrum. We must not burden them with such a heavy load. This is why Sir Richard Eden will not go to his superiors about this – that really would be suicide – or should I say genocide?"

A low rumble of grim, forced laughter emanated from the small group.

Zaugg got up from his chair and walked silently to the window wall. It was almost totally dark now, and as he stared through the glass he no longer saw the little town below his mountain estate, but his own reflection – old, proud, scared.

"The legend says they were buried together..." he said quietly. His voice was thinner now, almost a whisper, as if his mind was drifting to some other place where he would much rather be. "If the Ionian Texts give us what I expect them to, then we will soon be in possesson of the vault of Poseidon and its terrifying secrets." He sighed and closed his eyes. He raised his wrinkled hands and placed them gently on the glass in front of him. "We will change the course of the entire world... and my destiny."

He breathed in deeply and let the air out in a slow, restful exhalation. He was calm again, happy, expectant. No, the world was not ready for such a thing, but he was.

CHAPTER FOUR

"Hello, again," said Sir Richard Eden. The English politician was sitting behind an old, worn desk in the study of his townhouse just a few streets from the British Museum. His crisp white shirt was still covered in blood from the earlier attack, and his face seemed to have aged several years in the short time since Hawke had last seen him.

Through the window they could still hear the sounds of the sirens as the emergency services dealt with the aftershock back at the museum. Eden rubbed his shoulder and winced before speaking: "Apparently you've already met, but please allow me formally to introduce you to Lea Donovan – she's the head of my personal security."

He gestured to Lea who was now standing beside his desk. She had changed and was now dressed in a black sweater and tight blue jeans, and her blonde hair was tied back less formally. They shook hands again.

"No disrespect, but maybe you should change your head of security?" Hawke said.

"What is that supposed to mean?" Lea asked sharply.

"Sir Richard nearly got killed today, is what I mean."

"You were the one supposed to be running security at the museum. If you'd done your job properly the shooter wouldn't have even been inside the building."

"And if you'd briefed me about Sir Richard's psychotic enemies I might have run tighter security."

"If you must know," Eden said, "Lea didn't know anything like this could happen."

"And what *did* happen?" Hawke asked.

Eden seemed torn between a reluctance to speak and the urge to request their help. For a long time he was silent, staring at the middle distance outside his window. "I'm not sure how much I can tell you," he said, turning to Lea. "Even you."

Hawke and Lea shared a concerned glance. "You're going to have to tell us more than that, Richard," Lea said.

"Bloody right you are," Hawke said flatly. "A woman you claim you know walks into the British Museum in broad daylight in the middle of a major exhibition, rambles incoherently about the ultimate power of Greek gods and gets shot dead right in front of the cream of the crop. I think you owe us an explanation."

Eden stared at both of them for a few moments before speaking. "Yes, I did know the woman – that much is perfectly true. Her name was Lucy Fleetwood and she was an academic working here in London."

"An academic?"

"That's right. She was a professor of ancient languages just up the road at University College London."

"And how did you know her?" Lea asked. "You should have told me about this."

"She was working for me."

"If you want us to help you, we need the whole story, Richard," said Hawke. "Spit it out."

Eden fixed his eyes on Hawke and seemed to acquiesce.

"Of course. As you may know, I run a highly covert section of the intelligence services, but my lifelong passion is archaeology. A few weeks ago my team found something potentially of very great value to the archaeological world – and perhaps to the wider world as well. I'm talking about the Ionian Texts." He looked at them hoping to see a flicker of recognition, but neither showed any.

"What's the significance of these texts?" Hawke asked.

"Until recently most people simply refused to believe they existed, and dismissed them as a fanciful legend and nothing more. A few of us, however, never stopped believing that one day they would be found. I have spent my life searching for them."

"Yeah, but.." Hawke was growing impatient. "What's their significance?"

Again, Eden's face was a tortured mix of reticence and desperation. Finally he spoke: "They are supposed to refer to the location of the vault of Poseidon."

"The what?" Hawke's voice was sceptical.

Lea's eyes narrowed with doubt as she looked at her boss.

"It's like a tomb," continued Eden reluctantly, "only it's supposed to contain not only the sarcophagus of Poseidon but also an enormous hoard of treasure, both his personal wealth but also that offered to him as a tribute by his worshippers."

"Sorry?" asked Hawke, perplexed. "I might not have had the best education in the world but even I know Poseidon was a god. How does a god have a tomb?"

This time the fight on Eden's face between reluctance and desperation for help went the other way: "There are some things I just cannot explain to you at this time about the nature of the tomb and its contents, and you'll just have to live with it."

Hawke was used to being cut-off – it was part of life

in the marines, but he realized that this was different. "Come off it, Richard."

Eden sighed. "You were a very accomplished Special Forces soldier for many years and you served on a great deal of top secret missions. We both know you would not have been aware of the strategic significance of many of them, and we both know you were able to work with that. You can consider this the same thing."

Hawke was hoping to hate Sir Richard Eden, but already the old man was making it difficult for him. He appreciated frank, honest talk, and it looked like Eden did too. "I can live with that – for now, at least."

"Good. I was impressed with how you handled yourself today, with the exception of that little stunt with the tour bus – we've already had the Japanese Embassy on the phone to the Home Office by the way, so thanks for that – and if you want to see your little jaunt it was recorded by dozens of tourists and it's all over YouTube."

"It was my only play..."

Eden sighed. "And as for the destruction of a police helicopter over the Thames in broad daylight, let's just say Prime Minister's Question Time is going to be a bloody nightmare this week."

"Like I said, we had no choice."

"If you say so, but either way I need someone I can trust to get to the bottom of this. I've known you all your life, Lea, and I trust you totally. Hawke – I've run a check on you and you seem like a solid type. I'm sure the two of you can work together on this."

"As one door closes..." Hawke muttered.

"We don't have much to go on," Eden said, "but thanks to the quick-thinking of Professor Fleetwood we do have something – both her translation regarding the ultimate power being buried in some kind of kingdom, and also her reference to New York and the amphorae."

"Which isn't much, let's face it," Hawke said. "And oh yeah – what the hell is an amphorae?"

"What the hell *are* amphorae – it's plural. They're vases."

"Vases?" Lea asked.

"Ancient Greek vases."

"That's still not what I would call a lot to go on."

"But it's a start," Eden said coolly, regaining a little of his infamous composure. "The Ionian Texts are supposed to confirm not only the existence of the vault but also its location. According to legend, a daring raid was made on the tomb thousands of years ago by unknown forces."

Hawke was starting to wonder what the old man was smoking, but kept his thoughts to himself.

"Afterwards the keeper of the vault – a worshipper of Poseidon whose name was lost to history, but we know he was a potter and we refer to him as the Vienna Painter – hid all traces of its location."

"Why?"

"It's possible that the tomb could guard one of the greatest secrets known to man."

"And what would that be?" Hawke asked, eyes fixed on Eden.

"For now, that will have to remain classified."

"Oh, come on..."

Eden was not moved. "The potter left only one small inscription to reveal the tomb, and according to legend he hid it inside a vase. We thought the Ionian Texts would confirm this and it looks like they have, at least if Professor Fleetwood was right."

Lea nodded. "So that's where we need to start. Finding these inscriptions."

"And I suggest you get moving. Professor Fleetwood's killers are clearly very serious about getting their hands on the vault and everything in it, and I just can't let that happen."

"Do you have any idea who's behind this?" said Hawke.

Eden nodded. "A few days ago a man named Hugo Zaugg was released from a prison in Zurich where he had been serving a two year sentence for perjury and perverting the course of justice during a famous tax evasion trial in Switzerland."

"Sounds like a charmer," said Lea.

"He is a recluse and the world knows very little about him, except for the fact he has practically limitless wealth, very powerful connections in international agencies like the IMF, and also..."

"And what?" Hawke asked, sensing yet more reluctance on Eden's part.

"His father was Otto Zaugg."

Hawke shrugged. "Never heard of him."

"Unsurprising, but you would have had you lived in Greece during the Axis occupation in World War Two. He was a ruthless SS tank commander and went on to be a very high-ranking member of the Nazi Party before fleeing to Switzerland at the end of the war where he lived out his life in search of..."

"Let me guess – the vault of Poseidon?"

"Exactly."

Hawke studied Eden's lined face. "But what interest would a man like that have in an archaeological find? Sounds like a mystery to me."

Eden looked away from his desk. "Quite, yes."

"Are you sure you don't want to tell me something?" Hawke said.

"Only that if it really is Zaugg behind this then

watch out. He has extensive contact with the European underworld and among his associates are these two men."

Eden swivelled the computer monitor on his desk and showed Hawke and Lea grainy black and white photos of two men taken from a distance. "The man you see coming out of the gambling den is Kaspar Vetsch. He's a dangerous psychotic with no fewer than three European arrest warrants out on him. His speciality is torturing people for information and he's been known to work for Zaugg."

"He looks like a proper psycho," Hawke said.

"Creeps me out," said Lea, sincerely hoping their paths would never cross, but knowing if they did that he would come off worse.

"The other man – the one climbing into the back of the cab in this picture here is Heinrich Baumann, former Kommando Spezialkräfte – the German Special Forces. A sergeant with a lot of experience and a penchant for killing people in amazingly original ways."

"He looks even worse than Vetsch," said Lea.

"He has one eye?" Hawke asked.

Eden nodded. "Lost the other in a knife fight in Mexico City. The attractive metal hand is courtesy of a machete-wielding people trafficker in Budapest. We know more about these two than we do about Zaugg himself, so that's the only briefing I can give you at this time."

Hawke sniffed. "I've had worse."

Eden rose from his desk. "When you arrive in New York, you're going to have to work fast. I've already asked a contact in MI5 if they've heard any chatter regarding any of this, but they've drawn a blank so whoever it is knows how to dodge the security services.

That tells me they're powerful, rich and clever, which makes a formidable enemy. My money's on Zaugg."

"The bigger they are, the harder they fall," Hawke said.

Lea looked at him. "Maybe not this time."

"She's right – don't get cocky or you'll get dead," Eden said bluntly. "We don't know who they are, but we do know they've killed an innocent woman, stolen the Ionian Texts and their translations, and are probably already on their way to New York to search for the vase."

*

"I just need to make a call," Hawke spoke as they waited for a taxi. He stepped across the road and sent a text to an American cell phone number: *Are you there, Nightingale?*

A few seconds later came the reply: "*What do you want, Joe?*"

He texted back: *"Can you do something for me?"*

"Oh God."

Hawke could almost recognize the tone behind the text – she was in one of her moods. He only knew the woman by the codename Nightingale. She was former CIA in the way he was former SBS. They had worked together on many cases back in the old days, but never met, and she remained a mystery to him. But she had saved his life more than once, and he had saved hers once in Cartagena, so they trusted each other totally.

"*Please?"* Hawke texted. *"I almost just got killed."*

"Rlly? Cool," came the reply. She was *infuriating.*

Hawke needed this to move faster, so he dialled her number and two seconds later she picked up the phone.

"You nearly just got killed? Really? I was going to

say I miss that…" she said, and paused, "but I don't think so."

"Just check something out for me, Nightingale."

"Sure. I'm just about go to bed. What time is it in England?"

"Daytime."

"Cute. You know, I have a terrible headache and maybe the flu and I just had the day from hell. Literally just a second ago I just said to myself that I really, *really* hope Joe *Goddam* Hawke calls me and asks me to check something out for him."

"Thanks, I need you to get me some info. Not the sort you can pull off Wikipedia if you get what I mean."

She sighed. "What is it?"

"I'm working for a man named Sir Richard Eden."

The sound of typing.

"Okay, here it is: Member of the British Parliament, works for various national security subcommittees and has close links to MI5. Served fifteen years in the British Army and an obsessive collector of archaeological artifacts. You're not risking your life for this guy are you, Joe?" She sounded unusually concerned.

"What about a Lea Donovan, his personal security. Is there anything else you can tell me about her?"

More typing, this time accompanied by sighing.

"Sure – I just hacked her CIA file."

"She has a CIA file?"

"She surely does, Joe."

"That doesn't sound right to me. She works security for an MP."

Nightingale laughed. "You're so naïve, baby."

Hawke ignored this. "You were telling me about her CIA file?"

"She was involved in some anti-terrorism operations when she was in the Rangers."

"The Rangers?"

"Sure, the Army Ranger Wing of the Irish Army – they're called the *Sciathán Fiannóglaigh an Airm.* I probably didn't pronounce that right but in English they're called the plain old ARW. They're an elite special operations force into sabotage, ambushes, gathering intel, you name it."

"They let women in that?"

"You are such a sexist bastard, Joe Hawke. As a matter of fact she was one of just three women with them, according to what I'm reading right now."

"She told me she was in intelligence, so I assumed an intelligence corps officer."

"And you know what they say about assuming…"

"Yeah, yeah."

"I bet she could kick your ass."

"And that's why the CIA has a file on her?"

"Because she could kick your ass?"

"Funny. I mean because she was in the Rangers?"

"Uh-huh. Listen, gotta go, Joe. Call me if you need me."

She disconnected, and the taxi pulled up.

Hawke crossed the street and opened the taxi's door. They both climbed in and the taxi joined the traffic. "What are you doing?" he asked as Lea took out her mobile phone. She quickly jabbed a number into the pad and held it to her ear.

"Now it's my turn to make a call."

"Who are you calling?" Hawke asked.

"A friend. We're going to need all the help we can get and Ryan's a sharp cookie."

"Who's Ryan?"

"My ex."

An hour later, the taxi pulled up outside a large gray factory where a lone man dressed in a black trench coat and scarf was patiently waiting for them.

"What the hell is this place?" Hawke asked.

"They used to make paint here, a long time ago, but today it's occupied by squatters. It's where Ryan lives. That's him right there."

"And what does *Ryan* do?" Hawke asked sceptically.

"Sort of a student, I guess you could say. Oh yeah, also hacks computers."

Ryan opened the door and climbed in. A cold breeze of icy air blasted against them through the open door.

Lea glanced at him. "Ryan, hi." A kiss on the cheek. Cold and quick.

Ryan Bale climbed into the back seat beside Lea and offered everyone an awkward smile. He had scruffy, curly hair cut just above his shoulders, and Hawke turned to see he was wearing a Mickey Mouse t-shirt beneath the trench coat.

Hawke laughed. "You have to be kidding. He's fifteen."

"I'm not fifteen," Ryan said indignantly. "I just have a young face."

"A face they could use to sell nappy rash cream."

"Better that," Ryan replied calmly, "than a face that looks like a welder's bench."

"Hey!"

Ryan simply smiled, gave a condescending nod of the head and turned to Lea. "When you called you said nothing about bringing another one of your monkeys along."

"He's not a monkey, Ryan. His name is Joe Hawke and he's a security guard."

"Oh God, you're finally slumming it. I knew this would happen – but so soon after we broke up?"

"Cut it out, Ryan. We saw a woman murdered this morning, if you must know."

"You did?"

"People shot at us, Ryan."

"With guns?"

Hawke sighed. "No, with peashooters. Can we move this along please?"

"Oh no," Ryan said, sighing dramatically. "Another He-Man compensating for his lack of IQ with aggression and steroids."

Lea sighed. "This is why I divorced him."

"You divorced me? What a joke! I was the one who divorced you!"

"Yeah, you tell yourself that, Ryan."

"You two were *married*?" Hawke asked in disbelief.

"Sure, why not?" Ryan said smugly.

"It's not a part of my life I like to think about," said Lea.

Ryan peered out the window as they joined the M25 and drew closer to Heathrow Airport. He leaned closer to Lea and lowered his voice. "This guy got any cameras on him, or wearing any wires?"

"Oh, not this again."

"What's up?" Hawke asked.

Lea sighed. "Ryan's a bit of a conspiracy theorist."

Hawke laughed again. "A tin foil hatter?"

"You can laugh all you like," Ryan said, offended. "But like the mighty Kurt Cobain said, just because you're paranoid doesn't mean they're not after you."

"If you say so," Lea rolled her eyes.

"Well they are after you, now," said Hawke.

Ryan looked nervous. "What do you mean?"

"Are you not following the narrative, Ryan?" Hawke said. "We're racing to New York to stop the people who just killed a professor from getting their hands on what has been vaguely described to us as the tomb of an ancient god. That's not the sort of thing you do without upsetting people and they're not going to take it lying down."

"Don't be absurd," Ryan muttered. "Gods don't have tombs."

"That's what we're going to find out."

Ryan, now uncharacteristically quiet, paled slightly and sank silently into the folds of his sumptuous silk scarf. In the front seat, Hawke was desperate to get to the airport.

CHAPTER FIVE

New York

Hawke peered out the window of the Boeing 777 as it banked to starboard and descended into the clouds above Long Island. According to the screen on the back of the seat in front of him, they were at five thousand feet and would be on the ground in La Guardia in less than twenty minutes.

He turned to Lea who was still sleeping beside him, and nudged her awake.

"Time to reset your watch to East Coast time," he said. "We're here."

"Didn't you sleep?" she asked, rubbing her eyes and hoisting herself up in the seat. "I always sleep on planes." She glanced surreptitiously at Ryan.

"I never sleep on planes," Hawke said. "Especially if I'm expected to do a halo jump out of one."

"What's a halo jump?" Ryan asked. He was sitting on the aisle seat on the other side of Lea, ogling one of the flight attendants.

"High Altitude Low Opening," Lea spoke before Hawke had a chance to respond.

"Sounds cool, actually," said Ryan.

Hawke smirked. "It usually is. At thirty thousand feet it's around minus thirty-five degrees or thereabouts."

"No, I meant..."

"He knows what you meant, Ryan."

"Ah... well, I knew that," Ryan said, embarrassed.

"Of course you did," Hawke said. "To be honest your lecture about ancient Greece and the Ionian Texts back over the Atlantic almost put me into a *very* deep sleep."

"Hey, you asked me if I knew anything about it."

"And the problem with that," Lea said, smiling wearily, "is that Ryan Bloody Bale knows everything about everything."

"Except about how to keep a woman happy, apparently," Hawke muttered.

"What was that?" Lea asked.

"I was just saying that ancient Greece is a fascinating subject."

"Ah – yes, indeed!" Ryan piped up. "Especially the gods. Poseidon, of course, was one of the twelve great Olympian immortals of the ancient Greek Pantheon. The people feared him so much they called him the earth-shaker because of his ability to create earthquakes and massive tsunamis with his trident."

"So not a great bloke to invite to your average beach party then?" Hawke said.

"The gods are not to be mocked," said Ryan, pushing his glasses up on the bridge of his nose. Hawke wasn't sure if he was being serious or not.

They left the airport and hailed a cab. Moments later they were driving through a crisp New York afternoon. Lea instructed the driver to go to the hotel Eden had booked for them before their flight.

Hawke was already switching back into SBS mode and wondering if the people who killed Professor Fleetwood and stole the Ionian Texts might have prepared a welcoming committee for them here in America.

Presumably they had the same information that Fleetwood had given to Eden and possibly much more, but when they arrived at the Hotel Plaza Athenee there was no one waiting except the front desk clerk and a young bellhop.

Upstairs, Hawke was less than impressed.

"Hang on – so Eden only booked two bloody rooms?"

"Government budget." Lea shrugged her shoulders and smiled.

"You're sharing with your ex, right?" Hawke protested, nodding his head in the direction of Ryan, who was struggling to open the window.

"Get out of it, Joe Hawke! You two are sharing, and that's my room over there." She pointed across the corridor at the door opposite theirs.

"Talk about motivation to get out of here before nightfall..."

Ryan sat at the table by the still-closed window and took a MacBook Air out of his luggage.

"So what do we know, then?" Hawke asked.

"Not much," said Lea. "All we have is a vague reference to New York, and the fact a potter left a map to the tomb inside some of his work thousands of years ago."

"And don't forget Fleetwood's cryptic last words," Hawke said.

"I've been thinking about those," Ryan said. "Her reference to the 'ultimate power' probably has something to do with Poseidon's trident."

"The trident?" Hawke asked. "Maybe that's what Eden was being so coy about. What about the vase – anything on that?"

"The vase in question is probably one called the Poseidon Vase by this Vienna Painter Eden told you about. Greek Attic vase creators are named after various things, one of which is often large collections around the world. The Vienna Painter is named after an amphora in the Kunsthistorisches Museum in Vienna."

Hawke smiled. "I wouldn't want to say that after a couple of pints."

"Like I said," Lea muttered. "Not as funny as you think you are."

Ryan continued without replying. "It's one of a pair, the other featuring Amphitrite. They make a set because the scene is one of Poseidon fishing, and then the other has Amphitrite holding the fish. The obvious corollary is that the Vienna Painter hid the location of the vault in either one or both of these vases."

Hawke mouthed the word *corollary* to Lea behind Ryan's back and winked.

Lea smiled at him as Ryan continued, oblivious. "*Amphitrite* – who would have thought it?"

"So who was Amphitrite?" Hawke asked.

Ryan stared at the MacBook for a few moments as he flicked through a few pages before winding up on Wikipedia. "Amphitrite was an ancient goddess, originally the wife of the great sea god Poseidon, one of the twelve great Olympian gods of the ancient Greek Pantheon. She was a nereid, which was a sea nymph a little like the sirens."

"The ones that used to sing sailors to their deaths by making them sail into rocks?" Lea asked.

"Uh-huh, but nereids were good and they used to help sailors make safe passage through dangerous storms. According to ancient Homeric scripture, all this starts with Kronos."

"Who?" Hawke asked. "Sounds like an aftershave."

Lea sighed. "Only the kind *you* would buy."

Ryan sighed and shook his head in disappointment. "Kronos, he was a Titan who descended directly from the ultimate divine beings – Uranus, who was the sky, and Gaia, who was the earth. Kronos had three divine children, Poseidon, Zeus and Hades."

Hawke frowned. "This is getting complicated."

"Hardly. Poseidon inherited divine power over the sea, Zeus got the sky and Hades got the underworld. Simples."

"What else does it say about Poseidon in particular?" Hawke asked.

"With the exception of his father Zeus, king of all gods, he was the most powerful god the earth has known. As I say, he was once called the earth-shaker because of his ability to cause earthquakes and tsunamis. He was also known among the ancients for his unpredictable temper and wild nature. He was not a god to displease, it seems."

"But the ancient gods were myths." Hawke said. "This is what I'm just not understanding." He walked to the door and checked the spyhole to make sure the corridor was still empty.

Ryan continued. "According to this, the myth of Amphitrite is..." he squinted through his glasses at the screen. "Er... the process of deification in reversal. In the earliest days she was understood to be a sea-goddess, but the Olympian pantheon reduced her status to Poseidon's consort – a bit like when Princess Diana was stripped of her HRH status."

"Nice topical analogy, Ryan." Lea shook her head and sighed.

"He likes keeping it simple, I can see that," said Hawke.

"Hey, if it helps proles like you to understand, then I'm happy with it."

"Hey, Hawke is not a prole," Lea said. "He's a pleb."

Ryan continued. "Anyway, much later, the ancient poets and storytellers reduced Amphitrite once again to a metaphor for the sea itself and – wait – this is important."

Lea looked at him. "What?"

"We need to make sure Hawke knows what metaphor means."

"Get on with it, Rupert," Hawke said. "Unless you want a knuckle sandwich."

"Oh you *do* know what a metaphor is, good. Anyway, in other words, as time passed the absolute certainty that she was a real goddess – breathing, and walking on earth – was slowly diminished in gradations until today we see her as a myth. Shit! I'm really good at researching this ancient Greek stuff."

"A myth like Jesus, you mean?" Hawke said, ignoring the hubris.

"Many high-profile atheists believe Jesus was a real man who walked the earth, even if they dispute he was the son of god. Why is it possible for so many of us to accept Jesus was really on earth, and also a god, but not for us to believe that the ancient gods of earlier cultures were also real, and had a physical presence here on earth?"

"Because there's no evidence of it."

"In the last few minutes I've been to more than one website which claims there is solid evidence of it."

"You mean tin foil hat websites?"

"Not necessarily, no."

"So why has no one ever heard of this evidence then?" Hawke asked.

"I'd imagine there aren't many people willing to risk their careers for the truth. It's probably almost impossible to prove, I'd bet. Either the cultures in question are so old they have turned to dust, or the authorities work hard to suppress the truth in order to keep control of the current narrative."

"You mean the history we all know?" Hawke asked.

"The history you think you know, yes," Ryan said with a smile.

Hawke turned to Lea. "I know you said this guy was a bit of conspiracy theorist but you never said he was a total nutcase."

"Excuse me," Ryan objected, "but evidence of antediluvian civilizations is probably out there for those who care to look. The scientific community regard some believers as conspiracy nuts and maybe that's their loss – or perhaps their discrediting of those people is more than a simple dismissal of the unlikely – we may never know."

Hawke thought things through for a second. He felt like his mind was melting. "So where do we find this Vase of Poseidon?"

"The Met," Ryan said.

*

Under the pretext of grabbing a coke from the vending machine, Hawke took a walk and put a call through to Nightingale. He was still concerned about whatever it was Sir Richard Eden was keeping from him.

"It's this trident that's bothering me,' he said to her. "What can you tell me about that?"

Nightingale worked fast and was soon hacking through secret government documents. "The legend says that the trident was pretty much the most powerful weapon possessed by any god. Apparently it had some kind of power that enabled Poseidon to cause earthquakes and tsunamis at his command anywhere in the world at any time… but there's some other stuff in here about the contents of the vault."

"And?"

"And it's blocked."

"I thought you hacked it?"

"Sure did, but this is a PDF of a scanned letter, and someone's blocked out a few lines with a black pen. Whatever it is, they don't want anyone to know about it. I guess that explains why Langley is keeping an eye on this."

"Langley believes this crap?"

"Joe, the US Government is heavily invested in the esoteric – MK Ultra, teleportation experiments, telepathy experiments, you name it. If they thought there was even the slightest possibility that something like the trident really existed, believe me, they would want it."

"This just gets worse."

"As for the stuff that's blacked out… who knows? Back when I worked for them there was even a rumor they took the Ark of the Covenant from the Nazis way back in World War Two and hid it in a giant storage facility, but none of us ever bought that one – some things are just too ridiculous to believe, you know?"

"Yeah, that *is* ridiculous." Hawke's mind raced with ideas. "So let me get this straight – you're saying that Poseidon's trident really exists and is a weapon of mass destruction and that a Swiss megalomaniac is trying to get his hands on it and that there's stuff even worse than that because it's blacked out?"

"Pretty much."

At times like this, he missed the Special Forces. Life seemed somehow simpler back then. Less nuance and more black and white back in the old SBS.

The SBS were the Royal Navy's equivalent to the British Army's SAS, just as highly trained but much less comfortable in the public eye. Not being as well-known as the SAS didn't bother the men in this elite unit – it was a small band of soldiers of less than two hundred, and they lived by their motto: *By Strength and Guile.*

They were especially proud of the fact they had the only Victoria Cross in the Special Forces, won in 1945 by Anders Lassen who led a daring attack in the north of Italy at the end of the war.

But recently, the section had suffered a hammering to their reputation after a failed attempt to rescue hostages held by jihadi terrorists in Nigeria. Some had argued the SAS should have been used, but Hawke knew the situation would have been the same whoever was handling it. He had served in M Squadron, the Maritime Counter Terrorism sub-unit, and life there was unpredictable and dangerous.

But that was then and this was now. Like it or not.

Hawke thanked Nightingale and returned to the room. He put the cokes on the table. Ryan had packed up the MacBook and was flicking through the TV channels.

"We didn't pay for the porn option, sorry Rupert," Hawke said.

"Very funny."

"Listen," Lea said, rubbing her temples. "I'm going to grab a quick shower before we head over to the museum."

Hawke thought the two of them looked like they had been arguing.

"Do you need any help?" Ryan said, cockily.

"Those days are over, Ryan. You stay here with Joe and work on this."

Hawke watched Lea pull out her hair-tie and close the door behind her.

CHAPTER SIX

Lea closed the door of her room and turned on the shower. Steam filled the bathroom as she took off her clothes and wrapped herself in a towel.

She hadn't stopped since the shooter had killed Lucy Fleetwood back at the British Museum, and since then she'd been on a chase across London in a bus of terrified tourists and up the Thames on a speedboat. Avoiding talking to Ryan by pretending to be asleep for a few hours on the flight to New York was the last straw, and all she wanted to do now was relax for a while and freshen up.

She stepped into the steamy bathroom and dropped the towel from around her naked body to the floor. She felt the warm steam on her body, and while part of her knew it was good to be actually doing something besides guarding the old man, another part of her wished she was back in her flat in London just watching television and drinking wine.

Inside the shower she tried to wind down, but her mind raced with the events of the last few hours. She hadn't seen Ryan for several months and had wondered if maybe he might have changed, but as soon as she saw him she knew he was the same person she had divorced, and with good reason. Was it the perils of marrying someone younger, she wondered, or had it really been all her fault?

As for the other guy – she had no idea what to make of him. He seemed to walk the walk, but between the jokes and the bravado she recognized the type from her days in the Irish Army. No, she wouldn't go there, either. *"Why is my life such a damned mess?"* she whispered to herself, gently taking the shower gel from the shelf.

The soap ran through her hair and down her face. She closed her eyes tight to stop the suds from getting in and stinging, and that was when she thought she heard the hotel room door open and click shut again. Did she lock the door? Securing a room was an old habit, but she was just so out of shape these days, not to mention exhausted.

Then, the door to the bathroom opened, and she spun around to see the figure of a tall man entering the room. The soap stung her eyes, and she tried to rub it away while simultaneously tracking the path of the man as he approached through the steam.

He swung open the door and lunged at her. Dressed in black, stubble. Not Ryan or Hawke. She reacted fast, but slipped on the water and fell over backwards, almost knocking herself out.

The man pulled a knife from his belt and thrust it forward. Lea screamed and lashed out, landing a solid kick in the man's groin.

He doubled over reaching instinctively to protect his balls, but Lea's army training kicked in and she grabbed the shower gel bottle and rammed it into his face, splitting his lip and ramming hard into the columella of his nose. Blood sprayed out into the tiny cubicle and over her naked body.

The man lurched back now reaching for his lip, cursing. He waved the knife blindly in the steam as she slipped out of the shower and into the hotel room. She tried to open the door but the man grabbed her arm and yanked her back onto the bed.

She screamed and punched the man in the throat.

He gasped and strained to suck air into his lungs.

She screamed again, and tried to bring her knee up

into the man's groin a second time, but this time he was ready, grabbing her knee and almost crushing it as he forced it to her side.

He gripped the knife and pushed it towards her throat.

Then the door smashed open. It was Hawke.

He grabbed the assailant by the shoulders and pulled him away from her, spinning him around and landing an eye-watering punch in his nose which gave away like papier-maché under the force of his heavy fist.

Lea scrambled to cover herself with the nearest thing to hand – the duvet.

The man staggered back until he struck the windowsill.

Hawke stormed forward, pulled his hands away from his broken nose, and hit him again, this time breaking his cheekbone. "Who sent you, you bastard?" he shouted. The man didn't reply.

So Hawke opened the door and pushed him onto the balcony.

The man, still in a daze from the vicious assault was helpless as Hawke picked him up in a fireman's lift and then dangled him over the balcony. He screamed and flailed about like a rag doll in the cold wind.

"Who sent you?" Hawke shouted. "That right there is the last time I ask before dropping you on the street down there and turning you into a puddle of gravy, get what I'm saying?"

The man stared at the ant-like people and tiny toy cars driving along the street fifteen storeys below and got what Hawke was saying: "Vetsch. His name is Vetsch. Please don't kill me, man. Not this way, man, please."

"Who and where is Vetsch?"

"All I know is the name, Kaspar Vetsch – that's it, I swear. I never met him, and I never saw him. He paid me to kill you all. That's all I know."

"You're not very good at your job, are you?" Lea called out from inside the room.

Hawke pulled the man off the balcony and threw him back in the room. He scrambled to his feet and Lea thought he was going to run, but instead he picked up the knife a second time and made another move towards her, pulling the duvet off and lunging at her with the knife.

Hawke sighed, and stepped into the fight, tossing Lea a hand towel to cover herself and disarming the man in a second with a hefty downwards chop on his forearm. They struggled and ended up crashing into the bathroom where Lea could hear various grunts and punches and then the sound of breaking glass. She got up. Ryan stepped cautiously into the room.

"What's going on?" he whispered. "When Hawke heard you screaming he told me to stay in the other room. I wanted to come, honestly."

"Save it, you weasel."

Hawke emerged from the bathroom rubbing his fist.

"Are you all right?" Lea asked.

"You should see the other guy," Hawke joked.

"I could have taken him, by the way. You should have let me finish the job."

"Sure," Hawke said doubtfully.

"I guess this means we're on the right track, at least," Ryan said.

They peered in the bathroom. The assassin lay unconscious, face down in the shower, with the hot water running the blood from his broken nose down into the drain. "I guess his career as an assassin is all washed up," Hawke said.

Lea ignored it. "So would you two just get out of here please! If you hadn't noticed I'm actually completely naked apart from this ridiculous hand towel."

"*I* noticed," Ryan said keenly.

"Out!"

*

They took East Sixty-Fourth Street until Central Park and then turned right on Fifth Avenue which they followed all the way to the Museum Mile and then the Metropolitan Museum of Art itself, set in the east side of the park. A light snow shower began to fall and they started to wish they'd taken one of the many famous yellow cabs, but it was a short walk taking less than twenty minutes.

All the same, they were grateful to step off the cold street and into the heated building. "So this is where we start?" Hawke asked, casting a skeptical eye over the sheer size of the place.

"It's our best chance," Ryan said. "If we knew why these people wanted to find Poseidon's tomb in the first place it would make things a hell of a lot easier."

They explained to a security guard what they were doing and moments later Hawke saw someone approaching. "This must be our babysitter," he said.

The young man walked across the imposing Great Hall with a spring in his step.

"Welcome to the Met," he said cheerily, shaking their hands. "You must be the Eden Group?"

Hawke frowned. "I've never been called that before."

"I'm Mitch McKay and I'm one of the curators here."

"Nice to meet you, Mitch," Hawke said, disappointed with the limp handshake – always a bad sign.

"I must say we were surprised to get a call from your

Government but we're only too happy to help in any way we can – especially if there is any kind of threat to one of our pieces."

"Looks like an amazing place." Lea looked at the vaulted ceiling high above them.

"Sure is," Mitch said, beaming. "This was all built in 1902 and is some of the finest neoclassical design in the entire world. The façade is all limestone, you know. All absolutely priceless, naturally."

Hawke nodded. "*Naturally*."

"The department you want is on the first floor."

"You mean ground floor," Ryan said chippily.

"He means first floor, Ryan," Lea said. "And stop being such a fool."

"If it's on the ground level then it's the ground floor."

"In America," Mitch chimed in with a warm smile, "we call the ground level the first floor."

"Yes, but that's not logical because..."

"Enough, Ryan." Lea elbowed him gently in the ribs.

Mitch steered them to the left and talked more about the history of the museum with so much personal pride Hawke wondered if he thought he owned the place.

"Well, here we are," Mitch said at last. "This is the Greek and Roman Art section right here, and what you want is up on the mezzanine – up there. Please, follow me."

They stepped into the large atrium and wondered among the many statues from the various ancient Greek and Roman periods. Mitch nodded his head in appreciation as if they were his children.

"Upstairs here is the mezzanine, and that's where we keep the vases. Do you know which one to look for?"

"Yes. It's one of a pair created in around 400 BC, we think. Poseidon and..."

"Poseidon and Amphitrite," Mitch said. "I know it

well. It's one of my favorites." He turned to Lea and lowered his voice, suddenly all business. "You know, what I wouldn't give for the other half of that pair!"

"And where is the other half?" Hawke asked.

"Athens. National Archaeological Museum. A damned shame, if you pardon my French."

"Consider yourself pardoned," the Englishman mumbled.

They reached the top of the stairs and walked along the mezzanine. It was lined with six foot-high glass cases filled with ancient artifacts from plates and bowls to flasks and vases. Some even contained jewellery and weapons, and all lit by tiny ceiling lamps which shone bright white lights on everything.

"Here it is," Mitch said.

The Poseidon Vase.

"Is that what all the fuss is about?" Hawke said dismissively.

The vase was less than a foot high, and not dissimilar from all the others in the room. It was a simple black and orange-red vase depicting a figure holding a fishing rod in the ocean.

Mitch said: "It's unusual because it's rather late for the black-figure style."

Hawke stepped forward. "Eh?"

"I'm sure you noticed," Mitch began, "that some of the vases depict red figures on a black background, while others depict black figures on a red background."

"Yeah, sure," Lea said. "We noticed that."

Mitch gave her a withering glance.

"This is what we call the bilingual painting style because of the red and orange. The red-figure style started around the fifth century BC through to the second century BC, while black figure was much earlier. This vase is black-figure, but dates to the fourth century

BC. We have no idea why the Vienna Painter did it this way."

"Fascinating." Hawke looked at his watch. "Can we look at it now?"

"You are looking at it," Mitch said.

"I mean really look at it. Hold it."

Mitch looked uncomfortable. "I'm not sure..."

"Open the case, Mitch," Lea said, stroking his forearm. "For me."

Behind Mitch's back, Hawke rolled his eyes at Lea.

Mitch opened the case and handed Lea the vase.

She looked at the vase and handed it to Hawke. It was light in his hands and painted in a simple style to depict a black Poseidon sitting on a rock holding a fishing line which dangled into a black ocean.

"So this was one of a pair discovered on Crete in the eighteenth century?"

Mitch's eyes widened. "You're remarkably well informed."

"Yeah." Lea jabbed her thumb over her shoulder at Ryan. "Thank the nerd, not me."

"Someone taking my name in vain?" Ryan asked, walking over to them from the mezzanine. "Some amazing artifacts in here, Mitch."

"Gee, thanks. We like to think so."

Ryan's gaze was immediately drawn to the Poseidon Vase. "Now that really is beautiful."

Lea nodded. "But how can it help us?"

"Give Uncle Ryan a look," he said, snatching the vase from Hawke's hands.

"Hey, watch out!" Mitch snapped. "That's worth hundreds of thousands of dollars!"

"It's fascinating," Ryan said, pushing his glasses up on the top of his head and peering closely at the artwork. "Rather late for a black-figure work, isn't it?"

Mitch nodded appreciatively, now calm in the knowledge that anyone who knew such a fact could not possibly drop such an ancient piece of art.

"So what's the deal, Sherlock?" Hawke asked impatiently. "What has that vase got to do with Professor Fleetwood's dying words?"

"Dying words?" Mitch went pale. "What's going on here, exactly?"

"Nothing for you to worry about," Hawke said reassuringly.

Lea looked at Ryan. "Well?"

"I have no idea..." Ryan said. "I need more time. All I see is an ancient vase painted in the bilingual style, featuring Poseidon holding a damned fishing line."

"Is there anything written on it?" Hawke said.

"Look underneath," said Lea.

Ryan turned it upside down but drew a blank. "Sorry, nothing – look."

The others peered at the bottom which was a standard, unmarked base, not glazed.

"I could have told you that and saved you a flight," Mitch said. "And no, before you look there's nothing inside either."

With these words, the three of them peered into the vase, maneuvering it so one of the spotlights illuminated the interior. Nothing.

Lea sighed. "What was that damned quote again?" she said.

"I think you mean quotation," said Ryan. "A quote is what the plumber gives you to fix the toilet."

"Shut up, Ryan," Lea said. "You know what I mean."

"All right – the *quotation* was *Those Who Seek His Power, Will Find It Buried In His Kingdom.*"

Mitch scratched his head.

Hawke and Lea stared at the vase in Ryan's hands.

"Quite the riddle," said Ryan.

"*Those Who Seek His Power, Will Find It Buried In His Kingdom*," Hawke repeated, staring at Poseidon, sitting on the rock, fishing, looking into history. Casually ignoring their plight.

Lea looked at it again. "Maybe there's some kind of code hidden in the picture."

"What do you mean?" Hawke asked.

"Like if you look at it upside down or in a mirror or something."

Hawke shook his head. "Look at him, sitting on his rock with all his future ahead of him. Immortal."

"Actually," Ryan piped up, "the ancient Greeks saw time the other way around to us. For them, the past receded away in front of them, while the future was approaching them behind their backs, which makes a lot of sense when you consider you know your past but not your future."

"How has this guy not got a girlfriend?" Hawke said.

"Hey!" Ryan said. "And who says I haven't got a girlfriend?"

"Inflatable dolls don't count," said Hawke.

Lea rolled her eyes. "Save it, Joe."

"I'm just saying how does that help us right now?" said Hawke, backing down.

Silence all round. Now it was Mitch looking at his watch. "Listen, if you guys have finished I'll have to ask you to hand the vase back to me so I can lock it up again."

Then the sound of screaming echoed up through the atrium into the mezzanine level.

"What the hell?" Mitch said, stepping forward to take a look.

"Why do I get the feeling this whole thing's about to go arseways, Joe?" said Lea.

More screaming, and then a man shouting orders at people, followed by several gunshots and the sound of smashing glass. Chaos had come to order at the New York Met.

CHAPTER SEVEN

"Oh my God!" Lea craned her head over the mezzanine rail and then back to Hawke. "They're here."

"Who are here?" Mitch asked, confused.

Hawke turned to Mitch. "You don't want to know. Suffice it to say they want that vase and not for its aesthetic value, either."

"This vase?" Mitch asked, turning the pottery over in his hands. "I don't understand. It's unique but hardly the most expensive item in the collection. There are artifacts downstairs worth millions of dollars – some are priceless."

"They don't care about money," Hawke said. 'They already have that."

Another round of gunfire, this time automatic rifles, filled the atrium and then the sound not of screaming but terrified silence. Lea's mind raced with possible options, but with a museum gallery full of frightened civilians the choices were limited.

"Mr Hawke!" shouted a voice from below the mezzanine. "I know you are here with your friends, so don't be shy."

Lea looked at Hawke and could see he was considering options just as she had done. She was aware of the others staring at him, looking desperately for some kind of lead. She thought about the accent of the man who was shouting – definitely Germanic, probably Bavarian or Swiss, she thought.

Hawke and Lea stepped closer to the mezzanine and

saw several masked men holding the lower level of the Greek and Roman Gallery hostage. Behind them two security guards lay dead, their weapons still holstered. It must have been a lightning assault.

"Who are you?" Hawke shouted.

The man chuckled. "You know who I am. You are responsible for the death of one of my employees earlier today."

"Kaspar Vetsch!"

"The very same."

"And I didn't kill your man, Vetsch."

"No, I did, for failing me."

Hawke looked at the others. Mitch was nervous, but still standing. Ryan looked like he needed to sit down. Lea spoke next: "If only we had some weapons."

Hawke nodded in agreement and turned back to face Vetsch. "What do you want?"

"Don't stall for time. You know what I want, and you will bring it to me immediately or I will shoot a hostage every ten seconds, starting with this security guard."

One of Vetsch's men dragged a guard into view. He was bloodied and bruised and holding what looked like a fleshwound on his arm. Vetsch began counting to ten.

"We can talk about this, Vetsch," Hawke shouted. "Just let the women and children leave."

A single gunshot ripped through the silence and the security guard fell to the floor, dead. Vetsch waved his pistol and a man in a suit was dragged off the floor.

"Oh God!" Mitch said. "That's Dr Peterson, the curator of Medieval Art."

"Don't waste my time, Hawke. My employer is not a man to play with."

"And who's that?" Lea whispered. "Baumann?"

Hawke nodded. "I think so." He turned to Mitch. "Hand me that thing."

Mitch handed the vase over without question, nervously peering down at Dr Peterson. Vetsch had counted to seven.

"All right, stop counting Vetsch," Hawke shouted over the balcony. "I'm bringing the vase down."

Vetsch smiled and Peterson was pushed back to the floor where he collapsed in a heap on the parquet tiles, sobbing.

"Are you crazy?" Ryan said. "He'll shoot you. He's obviously a complete psychopath."

"I have no choice," Hawke said. "He'll kill those people without blinking."

He took the vase in his arms and walked towards the stairs.

Lea watched Hawke walk slowly along the mezzanine to the steps, cradling the vase carefully in his arms the way he might hold a baby.

"Oh, sodding hell I am such a moron!" Ryan said.

"What are you talking about, Ryan?"

"The line from Fleetwood's translation – "*Those Who Seek His Power, Will Find It Buried In His Kingdom...*"

"What about it?"

"It's Poseidon – his kingdom was the ocean."

"So what?"

"So the bottom of the vase was represented to portray the ocean, wasn't it?"

"And?"

"So the Vienna Painter wasn't giving us a clue to crack a code in the picture of Poseidon himself, but telling us that whatever we're looking for is hidden actually inside the vase."

"We looked inside the vase," Lea said.

"No, not its interior. I mean actually inside it – baked into the pottery itself, down at the base where the sea was painted. Those who seek his power will find it buried in his kingdom – buried in the sea. Do you see now?"

Lea nodded. "Excellent work, Ryan," she whispered in her Dublin drawl. "You're a great guy to have around five minutes after a crisis."

"At least I thought of it!"

"A shame you couldn't have thought of it before these maniacs turned up. Now they've got Hawke."

She heard Vetsch laugh again, and then shout more orders. "All of you are to come down please, not just Hawke – and with your hands up."

"Shit," Ryan said. "I thought we were going to get away with that."

"He's... he's not going to kill us, is he?" asked Mitch.

"Not if I have anything to do with it," Lea said. "Just follow my lead."

"Quickly please," Vetsch shouted. "We don't want to wait for the police to arrive, do we?"

Lea and the others soon caught up with Hawke, and the three of them were now standing together at the bottom of the mezzanine stairs.

One of the men stalked over to Hawke, grabbed the vase and pistol-whipped him across the face, almost knocking him to the floor. Hawke kept his balance, tensing with anger at the vicious assault. The other men laughed and the museum visitors looked on, horrified at what their day had become.

"Give it to me!" barked Vetsch, and the man handed him the artifact. "Ah! The Poseidon Vase – we meet at last."

Lea watched Vetsch caress the vase with his gloved fingers, grinning and nodding his head in appreciation.

"Such a beautiful object as this," he said, "deserves to be treated with respect." As he spoke, he held the vase out on one hand at arm's length and let it wobble from side to side, pretending to let it fall and then catching it again. His men laughed. Mitch almost passed out.

"The truth is I know nothing about ancient Greece," Vetsch said, looking at his watch. "Nothing about their bizarre little rituals and orgies, nothing about their myths, legends and deities, and certainly nothing about their damned pottery."

"You've got what you came for, Vetsch!" Hawke shouted. "Just let these people go."

"Silence!" he screamed, his eyes almost popping from his head. "This vase is irreplacable, am I right, Mr Curator?" Vetsch pointed the gun at his head.

Mitch nodded, terrified. Lea saw he was sweating with fear.

"But sadly, orders are orders, and you don't disobey the man who gave me those orders." And just like that, Vetsch let the vase slip from his fingers and fall to the tiled floor where it smashed into dozens of pieces. They scattered across the floor, ancient orange dust rising from them into the air where the sun illuminated them like tiny dust motes.

"Oh dear God!" Mitch said, shaking his head.

Then Lea saw it. Among the fractured pieces of pottery was a golden semi-circle covered in strange carvings.

Vetsch saw it too, and leaned slowly forward to scoop it up in his gloved hand. He held it aloft theatrically where it caught the sunlight and flashed in Lea's eyes.

Vetsch laughed as he turned the piece of ancient metal in his hand, and for a moment the room was silent and still until the peace was shattered by the sound of police sirens.

"Whatever that is," Mitch said, stepping forward, "the museum will pay anything you ask for it, I can assure you."

"Some prices are too high to pay," Vetsch said and raised his pistol. Hawke tried to tackle Mitch to the ground but it was too late, Vetsch had shot him through the heart and he dropped backwards against the pedestal of an Aphrodite statue. Lea watched in horror as Mitch slid down, smearing the pedestal with his blood as he sank lifeless to the ground.

All hell broke loose.

The hostages screamed and scattered in all directions to save their own lives. Ryan dived behind a statue of Dionysus while Hawke and Lea charged Vetsch and his men, but they were kept back by a hail of bullets as the Swiss team retreated out of the gallery and sprinted across the Grand Hall.

"What now?" Lea asked.

"I don't know about you," Hawke said, "but I'm going to grab a gun and chase after those bastards."

"Good plan – coming Ryan?"

"Well, I..."

"Get a move on, Rupert," Hawke shouted, tossing him a security guard's Smith & Wesson.

"What the hell is this?" he shouted.

"Damn it, Joe, he can't shoot that," Lea said, grabbing herself a pistol. "He couldn't hit a barn door with a Howitzer at ten yards."

"No one is going after them unarmed," Hawke said, and ran into the Grand Hall.

No sooner had they reached the Grand Hall when they were forced to turn back in the midst of a savage volley of automatic weapons' fire, shot indiscriminately in their direction. Large chunks of marble were blasted from the sides of a fluted Ionic column Lea was using for cover.

"Good job Mitch isn't around to see that," Ryan said.

"Poor taste, Ryan. Another reason why I divorced you."

"I think we established that, in fact, I divorced you."

Hawke sighed. "Please you two, not this again, and not now!" He returned fire and planted a neat line of bullets in the side of one of the cash registers now being used as cover by one of Vetsch's men.

One of the men began to spray sub-machine gun fire in a reckless arc around the Grand Hall just for the hell of it, and another threw a grenade into the center of the room as they ran out into the courtyard.

The grenade exploded and showered plaster and dust down on them. Hawke sat up and scrambled behind one of the Doric columns for cover while Lea and Ryan copied his lead and hid behind the next column along.

Hawke saw two more security guards run toward the assailants, with pistols raised and screams demanding Vetsch and his men drop their weapons and put their hands above their heads. He fired a few rounds in their direction to try and draw their fire but it was too late.

Vetsch raked them with his sub-machine gun and they both fell to the floor, almost cut in half with the number of rounds plowed into them. *They're not playing games,* thought Hawke.

With that final flourish, Vetsch led his men out of the museum and into the street. Hawke, Lea and Ryan pursued them as fast as they could.

CHAPTER EIGHT

"We need a vehicle right now." Hawke saw the quickest option ahead of the museum's Fifth Avenue entrance. An empty car was idling in a line of traffic – its owner had gotten out and seemed to be arguing about something with the driver of a cab parked behind him.

"That's our ride right there," Hawke said. "Come on, be quick and be quiet."

"This is beyond a joke," said Ryan as they climbed into the 1935 Ford hot rod, complete with flames painted on the hood, a visible engine and double exhaust cut-outs.

Ahead of them, Vetsch and his men were making their escape in a black Mercedes S-Class.

They climbed into the hot rod, Hawke at the wheel, and a second later were racing up Fifth Avenue, the roar of the twin exhausts making the owner and just about everyone else in uptown Manhattan turn in horror.

On the road, Hawke slammed the throttle down and was impressed by the Ford's sharp acceleration and the ludicrous roar of the suped-up flathead V8 engine. "I've never driven a hot rod before," he said, nodding with appreciation.

"Simple things amuse simple people, I suppose," sighed Ryan.

Lea smiled. "It's pretty cool, actually."

"Oh, come off it," Ryan said. "You're not actually impressed by this sort of thing, are you? You realize men drive cars like this as compensation for their inadequate penis size."

Hawke smirked. "Is that a fact?"

"A well-known one in certain circles."

"Circles of jealous losers, you mean?"

"Both of you, stop it," Lea shouted.

"I'm just stating a fact about men, cars and small penis size."

"Well, you would know, Ryan," Lea said, causing him to redden. A smirk spread on Hawke's lips.

Hawke accelerated the Ford and weaved through the traffic, leaving a sea of angry car horns and fist-waving in the rear-view. The Mercedes skidded around to the left and joined East Drive heading into Central Park where it sped up and overtook several slower-moving vehicles who swerved to let it pass.

Irate joggers waved their water bottles at him and swore brashly, but to no effect. Seconds later they were doing the same thing to Hawke and the hot rod as he tore past them and sharpened his pursuit of Zaugg's team.

It was now that the Mercedes slowed and skidded across the cycle lane to the left, mounted the grassed area and cut across the footpath. A man selling hotdogs jumped to safety before shouting abuse and angrily waving a pair of cooking tongs in the air.

"Where the hell are they going?" Hawke asked as passers-by in their path screamed and scattered.

"North Meadow – it's where the baseball fields are." Lea waved her iPhone at Hawke. "I just got a map of Manhattan up so we can see what's what."

"Ah," Hawke said, giving the phone a sly, sideways glance. "I was wondering how long it would take you to think of that."

The Merc left the meadow, smashed clean through a chainlink fence and accelerated in a violent swerving weave until it hit West Drive.

It chewed up great clods of frozen earth and muddy snow which sprayed up behind it as the powerful car raced forward. Finally it hit the tarmac and bounced violently up and down before settling into a renewed acceleration.

One of the men inside was now leaning out the rear window, his hair blowing wildly in the cold wind as he recklessly aimed an Uzi at the hot rod.

He fired off a few bursts. More screaming people dived for cover while others hurriedly dialled emergency services on their cell phones.

With the gap closing, Lea leaned out the right side of the hot rod and took a couple of shots at the Merc, missing with the first but taking out the rear window with the second.

Vetsch swerved in response but soon regained contol.

"You're getting there," said Hawke with a patronizing smile.

Lea was taking another aim and said calmly: "Were you smacked too hard as a child, Joe Hawke?"

Before he could answer she fired another two shots, this time taking out the rear left tire in an explosion of black, shredded rubber.

"Better," Hawke said. "Better."

The Merc swerved violently across West Drive before plowing across the western strip of Central Park, skidding uncontrollably on some snow and narrowly avoiding a high-speed impact with the bough of an oak tree.

Hawke smiled. "That's more like it. He nearly lost it then."

Vetsch fought to maintain control, over-revved and smashed through a low brick wall before finally hitting Central Park West.

He tried to corner too fast. His one rear tire broke

traction and after a moment of terrifying oversteer during which Hawke wondered if some pedestrians might get killed, the Merc rammed into a U-Haul truck at a busy junction and its journey was almost at an end.

The U-Haul's cargo trailer was badly smashed, but the Mercedes came off worse, spinning around like a toy car against the impact with the heavy GMC truck.

It slammed through a One Way sign before finally coming to a stop with its nose in the front window of a dry cleaner's store, burst radiator steaming in the cold air.

Realizing that the rot rod was only about five seconds from meeting the same fate as the Merc, Hawke hit the brakes and after an unsettling moment of sliding sideways in the snowy grass he steered into the skid until the tires got some traction back. He gently tapped the brakes and brought the hot rod to a stop.

"Is it over?" asked Ryan, peering over their shoulders from the back seat.

"Almost." Hawke pointed at the Merc. "Just be thankful it didn't catch fire."

Then the Merc caught fire.

Flames flickered out from beneath the hood and Vetsch and his men screamed and started to scramble to safety.

Hawke sighed. "Absolutely bloody fantastic. I hope the gold disc's not in there."

"That'll flush the bastards out though." Lea checked the Smith & Wesson. "Only three rounds left."

"I've still got all seven," Hawke said. "And Rupert here hasn't fired any either, have you Rupert?"

Pedestrians scattered away from the burning engine, but stayed close enough to film it on their phones.

Meanwhile. the stationary U-Haul truck in the middle of the junction was causing heavy tailbacks along

Central Park West. Drivers were getting out of their cars and leaning over their doors to see what was going on, expressing themselves with the usual New York niceties.

"And you can fuck off, too!" Hawke said to one of them as he climbed out of the ageing Ford. The man began to remonstrate with him until the moment Lea and Ryan got out to join him and all three brandished their Smith & Wessons, at which point he bid them good day and shrank back into his Chevrolet.

"They're trying to escape!" Lea shouted.

Vetsch and his men were now clambering dazed and confused from the burning wreck of the Mercedes. They fired a few shots randomly in the direction of the junction to keep Hawke at bay.

Hawke, Lea and Ryan ducked down behind the hot rod and winced as they heard bullets slam into the other side of the car with a deep metallic plunking sound.

"We have to get that golden fragment," said Hawke.

"Easier said than done," Lea said, craning her head over the hood and firing another shot at Vetsch and his men.

Hawke heard Vetsch screaming a command at his men, and seconds later they ran back to the burning car.

"They're trying to get the golden arc out," he said. "Now's our chance."

"What are you going to do?" Ryan asked.

"I want you two to put as much fire as you can on them," he said, handing Lea his pistol. "I'm going to get that piece of gold back. Whatever it is, we need it, and we don't want Zaugg to have it."

Ryan stared at his gun with incomprehension, while Lea leaned confidently over the hood, a gun in each hand, and started firing at the men.

She hit the man who had returned to the car, and he collapsed screaming to the ground, clutching his upper leg. Seeing his comrade fallen, the other man retreated, despite Vetsch screaming for him to return.

Hawke was in a forward position now, covered by a parked Toyota just a few yards from the Merc. He heard the sirens of the emergency services as they closed in on them, and doubted Sir Richard Eden had all that much influence with the NYPD but guessed he'd find out one way or the other.

One of the men stepped forward, but Hawke lunged toward him and grabbed the man's weapon in one hand, disarming him, while thrusting his other hand forward in a lethal tiger-punch which landed with a sickening crunch in his windpipe. He fell to the ground wheezing, purple-faced as the pedestrians looked on with a mix of horror and entertainment.

Another man ran toward Hawke, but the Englishman whirled around just in time to fire a classic double-tap into him and he lurched forward like a tailor's dummy, tumbling onto the sidewalk and rolling into the gutter.

Vetsch fired at Hawke, but he was prepared for the volley of Uzi fire and ducked behind another car for some instant cover. He raised the gun over the hood to return fire when he saw Vetsch was trying to take a passer-by hostage to save his own skin.

Vetsch's heavy hand gripped the woman around her waist and pulled her toward him with the ease of a bear flipping a salmon out of a river.

But seconds later she spun around, effortlessly slipping out of his grasp and brought her right knee up into his groin with eye-watering power and accuracy while simultaneously raising her clenched fist into the downward trajectory of his face.

The results weren't pretty, but she cleared things up with a well-aimed crescent kick that launched him backwards down the ramp of a multi-storey car park.

Hawke was speechless.

The woman shrugged her shoulders. "Self-defense classes," she said, and picked up her bag.

Hawke knew they had to get the golden arc and get the hell out of there before the cops came or they would be in jail until cockroaches took over the earth.

Lea fired and struck Vetsch's last man in the upper body, exploding his chest and throat and propelling him through the air like a doll until he crashed down on the hood of a silver BMW. Hawke whistled through his teeth: "*Remind me never to get on the wrong side of that girl.*"

With all of his men down and Lea's fire now turned on him, Vetsch cursed and ran deeper into the underground car park.

Hawke seized the moment and sprinted toward the burning wreckage. Dozens of people were filming him on their phones as he shielded his eyes from the heat and smoke and peered into the Merc for the golden fragment.

The sound of the sirens grew louder – *almost at the junction*, he thought. Then he saw the gold, lying on the rubber mat in the front passenger's footwell. The flames were now inside the car, licking at the walnut-veneer dashboard and leather steering wheel, and the cab was filling with pungent, toxic fumes.

He dropped the gun and leaned in to grab the fragment, shoving it into his pocket, and then turned to the pedestrians. "Get out of here before she blows, you bloody idiots!" And with that he sprinted back to Lea and Ryan who were waiting back with the hot rod.

He held up the piece of gold and smiled. "They were actually very obliging in the end."

"Are you sure about that, cowboy?" Lea gestured over his shoulder.

Hawke turned to see Vetsch exiting the car park at

speed on a vintage Harley-Davidson. He skidded to a halt alongside the body of his dead comrade and picked up his Uzi before turning the handlebars in the direction of the hot rod, his face a rictus of hatred and revenge.

CHAPTER NINE

"So you were right there and you forgot to pick up the Uzi?" Lea asked.

Hawke gave her a sideways glance, but said nothing.

"But I thought you were *perfect*, Joe Hawke. I'm so disappointed."

"I got this thing, didn't I?" he said, waving the strange golden semi-circle at her.

"Er, guys," Ryan said, pointing at Vetsch. "Psychotic gunman on a Harley coming this way fast."

"Sometimes he makes a good point," Hawke said.

They climbed back into the battered hot rod and mounted the sidewalk in order to get away from the traffic. A block later they were in another car park, which they traversed with as much speed as they could, but Vetsch was behind them and closing fast.

Hawke drove onto Columbus Avenue amidst a hail of automatic fire from Vetsch, almost upon them now as he easily outmaneuvered them in the faster and more agile Harley.

"Brace yourselves!" Hawke shouted. He slammed on the brakes, slowing rapidly and causing the Harley almost to go into the back of them.

"Get down, Ryan!" Lea shouted.

He ducked and a second later she blew out the back window. "Only two more shots left," she said coolly.

"And with your aim that's no joke," replied Hawke.

Vetsch dropped back, the deep tones of the Harley's shovelhead V-twin engine roaring against the Columbus

Avenue Brownstones. Somewhere behind him they heard yet more sirens as the NYPD worked out where the trouble was and gave chase.

They weaved the hot rod neatly in and out of the traffic on Columbus and then Hawke swung the wheel hard to the right and skidded into West 86th Street so fast they nearly tipped the thing over.

The Harley made the corner more easily, and seconds later was alongside them. Vetsch was laughing maniacally as he casually pointed the Uzi at the Ford.

Hawke waited a split second then skidded into the Harley. The gun fired, spraying bullets up the front wing and into the cab before they collided with the bike and sent it flying off haphazardly toward a line of parked cars on the right side of the road.

"Newton's First Law of Motion, baby!" Ryan shouted through the window at Vetsch who was now struggling to maintain control of the Harley. "You gotta love it!"

"Don't speak so soon, Ryan." Lea craned forward to look in her rear-view. "It's not over yet."

Hawke heard the rasp of the Harley as it accelerated once again.

"He's a determined little fellow," he said. "I'll give him that."

Vetsch pulled alongside a second time and fired a long burst of bullets up the side of the car.

"Everyone get your head down, now!" Hawke screamed.

A second burst – what the SBS called the old 'lead wasps' – smashed the rear window and whistled past Hawke's ear before thudding into the windshield with incredible velocity.

Ryan screamed again and put his head between his legs.

"Checking to see if you wet yourself, Rupert?" Hawke said.

"No I am not!" came the muffled reply. "And my name is Ryan!"

Lea sighed. "What is this, a dick-measuring competition?"

"He started it!" Hawke protested.

"I don't think so – I think Mr Testosterone here started it."

"Just pack it in, you two," she said. She turned to Hawke to reply, but something caught her eye. "You're hit!"

Hawke leaned forward to look in his mirror. "That's nothing," he said, wiping a line of blood off his cheek. "Just a flesh wound."

"Sodding hell, Joe," said Ryan. "You got shot in the face with an Uzi!"

"It's nothing," he repeated, keeping an eye on the traffic ahead while at the same time monitoring Vetsch's progress behind them.

Thanks to a UPS truck parked up with its hazard lights flashing, the road ahead narrowed and they only just got through the gap.

Lea took out her iPhone and flicked to maps. "Nothing ahead but water, Joe."

"Eh?"

"Those trees up there – see – that's pretty much where Manhattan ends and the Hudson River begins."

Hawke looked down at the speed – seventy-five miles per hour now, and racing in and out of traffic on West 86th. Behind them Vetsch kept pace, swerving from side to side like a madman, and then he fired another burst into the rear of the hot rod.

Behind Vetsch, Hawke saw the unmistakeable blue flashes of the police.

“When in doubt, go faster,” Hawke said, and stamped harder on the throttle. They all felt the jolt as the large engine instantly produced more power and the hot rod shot forward like a drag car. Hawke was beginning to enjoy himself again.

“Did you actually pass your driving test?” Ryan said.

“I’ve been driving since you were in nappies,” was Hawke’s blunt response. “If you don’t like it you can always get out and walk.”

Hawke dropped a gear and accelerated the Ford once again, haphazardly steering the old hot rod in and out of the busy Manhattan traffic in an attempt to lose the much faster Harley on their tail. The suped-up engine roared noisily as the car thundered forward.

“Watch out, Joe!” Lea shouted. “Lights!”

“Yes, thanks – I am looking out the same window as you are.”

They burned through a red light and skidded across a junction with seconds to spare, but Vetsch, insane in his pursuit of the golden disc fragment wasn't so lucky.

A Maybach pulled out on a green light and Vetsch rammed into it. As the old bike smashed into the front of the tank-like car, it stopped with a simple crunching sound and smashed into the wing.

Vetsch didn’t share the same fate. He was propelled from the seat of the Harley, Uzi still gripped in his hand, and flung like a stone from a caterpult through the air. He sailed across the junction and landed in the back of a passing garbage truck.

“Good riddance to...”

“Don't even say it, Joe,” Lea said, sighing. “Don't even think about saying it.”

“Sorry. But at least that’s one problem out of the way.”

They watched as Vetsch tried to scramble out of the

garbage in the back of the truck, his face twisting into a scowling mask of humiliation and revenge. His death threats were drowned out by the roar of the truck's engine as it accelerated away from the junction.

"So what's next?" Ryan asked.

They watched the garbage truck fade into the traffic beyond.

Hawke's eyes returned to the road ahead. "We go and take a look at that golden fragment. Then I want a steak and some beer before I go and take out every one of those bastards who have been trying to ruin my day."

CHAPTER TEN

Thanks to Vetsch's team infiltrating them at the hotel Eden had booked, they were forced to book a new room for the night, and it was several stars south of the Athenee, with a view of a side street and a brick wall instead of Manhattan's skyline, and a vending machine half-full of Dr Pepper replacing the luxury restaurant.

"I never met anyone like you before," said Lea as she wiped Hawke's grazed temple with an alcohol wipe.

"I'll take that as a compliment."

"Well don't. You're a total idiot who's going to get himself killed one of these days."

"I'll say," Ryan added.

"You attract bullets like you were a magnet, Mr Hawke." Lea gently cleaned the wound.

"Actually," Ryan said, perking up a little, "most bullets are made of lead, which doesn't have any magnetic qualities to speak of."

"Shut up, Ryan," Lea said. "I know that. It was just an expression. Weasel."

"Yeah," added Hawke. "Shut up, Rupert."

"Let me look at the fragment," Ryan said. He picked it up off the bed and turned it in his hands. It reflected the light of the lamp dully in the low light of the room.

"Anything?"

"There's writing on it, but it's in what I presume is ancient Greek."

Lea sighed. "And your language genius doesn't extend to that, am I right?"

"Partly. I can tell you this word here probably means *acropolis*, but other than that even I can't help on this one."

Hawke looked at the line of foreign letters neatly carved into the gold, unfamiliar and alien to him.

"Acropolis? That's in Athens, isn't it?" he said.

"There are many acropoles all over Greece as a matter of fact," said Ryan. "But yes, I suppose most ordinary people would leap to the one in Athens."

"I swear I'm going to punch him, Lea."

"Please, Joe – no. It's just what he is – like it or leave it." Lea turned to Ryan and shook her head at him, frowning. "*I* left it."

"No, I left you!"

"Not this again."

"Just, *please* Ryan," Lea said, "would you start working on the translation for us? Just for me?"

Ryan mumbled something about people using him only when they wanted something, and opened the MacBook, bathing his face in a bluish glow in the corner of the hotel room. "Luckily for you *heathens*, I happen to know an excellent yet sadly unvisited Ancient Green translation engine on here, and will endeavour to convert this to English for you."

"Thanks Ryan," said Lea, yawning. "It's been a long day."

"Yeah," said Hawke, "I'm being sincere when I say thanks too, Rupert."

"Listen, I guess we're making progress," Lea told him. "So I'm going to check that bar downstairs for a beer or something."

She returned a moment later holding two bottles of Rolling Rock.

Rolling Rock. The last thing he and Liz had shared before the terror that unfolded on his honeymoon in

Vietnam all those years ago. The day when he lost his beloved wife in a vicious drive-by shooting in Hanoi's Nha Tho Street, just outside a small bar they had just discovered together.

He knew the bullets were meant for him, but in the chaos they had ripped through his new bride, and left her dying in his arms on the sidewalk. Hawke had vowed revenge, but days after the attack a senior SBS officer had informed him the killer had died in an ambush by the Thai Special Forces in Bangkok, and so he was forever denied the closure of avenging his wife.

"What's the matter, you don't like beer?" Lea asked, handing him a bottle.

"Sorry, of course I do." Hawke took the beer and downed half a bottle in one swig. "I'm going to grab a shower and then we should get something to eat while Rupert here translates the fragment."

*

In the restaurant, Hawke bought Lea a steak and fries and they shared a bottle of wine. After she had drunk three glasses, Hawke asked her a question he'd had on his mind since the very beginning.

"Are you and Eden keeping something from me?"

She looked shocked and sat back in her chair. "I'm sorry?"

"Call me insane, but I'm sure there's more to this whole business than meets the eye, or my eye, anyway."

"I don't know what you mean."

"It's like you're holding something back from me – you and Richard."

"Don't be silly, Joe."

Hawke reconsidered. "It just seems like you seem to know more about this than I do. That's all."

"I told you, don't be silly."

He took a sip of wine and put his hand on Lea's but she pulled it away.

"I'm sorry," he said. "I just thought..."

"Forget it."

"There's someone else?"

Lea shook her head.

"You're still in love with Ryan?" Hawke could hardly believe it was possible.

"Bloody hell, no. It's nothing, really. Listen, it's not you, Joe. I'm not ready for anything like this. Something happened to me, all right? Something a long time ago, and it nearly destroyed me. That's part of the reason things didn't work out with Ryan."

"And I was thinking it was because he was an annoying little..."

"Please, Joe I'm trying to be serious here."

"Forgive me," he said sincerely.

"For your information, Ryan was actually very different when we were married. He was a very caring guy, you know? And so bright it's scary – that much stayed the same, of course, but he changed after the divorce and in a way I blame myself for that. I think I wrecked his life when I divorced him. It's all my fault you see..."

"You don't have to tell me this."

"Not now, no. But one day I will. And when I do, you have to promise me you won't judge me."

"That's fair enough."

"Tell me," she asked. "Who is this mysterious Nightingale?"

"Just a woman."

"How long have you known her?"

"I don't think anyone truly knows her."

"You know what I mean, Joe."

"I was in Bosnia during the war – behind the lines, covert ops with a squadron of SAS and some US Delta Force. My squadron was teaching that lot a few things about covert warfare."

"My God, you really do love yourself…"

"It was a lot of fun for a while. Then I was selected to go dark for a few months and infiltrate a group of Serbian radicals – my cover was being a journalist for an Argentine newspaper – I'm fluent in Spanish – and things were going well until my cover got blown."

"It happens, I know…"

"We don't know how it happened, but I lost all comms with my team. Agent Nightingale, who'd been supporting the Delta lads, literally talked me out of their interrogation HQ with a schematic of the building she had pulled up from somewhere. It took an hour, and we talked for a long time – it was her training to keep me calm, not that I needed that, of course, but it brought us together. She saved my life that night. We keep in touch, and that's it."

"But you've never met her?"

"Nope. All I know is she lives in New York. She's a very private person and she has the skillset to keep it that way – I don't even know her name. She makes J.D. Salinger look like an America's Got Talent contestant."

Lea laughed. "Well… she sounds mysterious to me."

"All I know is she left the agency a couple of years ago and that she lives in New York City – that's it."

"But you want to know more about her?" she asked. Hawke now wondered why Lea was asking so many questions about her.

"Well, *do* you?" she repeated.

He shrugged his shoulders and took a sip of the wine.

*

Back at the hotel, Hawke checked the place over for anything suspicious, and then pulled a miniature vodka from the minibar before crashing on the bed and flicking the television on.

"Any progress with the golden arc, Ryan?" Lea asked.

"Er, so I worked it out, yeah," he replied.

"You mean Google worked it out," Hawke said, sitting up again.

Ryan sighed. "Do you want to know or not?"

Hawke smirked. "Hit me."

"Don't tempt me, Big Fella."

"I would pay good money to see you try." Hawke pulled twenty dollars out of his pocket and waved it in the younger man's face.

"And I would pay for you both to shut the hell up," Lea said. "Ryan, what's the damned translation?"

"It's cryptic, I'm afraid. It reads *Beneath the Highest City, Where The Samian's Sacred Work Shall Guide*."

"Oh, that is just bloody fantastic," Hawke said. "More word games."

"And it gets worse. It seems to me that the way this sentence was phrased and inscribed, it's only a fragment of the original inscription."

"How do you mean?"

"I think this fragment is only half of what should be some kind of golden disc – maybe even some kind of technical machinery, so somewhere is the other half, and on that half is the second part of this inscription."

Hawke took a deep breath and walked to the window. He felt the vodka burning its way through him. He watched the traffic trundling along the street, stopping at red lights and moving off again when they turned green. A light flurry of snow blew down the street and dusted the sidewalks with a fine white powder. "I thought you said the word acropolis was on it?" he asked Ryan, thinking about the translation he had just read out.

"It is, acropolis means highest city."

"I'll let you off," Hawke said, irritated he had let Ryan humiliate him in front of Lea. "Tell me - what did you mean, exactly, when you were talking about out-of-place artifacts?"

Ryan spun around and rubbed his hands together, clearly enjoying the research. Hawke didn't imagine squatting in an abandoned paint factory, hacking computers for a living was much fun. "Many strange objects have been found that don't belong – like this which was blown out of the side of a hill with some dynamite. Wait a sec..." He looked at the MacBook again. "Here it is - Meeting Horse Hill in Massachusetts. They discovered a metallic vase in the earth there in 1951."

Hawke sat forward. "You're telling me these things are actually real?"

"Some say so. Check this out." He clicked his way to another page. "This is called the Dorchester Pot, it's the classic out-of-place artifact."

"What is it?"

"A sort of bell-shaped, metal vase." Ryan began to read the information on the screen to Hawke and Lea. "According to this, it was extracted from the Roxbury Conglomerate, a form of puddingstone rock formation nearly six hundred million years old and it was recovered in two pieces, both of which now sit, again according to this, in an alarmed glass museum case in Zaugg's library. Mainstream academics dismissed the pot finding as a Victorian hoax, but maybe Zaugg knew better."

"Why am I only just hearing about this?"

"Some will tell you that these discoveries are

suppressed by the governments via their puppets and proxies in the academic community. They consider such knowledge would be highly detrimental to the public. If you ask me, I would say it's because no one gives a shit."

Hawke smiled. Maybe he could warm to Ryan after all. "And Zaugg?"

"He's obviously a believer, but for his own reasons."

"And he has this evidence, you say?"

"Yes. Beside the Dorchester Pot he also has other precious discoveries that he either made or bought, including the Kingoodie Hammer, a corroded manmade iron nail found embedded in Devonian sandstone four hundred million years ago, a Norwegian silver penny from the reign of Olaf Kyrre in the 11th Century, discovered at an old Native American settlement in New Hampshire, and his prized possession – the Antikythera Mechanism."

"Sounds dangerous."

"Only in terms of its sheer existence. It's an ancient analog computer designed and built to make accurate astrological predictions such as eclipses. The mechanism was dated to at least one thousand years before clock mechanisms were known to have been built, and many people, including presumably Hugo Zaugg are convinced it was made not by man, but by a higher intelligence, perhaps even the ancient gods themselves. Zaugg paid the National Archaeological Museum of Athens a massive sum of money for it and it took pride of place in his collection – until now."

"Now?"

"I mean now the way is clear to obtaining the vault of Poseidon, Joe. If it was found to exist then it would prove our understanding of time was all wrong – that our interpretation of history was totally wrong – and then all the out-of-place artifacts around the world would assume a new legitimacy."

"I don't recall saying you could call me Joe."

"Er, sorry, I..."

"I'm just kidding, Rupert. Relax. Zaugg can't be the first person to look for this?"

"He isn't – I've been reading about it. Many people have tried to find it throughout history, including an attempt in 1887 by a Turkish archaeologist named Mustafa Özal, and another one in 1911 by a team of Russian treasure hunters in the Aegean."

"Interesting."

"They claim to have found conclusive evidence of it and given it to the Czar but after the revolution in 1917 it was seized by the Bolsheviks and moved to the State Hermitage in St. Petersburg. That turned out to be a hoax."

"I can hardly believe any of this." Hawke thought he maybe needed another vodka.

"The third attempt was in 1925 by a Greek shepherd who became very rich indeed when he successfully sold what he claimed were relics from the tomb to a private collector in Athens, but that turned out to be yet another hoax."

Hawke shook his head in disbelief.

"The fourth attempt was after the war in 1946. It was made by Bernard Decaux, a French amateur collector. He was very rich and no one knows what happened there – he disappeared."

"I don't like the sound of any of this," Lea said. "What happened to this Decaux character?"

"The last place he was seen was in Marseille in the south of France. He disappeared off the face of the earth in 1948. The final attempt – until Eden's effort this year – was an excavation funded by J. Paul Getty in the

1950s. Again, no one knows if he really discovered anything or not."

"And they were all searching for the lost tomb of Poseidon," Hawke said, his mind slowly coming to accept the idea. "So these vases – what's the deal?"

Ryan sighed. "From what I can tell, the Poseidon and Amphitrite vases are just regular works of pottery from the fourth century BC, and so is this inscribed golden arc that now we know must have been a disc which was broken into two halves and hidden in them."

"But the vault of Poseidon is much older?"

"It must be. Poseidon was a god, and that would predate history as we know it. If we can work out the meaning of the inscription hidden in the vases by the Vienna Painter they could lead the way to the greatest treasure on Earth, something far older than even Hellenistic Greece."

"And this ultimate power I keep hearing so much about?"

Ryan shrugged his shoulders. "Got to be the trident, an awesome doomsday weapon by all accounts – one of the most powerful ever wielded by any deity."

Hawke took a deep breath. "And what does it do, exactly?"

"Oh, just the usual fire and brimstone stuff – earthquakes and tsunamis on an unprecedented scale. When Poseidon was insulted by the people he would strike the ground with it and cause terrifying earthquakes. He could flood any land, cause oceans to swell and smash ships but worst of all were the tsunamis."

Lea frowned. "I don't like where this is going, Ryan."

"Poseidon used the trident to create massive tsunamis that raced across oceans and decimated entire coastlines."

Hawke frowned. "I begin to see why Hugo Zaugg is

so keen to find the tomb if it's got that bloody thing in it."

"Not to mention the gold."

"Gold?"

"Naturally, any tomb like that would contain almost unbelieveable amounts of gold, both that collected by Poseidon himself and also the massive amounts given to him in tribute over the years."

"This just gets better."

Lea's mobile phone rang. She took it into the bathroom, pausing in the door to say: "It's Sir Richard."

Moments later she returned.

"What's the news?" Hawke asked.

"He's pleased we got the gold fragment," she said. "And he says we need to meet him at once."

"Back in London?"

"No, he wants to meet in Geneva. He says he has a lead for us there, and he wants us to talk to someone. He sounded worried."

Hawke was considering these words when they heard screams outside their room and men trampling along the corridor. He reached for a weapon but before he got his hands on it the door was smashed open and officers from the NYPD rushed into the room.

"And we were having it so easy," Lea said.

CHAPTER ELEVEN

They were sitting in a drab holding room somewhere in the undercover CIA station in Manhattan. Hawke had been in places like this before, and maybe Lea too, but he was sure this was Ryan's first experience.

A tall man with a square head, bright blue eyes and the mother of all five o'clock shadows closed the door on his way in and fronted up to them with total confidence. This was his space and his time, he was saying, and you'd better not mess me about.

"Doesn't look like he suffers fools gladly," Ryan whispered.

Hawke coughed. "That's you out of luck then."

The man introduced himself as Agent Edward Kosinski, and spent a long time going through a manila folder on the desk in front of them. He was making them stew, Hawke thought, reading histories, raking over any old dirt the agency could wrap its long arms around.

"So you think you're smart, huh?" said Kosinski finally. He closed the file, sniffed hard and stared at Hawke, right in the eyes. "You think you just fly into my country and start shooting the place up and exploding things?"

"You have your own country?" Hawke said.

"Answer the question, smart-ass."

"It was self-defense," said Hawke, taking a long look back at his interrogator. "Besides, they were Swiss – and honestly, how much do any of us really know about the Swiss?"

Kosinski was undeterred. "Why are you in America?" he asked firmly.

"I love surfing."

Ryan chuckled but was brought back to reality by a sharp look from the much older Kosinski.

"Seriously, Mr Hawke, this is a big deal. I could charge you with about a hundred terrorism-related offenses and you wouldn't see the light of day until the next millenium."

"Do you think CIA agents will have evolved personalities by then?"

Kosinski ignored him. Hawke was sure if this turned into a battle of wits the CIA man would lose. Hawke had been interrogated before, and in far less savoury circumstances than this. He doubted the CIA would be resorting to waterboarding and electrodes in their case.

Kosinski continued. "You will answer my questions sooner or later, I assure you. In fact I have one particular question I'm very serious about getting an answer to."

"I'm flattered, really I am," Hawke said with a smirk, "but after my wife died I promised myself I'd never marry again."

Kosinski sighed and shook his head. He looked more weary than disappointed. Clearly he had been around this block just as many times as Hawke. "You really want to play it this way?"

"What way?"

"Listen – it doesn't have to be this complicated. I ask a few simple questions and you answer them, and then maybe we can smooth all this out. What do you want here in America?"

"Some black coffee and a doughnut would be wonderful, thanks for asking."

"All right, we're done."

Kosinski turned to Ryan Bale. He looked like he

would be easier to crack than a monkey nut.

"You're in a shit load of trouble, young man," he said. "You all are."

"Whatever," Ryan said. He was trying to sound defiant in front of Hawke and Lea but his wobbling voice broke the illusion.

"You guys are going to get broken up and taken to separate rooms. I'll keep you up all night until I get some answers."

"I know my rights," Ryan said flatly.

"Yeah, sure you do."

"What does that mean?"

"Your rights are malleable, let's just put it that way. Besides, you're not even American. What do you know about our rights?"

The young Londoner pushed his curly fringe out from his dark eyes and shifted confidently in the little plastic chair. "We could start with the fact you've already breached my sixth amendment right to be informed of the nature and cause of the accusation," he began, quoting the sixth word for word.

Kosinski raised his eyebrows. "So you've studied the Constitution – big deal."

"I read it once when I was bored at a bus stop. That was ten years ago."

"You read it once a decade ago and you can quote it verbatim?"

"Let's just say I remember things."

Kosinski studied the young man silently for a few moments before speaking. "Sure, fine. The accusation is that you are involved in a terrorist activity."

"How absurd. I should just plead the fifth and demand a lawyer."

Kosinski sighed. The young man wasn't playing ball in the way he'd hoped. Hawke noticed this was the second time he had glanced at his watch. Maybe he had a dinner date.

"What about you?" Kosinski said, turning to Lea. "I know you're here to make trouble," he said. "I can smell these things." He tapped the side of his broad nose. "I have a sixth sense for these things. Maybe you could fill in some of the blanks?"

"I don't know anything."

"Why are you in the US, Miss Donovan?"

"I'm on holiday."

"I ran a check on your passport with the Irish Embassy. I see you were an officer in the Irish Army for several years."

"So what?"

"So maybe there's a terrorist link in here somewhere."

Lea laughed. "Don't be ridiculous. You're not getting the Irish Army and the Irish *Republican* Army confused are you, you silly man?"

"I'm aware of the difference, thanks. Just tell me why you were shooting up Manhattan Island and maybe we can speed this along. Seems to me something's up, and I want to know about it."

"I have a right to silence you know!"

"Oh, not another one! You're just like these two. Can't you see how much shit you're in?"

Kosinski stared at her long and hard for a moment, wondering how to make her speak.

Then a middle-aged women with short, brown hair opened the door and gestured for Kosinski to talk to her. He rose from his chair and stepped out to the corridor.

"What is it?" he said as he closed the door gently behind him.

"Phone call."

Kosinski left the room for a few moments and

returned with a different expression on his face.

"I just had a very interesting conversation with my boss about you all. He had a very interesting conversation about you all with *his* boss. And you know what just happened to *his* boss's boss?"

Hawke, Lea and Ryan said nothing.

"His boss's boss just had an interesting chat with *his* boss – are you following me?"

Hawke frowned. "You lost me somewhere around the third boss."

"Let me help you with that, the third boss is the Deputy Director of the CIA."

"Ah, so quite bossy then?"

Kosinski smiled coldly. "He tells me that the British Government has instructed us to release you on national security grounds. Something about grave consequences for humanity. Ring any bells?"

Hawke studied Kosinski's face. He was trained in neurolinguistic programming and knew how to read tells that might give away when someone was lying. A good way of telling, though not always accurate, was the direction the eyes looked in when a person was speaking.

As you faced the person you were talking with, if they looked to the right it meant they were remembering actual memories, things that happened, things they once said or heard or saw. If they looked to the left it meant they were constructing things – lying, in other words. Right now, Kosinski was looking to the right – telling the truth.

"A man's got to do what a man's got to do," Hawke said. "And it sounds like you've got to take these handcuffs off, mate."

Scowling, Kosinski had no option but to agree.

"You haven't heard the last of this," Kosinski said. "I know you're up to something big and I'm going to start poking around."

"Please, Eddie, not in front of the lady."

"We're not done, Hawke – not by a long shot. I have reach."

"And we have a flight to catch."

CHAPTER TWELVE

Geneva

Their arrival at the Richemond hotel was met by Sir Richard Eden himself, who had flown into Geneva an hour earlier. Switzerland felt small and claustrophobic after the United States, but they were glad to have some time to regroup.

They took the elevator to the top floor and followed Eden to his room. Hawke noticed that the Member of Parliament's door was guarded by more security than he would expect, and was immediately suspicious.

"What's with the goons, Richard?" he asked.

The two men with ear-pieces turned to look at Hawke with sour expressions on their faces, and took a step towards him before being ushered away by Eden.

"Inside, now."

Hawke, Lea and Ryan followed Sir Richard Eden into the room where another two armed guards were standing in the hall area. They parted to reveal a man Hawke recognized immediately as the British Foreign Secretary. He stepped towards them.

"I'm James Matheson," he said, shaking their hands.

"My name's Joe Hawke, and this is..."

Eden stepped up. "The Foreign Secretary doesn't meet people in hotel rooms unless they've been fully vetted," he said. "He knows who you all are."

Ryan suddenly looked nervous.

"Don't worry, Mr Bale," Eden said, frowning.

"We're not interested in your creative tax situation."

"Please," Matheson said. "Do sit down, all of you. We have tea."

Hawke watched one of guards lay a tray laden with tea cups on the table in front of them and begin to pour. The steam rose up into the air. For a moment in the heavy silence, the only sound was the reassuring chink of silver teaspoons against expensive china. Matheson glanced at Hawke and seemed anxious.

"I haven't the time to beat around the bush," Matheson said. "I've been apprised of the situation by Sir Richard here, and we've taken steps to ensure Hugo Zaugg desists in his attempts to locate the vault of Poseidon and take control of its contents."

Blunt and to the point, Hawke thought. He sipped his tea and wished it was a whisky. The moment seemed to call for something stronger than Earl Gray. Not too long ago he had been running parkour and looking forward to a new job and a fresh start, but now he was having tea with the British Foreign Secretary and talking about Top Secret threats to international security.

"What's your take on the situation, Hawke?"

"It's obvious this Zaugg character has serious reach, sir," Hawke told Matheson. "And you're frightened of him."

"What makes you say that?"

Hawke jabbed his thumb over his shoulder at the view of Lake Geneva. "Don't think it's gone unnoticed that you've put the three of us against the window while you sit further inside the room, Mr Matheson. You're afraid of snipers out on the water."

"Standard safety protocol," said one of the guards flatly.

"Yeah, sure. Listen, you obviously need us or we wouldn't be here, so get on with it."

Matheson raised an eyebrow. "I'm not going to lie to you – we know we need some help on this. There are agencies inside the government who are not convinced Zaugg is a genuine threat, and so it's going to come down to smaller units to handle the problem. Also HMG is not all that keen on this spilling out into the press."

Hawke sniffed. "Her Majesty's Government isn't that keen on lots of things."

"Listen, we're prepared to give you carte blanche to rein Zaugg in, and we can provide some extra assistance if you need it, but you'll need to work under the radar."

"I'm not sure..."

Eden spoke up. "Come on, Hawke. I've read your file and I know you're more than capable. Your commando work in the marines and SBS is first class. You really should have been decorated."

"I was, but I turned it down."

Eden looked confused, and opened Hawke's file a second time. "There's nothing in here about that..."

"There wouldn't be, and no – I don't want to talk about it."

Matheson shifted in his seat and cleared his throat. "Perhaps this is a discussion for another time? Right now we need to talk about Zaugg. I've spoken with some friends at the UN and also Interpol, and amongst us there is consensus that Zaugg is a threat and that he must be stopped. That is where you come in."

Hawke fixed eyes on Matheson: "Go on."

"We have some good news. We've had some intelligence from a reliable contact in Berne that Heinrich Baumann is the man who tortured Professor Fleetwood, but he sent Kaspar Vetsch to kill her when she escaped and tried to tell Sir Richard here of their plans."

Eden slipped a new black and white photo of Vetsch

across the table.

"That's the man who tried to kill us in New York," Ryan said. "I'd remember that face anywhere."

"This is a new picture, taken in here in Geneva less than three hours ago."

"He's in Switzerland?"

Eden nodded sternly. "We can only presume that he was recalled by his handler, Baumann, after his failure to retrieve the golden arc from the Met in Manhattan. I doubt Zaugg would be involved at such a low level."

"Where was this picture taken?" Hawke asked.

"Outside the airport here in Geneva."

"You think he's the type to talk?" Lea said.

"I do wonder if he might be, yes."

"But you're not sure?"

"You have to remember Kaspar Vetsch is not only a hitman, but also a complete sadist. Zaugg employs him to get information from nuts that are tough to crack. Whether or not a man like that is more or less susceptible to persuasion, as it were, only time will tell."

"What do we want to get out of him?" Ryan asked, causing much eye-rolling around the room.

"We need information to lead us either to Baumann or directly to Zaugg if possible. Vetsch could be our way into that particular cesspit."

Matheson cleared his throat again. He seemed anxious. "I can give you some assistance with this operation," he said calmly, "but it's all hush-hush, and if your cover's blown we never knew you, understand? HMG cannot be seen to be working against a man like Zaugg in this way. He might be a recluse, but he's also a high-ranking Swiss citizen with considerable influence in the government here. I'm sure you understand. The situation is delicate."

"That's *very* nice," Hawke said.

"I'm sorry?" Matheson said sharply.

"Get us to do your dirty work and if we get into trouble pull up the drawbridge."

"We got you out of New York, didn't we?" he replied coolly. "And that wasn't easy. You brought half of Manhattan to a standstill. The CIA were fuming."

"I'm just along for the ride." Hawke leaned back in his chair and put his hands behind his head. "This is really between Sir Richard and Herr Zaugg as far as I can tell."

"Well, on that you are quite wrong," Eden said. "The British Government might not formally recognize the threat to national security if Zaugg gets into Poseidon's tomb, but I certainly do, and so does the Foreign Secretary as well. So this is not some personal vendetta between Zaugg and me."

The English politician was clearly fired up by it all, but at the same time Hawke felt in the way he spoke the same reluctance that he sensed in Lea. There was something in their manner that made him feel as if they were keeping something from him – something big, and something he should know.

"So where is Vetsch right now?" Hawke asked.

"We don't know, but we do know the address of this man, Didier Martin." Eden slid another black and white photo across the table."

"Who is he?" Hawke asked. "He looks like a slug."

"Middle-ranking underworld figure who's made a lot of money selling drugs and so on. He supplies Vetsch with cocaine and is known to sell heroin as well. He should be a reliable lead to Vetsch."

"Where do we find this Martin?" Hawke asked.

"In the Old Town," Eden replied, turning to Lea. "The apartment is in the Place du Bourg-de-Four, a very upmarket area, so please refrain from blasting it to pieces when you get there."

Hawke smiled. "Who, us?"

"I mean it. I want this kept clean and sharp, all right? Here is the address, so get in and get out, preferably with both Didier Martin and Kaspar Vetsch alive and kicking into the bargain. They're no use to us dead, are they now?" As he said this he frowned and fixed his eyes on Hawke.

"Sounds like a plan."

"And there's something else," Eden said. "I think you're going to need more help, so I've organized a little assistance. She's former military, but SAS, not SBS."

"No one's perfect" Hawke said, smiling.

"But now's she MI5, so play nice," Eden added, smiling back.

"Where is she?"

"You're meeting her in an hour at the Grand Hotel Kempinski. She happens to be an old friend of yours."

*

Hawke stepped off the tram and emerged into a cold, overcast Geneva afternoon. An easterly breeze was blowing off the lake and cutting through the city like razors. Most people were obscured behind scarves or umbrellas.

He unfolded the piece of paper Eden had given him. Its message was simple: "Hotel Grand Kempinski. Midday. Cairo." He knew only too well what the last word meant, and it wasn't the Egyptian city. That one word had brought deep memories about his past flooding back.

The Hotel Grand Kempinski was less than two hundred yards from the tram stop, and he could see the traffic backed up along the Rue Philippe-Plantamour as he walked through to the Quai du Mont Blanc entrance. The aroma of fresh coffee and chocolate drifted over to him as he passed a small café.

He slowed to a casual walk as he cut through a line of taxis and briskly stepped up the polished steps of the east entrance of the hotel, flanked on either side by expensively manicured bay trees in art deco pots.

Inside he took the elevator to the famous rooftop restaurant bar, where he immediately saw Scarlet Sloane sitting on her own along the far edge. The Geneva skyline sprawled behind her, and he could see the mountains rise up into the bitter winter sky above the city to the west.

"Bonjour, Joe," she said, sliding a glass flute across the table. "It's their signature drink – white rum, Champagne, fresh grapes, cinnamon and vanilla. They call it the Marjad."

"It's a little early in the day for cocktails, don't you think?"

"That rather depends on what timezone your body's in," she said, smiling.

Hawke sat down and looked at her. She had aged a little, but on reflection not as much as he had. Her hair used to be red, and looked better that way – and it was longer once, but now it was short and blonde and had a vague military quality he wasn't sure he liked, which was ironic. He watched in silence as she pulled a menthol cigarette out of a silver case and lit it up, blowing a cloud of blue smoke into the cold air.

"What's this all about, Joe?" she asked.

"I've been sent here by Sir Richard Eden. I believe you know him, Cairo?"

"Cairo! I haven't heard *that* one in a long time."

"That's because we haven't spoken in a long time."

"No. Richard told me you were on the market looking

for trouble and asked me to meet you here. Being seen with you in public could put quite a dent in my image."

"Are you armed?" he asked.

"*Naturellement*."

Hawke drummed his fingers on the edge of the table for a moment, but stopped when he realized it was sending the wrong signal to her – nerves. He wasn't sure how to handle her. That was the sorry truth.

"So you work for Five now?" he asked.

She nodded.

"What happened to the SAS? Was it too boring for you?"

Just another smile. Only the mouth, not the eyes. "Humor never was your strong suit."

"How do you know Sir Richard Eden?" Hawke asked.

"Richard and I go back a long way, and the rest is none of your business."

"Why am I here, Cairo?" he asked. "Eden's keeping something from me, isn't he?"

He felt her shoe sliding up the inside of his lower leg, and he moved it away before it got too comfortable there.

"Don't you like it?" she asked.

"It took me the whole journey to remember who you were," he lied.

The woman frowned. "I'd hoped I'd left a greater impression on you than that."

"It's been a long time since Helmand."

"So you do remember. Tell me, did you ever marry, Joe?"

"Yes."

"And how is the little *darling*? At home knitting tiny booties for your three perfect children?"

"She's dead."

"Oh... I'm sorry to hear that. Truly. How?"

"That's not important right now, Cairo."

"There's that silly nickname again." She breathed a cloud of cigarette smoke into the air between them.

"Will you help me or not? Eden says you will."

"Eden doesn't tell me what to do. No one does." She got up to go.

"Please, Cairo – all he said was you're available for work."

Scarlet Sloane sat back down, graceful as a cat. He could hardly believe she was the same person he had almost fallen in love with all those years ago. Back then she was another woman. Now she seemed somehow different – embittered, angry, emotionless – working for the highest bidder, who this time happened to be Sir Richard Eden.

"What happened to you, Cairo?" He wasn't looking at her now, but staring at the floor. He was thinking about the damage the past does to the present.

"If I told you that it would keep you up at night, Joe. It's better you get your beauty sleep – you need it."

He raised his eyes to see her staring absent-mindedly across the Geneva skyline. The sky darkened with the threat of rain. A waiter dropped a plate and some cutlery and knocked her from her daydream. She focused on the man's behind as he picked up the knives and forks, and she grinned like a Cheshire cat.

Hawke smirked. "Same old, same old."

Scarlet simply shrugged her shoulders, closed her eyes for a moment and made a long, satisfied sigh.

She got up from the table and gently stubbed her cigarette out in the little ashtray. She turned and glanced over the rooftops. It was beginning to rain a little.

"I'll let you work with me on this," she said.

"I think you mean *I* will let *you* work with *me* on this."

"You wouldn't want to work against me, Joe."

“Why’s that?”

“You’re at such a disadvantage, darling.”

“How so?”

“You’re just a man.”

She leaned forward and kissed him gently on the temple, rubbing her hand slowly up the back of his head as she did it. Blood-red fingernail polish, expensive perfume.

“So you’re on board?” he asked, undeterred.

“I am, yes. But the question is – are *you* up for this?”

“What do you mean?”

“I mean, aren’t you a little over the hill? Perhaps you’d prefer to go home and relax. Get some of that aggression out on Call of Duty or something.”

“I’ll take that as a challenge,” he said, as she walked slowly away from their table. “You’re working for me,” he shouted after her. “Not the other way around, Cairo.”

She didn't turn back, but simply called over her shoulder: “No one calls me that anymore, Joe.”

“I do.”

“Are you coming or not?” she said.

Hawke smiled and got up from the table.

CHAPTER THIRTEEN

"Call me old-fashioned," Hawke said. "But my idea of a good night out is not sitting in a stationary Citroën, freezing my knackers off while waiting for a drug-dealing scrote to come home."

He was sitting outside Martin's apartment in the maze of winding streets that was Geneva's Old Town. They were parked outside an expensive café lit up bright orange in the wintry darkness, and a light snow was falling but not laying.

The apartment, just across a medieval square, was now and for the last few hours under the constant surveillance of Eden's makeshift team. Hawke yawned and grabbed a handful of peanuts. In the front, beside him, was Lea, while Ryan was in the back with Scarlet Sloane.

"As I recall," Scarlet said. "Your idea of a good night out used to be farting five pound notes into beer glasses in the sergeant's mess."

"Now that is simply not true," Hawke protested. "It was ten pound notes."

Lea rolled her eyes and shook her head in disgust.

Hawke was defiant. "It's not *true*. I was joking."

"You haven't changed, at least," said Scarlet.

Lea opened the file that Eden had given her back at the hotel. It was essentially the one Matheson had brought to the meeting but with several sections missing. Unlike Baumann, Vetsch was not former military, but just pure underworld scum with busts for everything from drug dealing to extortion to pimping.

How he had gotten out of prison for his last conviction was questionable, but most linked it to Zaugg's influence, running through Baumann. As for Didier Martin, he was simple pondlife and should crack like an Easter egg with the slightest application of pressure.

Scarlet finished her macchiato and tossed the paper cup out the window into a nearby trash bin.

"Good shot," Ryan said.

"I could hit you in the throat with a hunting rifle from half a mile away," she said flatly. "While you were jogging. That was not a good shot."

"Fair enough," Ryan replied, and sank back into his scarf. "Just trying to be nice."

"Cairo Sloane and nice?" Hawke scoffed. "Not so much."

"That's not what you thought back in Helmand that night."

Lea turned in her seat. "Oh yeah?"

"Forget it."

"I can't believe in a car full of ex Special Forces it takes me to point out that Martin has come back – look." Ryan pointed across the square where a man hunched into a dark raincoat was passing the marble medieval fountain. He spat into it, and looked over his shoulder before briskly jogging up the steps outside his apartment.

"Could be anyone, boy" Scarlet said dismissively.

"Hey, less of it, *grandma*."

"Grandma? I'm not even thirty."

Hawke nearly choked on a peanut. "Come off it, Cairo. Besides, he's right – the light to his apartment has just gone on."

"That's as maybe," Scarlet said, turning to Ryan and running her fingernails along his upper leg. "But you'd beg for it if you thought you had half a chance."

For once, Ryan was totally, completely speechless.

"And who's this, I wonder?" Hawke said.

A gold Lamborghini pulled up in the square outside Martin's apartment. The lights closed into the hood and the engine powered down. It was like watching a lioness go to sleep. The door opened and a man in a leather jacket stepped out, warming his hands with his breath.

"Vetsch!" said Lea.

"The very same," Hawke added, narrowing his eyes.

"You let a weasel like that chase you around New York?" Scarlet said.

"He had a team of Uzi-wielding maniacs," Ryan said.

"Basic training," said Scarlet. "Eden should have called me earlier."

Vetsch walked casually up the steps and moments later the two men were standing in Martin's apartment talking.

"Time to join the conversation," Scarlet said in her cut-glass Oxford accent. She pulled a small device out of her bag.

"What the hell is that?" Ryan asked.

"What the hell is what?" Hawke asked without taking his eyes off the apartment.

"Looks like a light sabre," said Ryan, clearly impressed.

Hawke heard Scarlet sigh. "It is *not* a light sabre, boy. It's a very high-quality laser microphone." She put on some headphones and opened her window, gently resting the mic on the sill to keep it steady.

Inside, Martin and Vetsch were now arguing about something.

"What are you getting, Cairo?"

"Sadly, not much – not unless you can speak whatever the hell they're speaking." She passed Hawke the headphones.

"It's Schweizerdeutsch," he said, passing the headphones back to her. "Swiss German."

"Sounds like a cross between Dutch and Klingon to me," Scarlet said. "I was hoping they might speak French. It's so much more sophisticated."

"That's your laser microphone in the jacks then," Lea said, smirking.

"I'm sorry?" Scarlet asked.

"Nothing."

"That's not really true about what happened in the sergeant's mess, is it?" Ryan asked, his face the picture of genuine concern.

Hawke smiled. "Why do you ask?"

"I just can't believe things get as bad as that in the army."

"Of course not," Hawke said reassuringly. "Things get much worse than that. And it was the marines, not the army."

"We wouldn't let a man like Hawke into the army," Scarlet said.

Hawke smiled. "Yeah, yeah. Let's not forget we've got a job to do."

Lea opened her door. "So let's do it. Ryan, stay here."

"Damn!" he said. "I was hoping to sneak into Martin's apartment and strangle him with his braces for information."

Lea glanced back at Ryan. "Very funny."

"But that's not how you get information out of a toerag like that," said Scarlet, opening her door.

"You too, Cairo. In the car." Hawke's tone was firm.

"Eh? Eden put me in here to fight, not babysit Ryan – no offence."

"None taken."

"We need a backup unit, and you're it. You know

how these things work."

"So put Miss Ireland in backup."

Lea scowled.

"In the car, Cairo. I mean it. Eden put me in charge and I want Lea up front with me. We've fought these guys before and we both know their moves."

Scarlet sloped back into the car, but this time in the driver's seat, and adjusted her black roll neck in the mirror. "If you say so, darling."

Hawke and Lea crossed the square and walked past two or three cafés and boutiques before reaching Martin's apartment. It was two storeys above a pharmacy which was closed for the night, the green glow of its sign reflecting in the melted snow outside in the street.

"We're opposite a police station." Hawke gestured over his shoulder.

"Great," Lea said. "Let's keep this quiet or it could get really out of hand."

"My thoughts exactly."

Hawke looked across the square where Scarlet and Ryan were sitting in the shadows of the side street in the Lexus. A fleeting doubt crossed his mind about whether or not he could really trust Cairo Sloane, but if Eden had vouched for her then he could live with it.

"You think Ryan will be okay back there?" Lea asked.

"Sure. Her bark is worse than her bite."

"I meant if anything kicks off with Vetsch, Joe."

"Oh sure – that too. She can look after him. Trust me when I tell you there's only one person in the world more ruthless than Cairo Sloane."

"And who would that be?"

"If you're nice to me I might tell you one day."

"What's his name?"

"Who said it was a man?"

They slowed up at the bottom of the apartment steps and rang the bell.

"Oui?"

"J'ai une pizza pour vous, monsieur," Hawke said.

Lea gave him an appreciative glance. "Not bad," she mouthed. Hawke nodded his head with exaggerated pride.

"Je n'en veux pas. Allez-vous en, maintenant." The reply was gruff and short.

Lea winced. "I'm guessing that's not polite."

Hawke thought again. "D'accord, j'ai besoin de la blanche, mec."

"What the hell does that mean?" Lea whispered.

"I think I asked him for heroin, but my accent is so bad he'll just think I'm a foreigner."

"Pas ici!" Then the door buzzed open.

Upstairs, it didn't take Vetsch long to recognize Hawke and Lea. He reached for his gun, but Lea had a Glock 17 in his face before he knew it.

"Forget about it, laddo, and hand the old shooting iron over before I blow your balls off."

Vetsch gave her his gun, a Colt 45.

"Now sit the fuck down." He did as he was told.

Hawke stepped forward and checked Martin for weapons, and after pulling a Heckler & Koch USP from a shoulder holster and a flick-knife from his rear pocket, told him to sit down next to Vetsch.

"You guys must be paranoid carrying all this junk around," Lea said. "And put your hands behind your heads."

"Baumann will gut you for this," Vetsch hissed in heavily accented English.

Hawke ignored him. "What do you know about Hugo Zaugg?" he asked.

The men gave each other an uncertain glance and

then looked at Hawke in terrified silence.

"Shoot that one in the knee," Hawke told Lea, pointing at Vetsch.

She stepped forward and cocked her gun for effect.

Vetsch was cool. "We both know I work for Baumann. No one gets close to Hugo Zaugg. Ever. I hear he was very upset about your activities in New York."

"What about Baumann?" Hawke said, ignoring his comment.

Vetsch's eyes crawled from Lea's Glock to Hawke's eyes. He grinned, his forehead starting to sweat. "Baumann has access to Zaugg, but that is all I know. Everything is compartmentalized."

"And where is Baumann?" Hawke asked.

"Herr Baumann is very hard to find."

"You mean he's wanted by every police force in Europe so he keeps a low profile." Lea said.

Vetsch shrugged his shoulders. He seemed to be re-evaulating the situation. "Baumann is not the sort of man you cross. He will kill me for telling you this."

Hawke moved closer. "I want to find Baumann."

"I will die first."

"Try that one," Hawke said, indicating Martin.

Lea pushed the Glock's muzzle into the top of his knee bone.

"Well, I won't die first!" Martin said, breathless with terror. "I can tell you how to find Baumann."

"Silence, you fool!" spat Vetsch.

"He can be found at..."

A second later and everything changed.

Vetsch moved like lightning, the hands behind his back pulling a knife from a shoulder holster and slashing at Lea's hand before spinning in his seat and cutting Martin's throat.

Lea recoiled instinctively to check the wound on her hand, dropping her gun. Martin slumped forward, eyes bulging with fear, and then collapsed on the wooden floor tiles where his blood spilled out in a large pool.

Vetsch picked up Lea's gun and sprinted into the kitchen, slamming the door behind him and wedging something behind it.

"Are you okay?" Hawke asked Lea.

"Yeah, sure. So stupid of me to drop that gun. I'm sorry, Joe – I guess I've been out the army for too long." Her hand was bleeding heavily.

"Forget it."

Hawke smashed in the kitchen door and saw the window was open. The drapes blew into the room with a gush of icy air. He went to the window and looked out. "A fire escape, but he's not in the street. He must have gone to the roof. You get to Cairo and get your hand fixed up, then follow me as best you can in the car."

"You're not going up there after him?"

"He's our only lead to Baumann and Zaugg!"

"If you're going, I'm going."

"With your hand like that?"

"Screw my hand!" she shouted, grabbing a towel from the side and wrapping it tightly around the wound. "I want my damned Glock back!"

They climbed up the fire escape to the next storey and clambered out onto the roof. It was below freezing now, and ice had begun to form on the tiles, making them slippery and their route across them dangerous and unpredictable.

Lea joined Hawke who was standing in between two tall chimneys and surveying the moonlit rooftops. His breath was visible in the cold night. Ahead, maybe two or three houses, Vetsch was crawling into the frozen darkness, his outline now a silhouette in front of the gentle glow of the city beyond.

"There's our man," he said.

"There's our *rat*, don't you mean?" Lea held to the bricks for balance in the rising wind.

"Let's get after him," said Hawke, setting out across the apex of the roof.

Lea followed, choosing her steps carefully as Vetsch's more desperate method widened the gap between them.

A blast of icy air rushed off the lake and cut into them. Hawke put his head down and tried to push on, but Lea slipped and fell backwards, her arms flailing helplessly in the cold night as her upper body tipped back over the edge of the roof. She screamed in terror.

Hawke spun around and grabbed her by the belt, pulling her roughly towards him and grabbing her around the waist with his other arm. His parkour had made him immune to the fear of heights and turned any urban environment into a playground for him, but he'd forgotten how any normal person would view running across rooftops in the middle of the night.

"Are you all right?" he asked, this time no jokes. Her face was lit silver in the moonlight.

She nodded, still pale with the fear of what had almost happened. A quick glance over her shoulder at the street below made her shudder as Hawke released her.

"Be more careful from now on, okay?"

Ahead, Vetsch was almost out of sight as he skipped fearlessly along a distant roofline, the ornate copper spire of St. Pierre's Cathedral rising behind him. For good measure, he turned and fired blindly at them, his bullets crackling away into the night.

"Damn it, Joe Hawke!" Lea said. "What the hell am I doing here? I could be at home, you know!"

"And miss all this? Where's your spirit of adventure, girl?"

They watched Vetsch descend on one of the fire escapes and hit the street. Hawke searched for the closest way down and caught sight of a much closer fire escape. It took them halfway to street level, where from his view on the lower roof he looked out across the streets of Geneva's Old Town and watched Vetsch sprinting into the night.

They jumped off the lower roof and gave chase.

Vetsch turned a corner and hit a busier road, with cars and mopeds moving slowly around the Old Town's ancient streets.

Hawke scanned the road in both directions. Which way did he go?

Then they saw him. He was running through a crowd of people gathered outside a café and trying to disappear into the cheerful throng. They gave chase once again.

Vetsch led them into a maze of backstreets. He turned and fired at them once more, warning them not to continue their pursuit, but Hawke felt differently about the matter, and so did Lea. Hawke returned fire, whacking a chunk of plaster out of a wall a few inches above Vetsch's head as he darted around a corner.

They raced after him, Hawke cursing himself for letting Vetsch get away, but using his anger to fuel the pursuit.

Around the corner, there was another small square ahead of them, centered around a small stone fountain behind which Vetsch vanished into an alley.

They followed into the darkness to find a dead end where there was only one door, but now closed. Hawke kicked the door hard and it burst open, hitting the inside wall with a loud smack. A staircase led to the next floor, and they could already hear Vetsch breaking his way through another door somewhere above them.

Hawke and Lea kept up their pursuit, and clambered up the stairs as fast as they could only to see Vetsch running through a cosy, well-lit front room of someone's apartment, screaming at them to keep away.

They followed him, apologizing to the confused and terrified occupants as they went. Vetsch exited the apartment, ran down the stairs and reached the next street.

"I want that little rat!" Lea screamed.

Hawke looked at her. She looked more determined than ever, and he cynically wondered if Lea was using this whole enterprise as a kind of path to personal redemption for whatever it was in her past that she was hiding. Whatever it was she had alluded to over dinner in New York, but then closed up again when he had gotten too close.

Outside, they watched as Vetsch dragged a man from his vehicle. He shot him twice in the head and climbed into his car, a silver Honda. A moment later he was zooming away into the night.

CHAPTER FOURTEEN

Hawke desperately searched for a vehicle as Kaspar Vetsch fled the street in the stolen Honda, its driver now lying dead in a pool of blood on the cold cobblestones.

"That'll be the easiest," he said, looking at a bright purple Renault Twingo.

He told Lea to keep watch while he took off one of the hubcaps and used it to smash the driver's window. Inside, he removed the vinyl guard under the steering column and located the wiring harness connector, a small coil of electrical wires.

"Faster, Joe. We're losing him."

"Oh thanks – I was planning on stopping for a tea break but since you mention it, I'll get on." Over his shoulder he heard her sigh.

He separated the little bundle which contained the battery, ignition and starter wires and used a piece of the smashed window glass to strip the insulation from the battery wires and twist the copper wiring together. This allowed electricity to flow to the ignition component so the engine would start when he turned the starter.

Then he connected the ignition and battery wires and watched as the dash lights all came on. Next he sparked the wires and the starter turned over. He revved the car gently for a few moments and then snapped the steering lock free with brute force.

"Ready for a drive?" he said, and winked.

"SBS training includes how to steal cars?" Lea asked.

"No, that little skill is courtesy of a misspent youth.

Now get in!"

"Something tells me I'm not going to like this," Lea said.

"Where's your spirit of adventure?" he asked.

"I think it flew away up on the rooftops."

"Nonsense. Buckle up," Hawke said. "But yeah, this could get rough."

Seatbelts on. First gear, and throttle down.

The Twingo lurched forward. Its 1.1 litre engine was cold and howled like a scolded cat as Hawke raced the small Renault along the narrow cobblestone backstreets of the Old Town. His eyes focused on the Honda in front, driven to its max by a desperate Kaspar Vetsch.

Then the Honda drove down a flight of broad stone steps leading into a medieval square. Hawke didn't hesitate, and piled the Twingo down the steps, the heavy impact of the descent rattling through the shock absorbers with terrific violence and reverberating inside the tiny cab.

Lea held on for her life, completely unable to take a shot with so much movement in the car. A brief respite as they raced across a cobblestone terrace before another set of steps caused Lea to fly up in the air and hit her head on the ceiling.

A string of exotic Dublin profanities filled the car and put a smile on Hawke's face, but it was only fleeting – the danger ahead of them loomed into his consciousness once again.

The Honda swerved violently, its right backside swinging out uncontrollably in the tiny square and almost plowing into a neat line of parked mopeds. But Vetsch regained control and accelerated into a side street, forcing people to jump to safety in a shop's doorway.

"Black ice," Hawke said, steering to avoid the same fate.

"I need to get a shot, Joe!" Lea said. "Could you at least try and get up close and calm things down a bit?"

"Please don't kill him – we need him alive!"

"Fine, I'll blow his tires. He must be getting used to that by now."

Vetsch careered around a streetlamp and accelerated into the Place du Molard, a broad pedestrianized area of elegant cafés where chairs and tables spill out onto the cobblestones during the day, but now the way was clearer, and Vetsch took advantage.

They followed the Honda into a wider street where Vetsch was skidding around to the right in a cloud of burned rubber smoke.

"We're going against the traffic, Joe!"

"Hold on!" Hawke shouted. Ahead, a tram was trundling towards them with its headlights on, its overhead contact system wobbling gently in the cold night as it moved along the street.

The Honda swerved to the left, mounting the sidewalk and smashing through a Vespa parked outside a Chanel store. A moped spun off to its right and struck the side of the tram in a blaze of sparks.

Hawke swerved left, narrowly avoiding a lethal impact with a large Jaguar and slipping out behind the tram to see Vetsch had gone left, still against the traffic and into a main thoroughfare.

The Swiss hitman mounted a traffic island opposite a taxi rank, smashing through a street sign before steering sharply to the right. He fired a volley of pistol fire through the passenger's window in a frantic attempt to slow the Twingo.

Hawke reacted in a second and swerved away from the bullets. Lea fired back, striking the Honda's right front wing and causing Vetsch to swerve into a line of Vespas, still firing, his bullets smashing the windows of another jewellery store.

"He's trying to get over the river." Lea pointed to the left where the Pont du Mont-Blanc stretched across the river Rhône, its streetlamps lighting up the Geneva night like a string of pearls.

Hawke pulled alongside Vetsch on the bridge and Lea fired a few shots from the Sig. Vetsch hit the brakes and dropped behind the Twingo, swerving in neatly behind it as he went and scraping the nose of the Honda against the Renault's rear fender for a few seconds before bringing the steering under control again.

He accelerated and rammed the back of the Twingo, which jolted violently forward with the impact from the much heavier vehicle behind it.

"That son of a bitch!" shouted Lea. She turned in her seat and fired the Sig through the back window, blowing the glass out and peppering the Honda's windshield with indiscriminate bullet holes.

Vetsch grimaced and swung the wheel hard to the left to avoid the volley of fire. Smirking, he then raised Lea's Glock over the steering wheel and let loose a long, rapid burst of fire, emptying the magazine into the back of the Twingo. One bullet got lucky and thudded into the plastic dashboard. Another got even luckier and blew the stuffing out of Hawke's headrest, narrowly missing him by centimeters.

The abrupt change in circumstances with Vetch switching from hunted to hunter had put Hawke at a disadvantage and he knew it. He also knew what to do about it.

"Hold on, Lea!" he shouted. "We're going for a spin."

He swung the steering wheel to the left full-lock and applied the hand-brake, bringing the Twingo to a terrifying and shuddering stop and spinning it violently to the left.

Vetsch could barely react in time, and the Honda nearly went into the back of them, but missed the impact when Hawke performed a speedy handbrake-turn with an impressive squeal of the tires. A great cloud of rubber smoke rose behind them on the bridge.

The Honda shot past them again, and Hawke brought the Renault three-sixty before slamming down on the throttle and taking the pursuit back up.

"You bloody maniac, Joe Hawke!" Lea was white with terror as she clasped the Sig in one hand and the door handle with the other, her knuckles white with the strength of the grip.

"Yeah – sorry about that," said Hawke. "Not done anything like that since we burned that doughnut on the local cricket pitch when I was a teenager."

"Literally unbelievable."

"Thanks."

"It wasn't a compliment."

Then, in the rear-view, he saw the first of the blue flashing lights and the familiar two-tone whine of the Swiss police as they pulled up behind him in a powerful Volkswagen Passat.

"Great, *les flics*," he said, jabbing his thumb behind his shoulder. He glanced at Lea as she turned in her seat to look at the cops, her face lit intermittently by the flashing blue of their lights. Even in the middle of all this he noticed there was something haunting her eyes that hinted of a long-ago tragedy.

Then more gunshots. Vetsch was firing blind over his shoulder as he raced through the night. A split second later the Twingo's windshield was covered in bullet holes, then it smashed completely and Hawke could see nothing.

"Kick it out!" he said.

Lea leaned back in her seat, raised her legs and kicked at the reinforced glass with everything she had, and four or five kicks later the shattered windshield flopped out of its frame and spun off to the right of the car, hitting the white metal fence at the side of the bridge and dropping into the freezing river below.

A rush of icy air hit their faces as they accelerated towards Vetsch, the annoying *nee-naw* of the Swiss police sirens getting louder as the much more powerful Passat behind them made short work of the Twingo's weak acceleration.

Hawke floored the throttle and the small car's runaround engine labored in response but the Honda was still getting way. Back on busier streets Vetsch had no advantage, but on the straight of the bridge the bigger engine was leaving them behind – with the police closing on them fast.

But now the bridge was coming to a close and Vetsch zoomed off the end, cutting in front of a bus outside the Four Seasons, and leaving Hawke and Lea far behind him.

By the time the bus had moved along and cleared the road, the Honda was halfway up a narrow road lined with boutique restaurants running parallel to the river.

"He's getting away, Joe!"

"Not if I have anything to do with it."

In the rear-view Hawke saw the police car get clipped by the front of the bus. It spun around in a circle several times before sliding down the riverbank.

"That's the rozzers out of the way," he said.

Ahead, Vetsch had met with similar misfortune and failed to avoid a large Kronenbourg truck which had turned the corner too fast and without warning.

Vetsch swerved to avoid it but his speed left no time to navigate a safe passage between the truck and a concrete lane divider, which he struck with considerable force.

The Honda's rear spun to the left and the car tipped on its side before coming to a steaming, smoking stop against an apartment block. Hawke pulled up a safe distance from it and they approached with caution.

The Honda's front wheels were still spinning by the time they reached the wreckage. Everything smelled of gasoline. Hawke leaned inside and saw at once that Kaspar Vetch was dead, hanging upside down in his seatbelt with a broken neck, eyes bulging in their sockets. His head lay on the deflating airbag like it was a pillow.

Hawke reached in and pulled out the Glock and Vetsch's phone. "His address will be in here," he said. "I'll give Cairo a call and let her know she's missed all the fun." He tossed the gun back to Lea, who caught it with ease and slipped it back inside her jacket.

"I told you I'd get my Glock back," she said.

CHAPTER FIFTEEN

Vetsch's apartment was a luxurious affair above a cyber café in Les Pâquis, a bohemian district on Geneva's right bank. Despite the cold and the hour, people milled about in the streets outside, laughing and joking. As Hawke and Lea climbed the apartment steps, a young couple stepped into an Italian restaurant opposite, kissing as they opened the door.

"Seems like too a nice place for such a scumbag," Lea said.

"All paid for by Zaugg, no doubt," said Hawke.

They opened the door with Vetsch's keys and took a quick look around – minimalist, clean lines, empty cupboards. On a glass coffee table was a copy of Plato's *Immortality of the Soul*. Lea picked it up.

"A little heavy for a man like Kaspar Vetsch, wouldn't you say?"

"De mortuis nil nisi bonum dicendum est," Hawke muttered under his breath.

Lea stepped into the back of the apartment, gun raised in defense, while Hawke began a search of the main living space. It was open-plan and had few hiding places. The search ended with a look through the kitchen cupboards.

"Anything back there?" he shouted.

"Maybe. You?"

"Nothing, Just instant coffee and some vodka – and a packet of old biscuits."

"Sounds like he was a real party animal," Lea said as

she walked back into the lounge. "I found this in his bedroom. Check it out."

She handed Hawke a manila folder three inches thick.

"What is it?" he asked, opening it.

"Looks like Vetsch's career. By the looks of the files inside I'd say it was a list of his hits."

Hawke looked through the folder. "This could be something," he said, passing a file back to Lea. It was a single sheet of paper with a black and white mugshot of a man in the top center. "All the others have a nice red line through their faces but not this guy – and check out his name."

Lea read the file. "Yannis Demetriou. Should I know him?"

"Look at his occupation." He pointed at some text at the bottom of the page.

Lea read on, her eyes widening. "Professor of Classical Antiquities at the National and Kapodistrian University of Athens. My God – this must be his next hit."

"I think so. And now Vetsch isn't around to do it I guess Zaugg will just hire someone else, maybe even this Baumann maniac. We have half the golden arc, but the other half is still in the National Archaeological Museum in Athens. Zaugg can't know that, because only we know that the Poseidon Vase contained only half the code."

"But he must know he needs a specialist like Demetriou to translate or he wouldn't have had Vetsch put him on his hit list. We have to get to him first, Joe. Heaven only knows what they'll do to him if they get their hands on him."

"You're right. We have to warn him. Get his number from the internet if you can."

Lea started searching on her iPhone.

There was a knock on the door and Scarlet walked into the room spinning the Lexus's keys on her finger. "Honey, I'm home," she said. "And I brought the kid, too."

"Who?" Ryan asked, looking over his shoulder. "Oh, very funny."

"Any news?" Scarlet asked, flopping into Vetsch's white leather sofa and quickly arranging her hair.

"You mean apart from Vetsch's tragic end on the banks of the Rhône?" Hawke asked.

"Of course."

"Just this," Lea handed Scarlet Vetsch's hitlist.

"Oh my goodness gracious me," Scarlet purred. "He *was* a naughty boy. He must have been one of the most active hitmen in Europe."

"Western Europe, actually," said a voice behind her.

They all spun around, guns raised.

Standing in the doorway was a young woman, standing alone, her hands raised in anticipation of their defensive reaction. She had dark brown hair, and was in her mid-twenties, tall and confident. Her eyes were intelligent and keen, but a weariness in them told Hawke she'd been around the block a few times.

"Who are you?" Hawke asked, Sig pointed squarely in her face, unwavering.

"My name is Sophie Durand," she said. "I'm with the DGSE."

"And who are they when they're at home?" Ryan asked, looking up from his MacBook.

"The DGSE," explained Hawke, "is the Direction générale de la sécurité extérieure, or, in English, the General Directorate for External Security. It's the French equivalent of MI6 or CIA."

"Oh, French secret service" Ryan said, going back to his computer. "What's she doing here?"

"She wanted to check out Kaspar Vetsch's interior design and ask him a few tips," Scarlet said. "What do you think she wants here?"

"And you've been following us since when?" Lea asked.

"Since your little escapade all over Genève," she replied. "The Swiss are watching you too."

"But they don't know you're here?" Hawke said.

Sophie shook her head. "Of course not. I am very good at what I do."

"We're going to need some ID here," Lea said.

Sophie opened her jacket so they could see the inside and slowly pulled out a thin black wallet. She held it forward and Scarlet casually took it and flipped it open. "In the old days this would have been enough," she said, passing it to Hawke. "But these days..."

"Cairo's right. Lea, take her picture and email it to the boss."

Lea snapped a picture of her face and moments later a text came back from Sir Richard Eden.

"He says she's legit," she said.

They lowered their weapons and Hawke patted her down. In her shoulder holster he found a nine millimeter semi-automatic PAMAS G1s.

"Anything else?" Lea asked.

"Just a Beretta." Hawke pulled it out of the holster and took a step back. "You can have this back when I trust you, and that's going to take some time. You can start by telling us everything you know and why you're here, exactly."

Sophie sank into the sofa opposite Scarlet, who then kicked Ryan's leg.

"Eh – what was that for?"

"Coffee, boy," Scarlet said, flicking her head at the kitchen.

"I'm not your coffee bitch, you know," he said.

"Sorry," she said, "but you really are."

"Just get some freaking coffee, would you, Ryan?" Lea said.

"And try and find some of those little French madeleine biscuits," Hawke said. "I like those."

Ryan flounced up from the MacBook and stormed into the kitchen, muttering to himself. He made no secret of his displeasure by slamming cupboard doors and cursing as he prepared the coffee.

Across the room, Sophie sat in the low light and started to talk.

"Paris knows Hugo Zaugg is up to something, but we also know how limited our understanding of him and his plans are. I have been cleared to make contact with you and ask if we can work together. My government has grave concerns about why Zaugg is so keen on finding the vault of Poseidon..."

Hawke and Lea shared a look at the mention of the Greek god. How much did other governments know about this? What were they keeping secret from the public?

"...and more particularly about what he might find inside it. And so when we detected your chatter – the buzzwords you used – I was put on your tail and so here I am. That is my story. What about yours?"

The others looked at each other for a moment. Hawke shrugged his shoulders and sighed. "Here," he said, handing her the folder. "As if my day could get any weirder than living Greek gods and trident superweapons. Knock yourself out."

"What is it?" she asked.

Hawke said: "It's a folder containing the hitlist of Kaspar Vetsch. You obviously know him from what you said when you made your introduction."

"Somewhat *melodramatic* introduction as well," Scarlet sighed, raising an eyebrow.

"Of course we know Vestch. All the security services know him, and Baumann too. They are both thugs, but Baumann is more strategic shall we say, and Vetsch was more tactical."

"In that folder is a list of all his hits, or what we presume to be his hits as they're all crossed through with red pen."

"This is true," Sophie said, pointing at one of the files. "This man is Bernard Dupont, a big hitter in the Marseille underworld – crack cocaine, prostitution – you name it. Last week he was found dead in his apartment, shot through the heart."

Hawke frowned. "Sounds like Vetsch. If you look at the back you'll see a file with a picture that hasn't been crossed out yet. His name is Yannis Demetriou and he works in Athens as a professor of classical antiquities. We think he was Vetsch's next job."

Lea spoke next. "He was probably going to kidnap him and torture him for information relating to the tomb. They did the same thing with an English professor called Lucy Fleetwood. They shot her through the heart and killed her."

"He was an absolute pyscho," Ryan said, arriving at the table and giving everyone an unimpressed look as he handed them the coffee mugs.

"If you think he was a psycho, you need to stay away from Heinrich Baumann," Sophie said, sipping the hot coffee. She peered into the cup and frowned.

"Don't blame me," said Ryan. "It was all he had, and sorry, Joe – but no madeleines. I did find a packet of macaroons, so you can try your luck on those. They're six months out of date."

"It's tempting, but no thanks."

"I'm going to have one," Ryan said, pulling the packet off the tray.

Hawke slurped his coffee. "Damn that's hot, Rupert."

"An inevitable consequence of having boiling water in it."

"Didn't you say the biscuits were six months old?" Hawke asked as he watched Ryan munching through one.

"That's nothing to him," Lea said. "You should see the fridge in his flat. They'll need to irradiate it before they dump it."

Ryan laughed. "It's not that bad, Lea."

"Nonsense – there's more culture in there than Geneva."

"You're so funny," said Ryan.

Hawke turned to Lea. "Any luck with Demetriou's address?"

"Not really, just his phone number at the university but it's too late for him to be at work now."

"We need to get our arses to Athens," Hawke said, finishing his coffee with a single gulp and setting the cup down on the table with a hefty smack. "We know the vase with the second half of the riddle is there and now we know Zaugg is somehow on the trail too because he was about to set Vetsch on Demetriou. He won't stop until he gets what he wants and that means Demetriou is in grave danger."

"How can we get there this time of night?" Ryan said.

"Leave that to me," Sophie said.

"So let's do it then," said Hawke.

"We're making progress!" Ryan said.

Hawke looked at him doubtfully. "I think the war with Zaugg is just about to start."

On the way to the airport, Hawke sent a text to Nightingale.

*

"I think that's our ride," Hawke said, pointing to a long, white jet. Some men in boiler suits were uncoupling a fuelling nozzle from its wing while the captain was conducting the pre-flight inspection of the aircraft, checking for fluid leaks and casting an expert eye over the pitot tubes.

The plane was a Cessna Citation X, a long-range jet with the distinction of being the fastest civilian aircraft on earth. How Sophie had obtained one at such short notice had not gone unquestioned by Lea, but she decided to leave it for later.

The main entry door at the front of the cabin featured an integral three-step airstair design and as they climbed up them the solid titanium blades of the twin Rolls Royce engines began to whir to life.

Inside, to the left, the first officer was beginning the flight plans and to the right was the passenger cabin. Eight white leather seats in dim blue lighting and a walnut-veneer drinks cabinet. The co-pilot pushed a button and all of the porthole covers gently opened.

They strapped in and the engines powered up. A few moments later they were racing from the ground, gear up. The Citation banked right hard and as the city lights of Geneva slipped away behind the aircraft, it straightened up and head southwest to Athens, soaring high above the clouds and racing toward the rising sun.

Lea Donovan drifted in and out of her nightmares as she watched glimpses of the Adriatic Sea through breaks in the cumulus far below. She felt a terrible sense of foreboding.

She looked over her shoulder and saw that Hawke was asleep. He looked younger now, taken away from reality by the soft glow of unconsciousness. She could see what his wife must have seen in him, but wondered whether a man like Joe Hawke could ever be happy in a real relationship.

He had mentioned Liz, but never discussed anything about her except the most casual detail, and then there was this mysterious woman in New York whom he claimed he knew only by her former CIA codename – Nightingale.

Even though she was more than a little intrigued by this strange American woman with no real identity, she would never give Joe Hawke the satisfaction of asking anything more about her than he had already volunteered. But that didn't stop her wondering if his story about not knowing her was a lie and whether they had ever slept together.

Next to Hawke was Ryan, her former husband – now a disillusioned dropout and hacker extraordinaire, who used his unfathomable computer skills to keep the wolf from the door. He was several years younger than her and the divorce had hit him like a truck, throwing him off the rails in a big way. Before that he was different somehow, more out-going and confident, but after their marriage collapsed he had changed. It was then he turned inwards and started hacking.

Lea once again blamed herself for everything that had happened between them and slowly fell asleep.

*

Hawke woke from his sleep and stared out the window of the luxury jet, but all he saw was Liz's kind, loving face. She had not found it easy to adjust when he moved from the commandos to the SBS. The demands were different, and so were the hours.

Worse, most of the missions he went on had secret or top secret security classifications so he couldn't talk to her about them, which made it hard on both of them as the years wore on.

But she loved him enough to marry him, and they were married in a small church on the southern English coast. They could never have known what would unfold twenty-four hours later in Vietnam.

When everything changed.

Hawke squeezed the soft leather armrest of his seat on board the Citation and nearly tore the stuffing out. His attention snapped back to reality. Somewhere forty thousand feet below them was the Adriatic Sea. Above a thin layer of cirrostratus clouds the light of the moon reflected back out into space, where thousands of bright stars sparkled more brightly than anything he had seen from the ground.

He turned back to Lea to see she was falling asleep. What was she thinking about, he wondered? Somewhere behind them he heard Ryan begging Scarlet for his MacBook back. Sophie was up front talking to the pilots.

Then his iPhone rang.

Nightingale.

"N, hi."

"Buenos noches, Joe."

"You're calling to teach me Spanish?"

"I'm calling because I've got that info you requested on your new friend."

"I didn't realize you could phone me on the plane," he said.

He heard her sigh. "Sure," she said. "High-capacity ka-band satellites have been in operation on commercial jets for ages. You can have phone calls, internet, whatever you like."

Hawke got up from his seat and smiled at Lea,

mouthing the word *Nightingale* as he walked past her to the rear of the plane. Lea rolled her eyes and nestled into her seat to go to sleep.

Hawke leaned against the toilet door.

"She has an interesting past. Last name Durand, born 29th June 1985, making her thirty years old. Former officer with the Direction générale de la sécurité extérieure, which is the French version of CIA or MI6."

"I know all this – I'm not a complete idiot."

"You're right, I'm sorry. You're only partially an idiot."

"We seem to be veering from the point…"

"Ah yes – Durand. She worked for DGSE for ten years, ending up a very senior rank, but then she left and I'll be damned if I can find where."

"She left the DGSE? When exactly?"

"About six months ago."

"So she's lying to us."

Hawke thought for a few moments, and frowned. "She never said anything to me about this – in fact she told us she'd been cleared by the DGSE to work with us."

"So maybe she's working alone."

"No way. She got us a private jet with no notice at all. She's working for someone powerful and now we know it's not the DGSE. Anything else?"

"Not really – both her parents are French, all from Marseille in the south – her address is Rue de Berceau in La Mulatière, and not much else, except – wait a minute."

"What have you found?"

There was a long pause.

"It could be nothing, but given what you're doing right now it could be relevant. I just took a look at her foreign missions that she undertook for the DGSE before quitting and it looks like she volunteered to work jobs in Switzerland and Greece. Like I said, it could be nothing, but then again…"

"It could hardly be a coincidence that those places are all related in some way to the search for Poseidon's tomb."

"Just what I was thinking – from Zaugg's pad in Switzerland, all the way to Athens, it matches up perfectly."

"You're not just a pretty face, N," Hawke said, deciding to keep the information she had just given him to himself for now. "Why won't you tell me your name?"

"Ah! This again…"

"We could have dinner. I promise I won't bring my Glock."

"What sort of use would you be without that?"

"You might be surprised. I'm serious. Tell me your name."

"How are you going to stop Zaugg, Joe?"

"You're changing the subject."

"Just interested."

Hawke sighed.

CHAPTER SIXTEEN

Athens

The journey from the airport into Athens was laborious and time-consuming, but it was warmer than Geneva and Lea was able to wind down the window of the cab and enjoyed the breeze until Ryan complained about the engine fumes. She knew what Hawke's response would be but he was on his way to the museum with Scarlet Sloane.

The taxi driver carelessly negotiated the gridlocked traffic and a couple of student demonstrations, slowly twisting into the ancient city and by the time they arrived at Demetriou's apartment the sun was high and it almost felt like a summer's day. She paid the driver and turned to look up at the white stucco façade of the apartment block. A few pots of red geraniums hung from one of the balconies above. It looked peaceful.

They climbed the steps and rang the bell. No one answered the door, but it took Sophie less than two minutes to break into the hall, and they were inside.

"This place is awesome!" Ryan said, marvelling at the bookshelves all around the expansive apartment. "There's his computer," he said, rubbing his hands together. "Should I?"

"I see no reason why not," Lea said. "We know Zaugg has an interest in Demetriou, and we know he's not answering his phone. There's no sign of him so either he's at the museum or maybe Zaugg's already got to him and we're behind a step."

"So let's get going," Sophie said.

"Agreed. Ryan – you get into the computer and Sophie can watch the door."

Lea watched Ryan turn on the computer and connect up the MacBook. Sometimes she wondered what she had ever seen in him, but other times she remembered what it was, and this was one of those times. He was out of his depth, surrounded by ex-military or secret service, in a dangerous environment, and yet he stepped up to the mark and got stuck in.

"Have you found anything yet?" Sophie asked. "We need to hurry things along."

"There's everything in here – loads of published articles in what look like highly respected peer-reviewed journals to me – all on subjects like the origins of Persian pottery and even one here on the early Roman oil trade."

"She means anything of use to us *today*, Ryan."

"Oh, sorry. Yes, I think so. I'm in a private folder – pretty rudimentary security, actually, which took me less than a minute to crack – anyway, some of it looks like his original research – all the stuff you might expect – ancient Greece, antiquities, artifacts of various kinds and also a pile of stuff on Ancient Greek – the language itself."

"That must be why Zaugg's so keen to get his hands on him," Lea said.

"You think?" Sophie said sarcastically.

Lea ignored it and leaned over Ryan's shoulder, squinting at the Greek letters on the screen, unintelligible to her. She leaned closer and touched the screen gently with her index finger. "What's that there – the one marked Fabula – it's written in English."

"It means fable, or legend in Latin," Ryan replied.

"A good place to start then."

Ryan clicked open the file.

"Shit – it's all written in sodding Latin," Lea said. "I thought it was going to be in English."

"It's his research into the Poseidon myth," Ryan said, casually reading the Latin as if it were his own mother tongue.

"Anything else?" she asked, once again impressed with Ryan's capacity to hold otherwise useless information in his head.

"Let's see..." he said. "It starts off simple enough – positing that Poseidon was more than a mythological figure, and that consequently his trident was also real."

"Not sure this is good news or not," said Lea. She sighed. "We know all this. Isn't there anything new?"

"Actually, yes – and this is weird."

"What does it say?" Sophie asked. She walked to the window and peered outside into the street.

Ryan translated. "He writes something here about the number seven having some important part to play in all this – something to do with seven levels."

"What's the significance of the number seven?" Lea asked, casting a suspicious eye across the room to Sophie.

Ryan's eyes crawled over the screen as fast as he could translate the Latin. "From Pythagoras onwards, the ancient Greeks were obsessed with numbers and numerology – and created something called isopsephy, where they attributed numeric value to letters and added them up to induce meaning," he said.

"So?"

"The number seven represented mysticism and magic. Clearly the Ancients knew they had something of terrible power in their grasp and perhaps in deciding to hide it behind seven levels they were obviously hoping to protect themselves from the wrath of the gods – presumably Poseidon himself."

"They thought that would protect them?"

"It's not so silly," Ryan said. "Using numbers in a divinatory way or a superstitious way like this was very common then. Even today some people are very superstitious when it comes to numbers – look at the way some people choose lottery numbers. The Ancients believed numbers were sacred, and that they formed a sort of bridge between mortals and the divine."

"But does it give us any more clues?" Lea asked.

"She's right, Ryan" Sophie said. "We need anything we can get our hands on."

Ryan continued to scroll though the chunks of Latin on the screen.

"Not really – it's just his thoughts on the subject which are surprisingly rambling, actually, and..." he slowed down and peered closer to the screen. "But this is odd."

"What?" Lea and Sophie asked in perfect unison.

"He's quoting Homer here, but I don't recognize it. I'm not altogether up to date with Herodotus but I know my Homer. He's from a much earlier period, of course."

"Of course," Lea said, smirking.

"But this isn't right – Homer never wrote this, I'm convinced of it."

"What does it say?" Lea asked, placing her hand on his shoulder. He looked up at her and smiled in return.

"Well, if my translation is correct it means – is that the ablative or locative declension?"

"We don't have time for this, Ryan!" Lea said. "We have to make sure we get ahead of Zaugg. For all we know Demetriou has already told them everything."

Ryan stared up at his ex-wife. "Do *you* want to translate it?"

"Sorry – I'm sorry, honestly."

Ryan stared at the simple sentence again: *"Take thine hands into the earth, and share the Victory of Theseus and Pallas."*

"What's that, a riddle?"

"I think it must be. It certainly isn't Homer."

"Fantastic – I was never any good at word games." Lea frowned.

"Perhaps if you could shoot it you would be of more use," Ryan said with a smug smile.

"If I could shoot you I would be of even more use," she said. "Something I should have done years ago," she muttered under her breath. "I was never any good at word puzzles."

"Luckily I was," Ryan said. "Pallas is just another name for Athena, the Greek goddess of wisdom and courage, so that bit's easy."

"Easy, he says!" said Lea. "I've never even heard of Pallas."

"It all just seems too weird to be true," he said, almost to himself. He stared at the screen. *"Take thine hands into the earth, and share the Victory of Pallas."* He repeated the sentence again almost in a whisper. "The only thing I can think of in terms of Athena and a reference to victory is the contest she took part in with Poseidon."

"Him again," Lea said. "He seems to be popping up a lot these days."

"We're talking about a contest that took place long ago even relative to ancient Greece itself – far back in the time of the gods. The first king of Athens was called Cecrops. He was half man and half snake."

"A lot of men are like that," Lea said softly.

Ryan ignored her, his eyes fixed on the little cursor blinking at the end of Demetriou's mysterious clue. "He decided he must find a deity for his subjects to worship, and he discovered that both Poseidon and Athena wanted to be their god, or goddess in her case. Poseidon and Athena were very ancient and powerful rivals, and they were on the cusp of going to war when Athena suggested they held a contest for the right to be worshipped by Cecrops and his subjects."

"So not unlike two politicians fighting for the leadership of their party then?" Lea said.

"You're not funny, Lea," Ryan said, sighing. "Beautiful, but not funny."

Lea looked at him from behind, unsure how to respond to such an obvious flirtation. She chose to ignore it and hope he moved on. He did.

"An enormous crowd gathered to watch the contest. It started with Poseidon – he was well known for his temper – he struck the earth with his trident. It broke the earth up and brought forth a spring, which became a flood, and that in turn became a body of water named the Sea of Erechtheus."

"A good opening gambit, I would have thought."

"Not really," Ryan continued. "The people were overjoyed until they tasted the water, which was salty because Poseidon was the god of the sea. They weren't happy."

"Bummer," said Lea. "Fifteen love to Athena then."

"Athena's approach was different. Instead of a dramatic event like the creation of a sea, she gently knelt on the ground and buried an unknown object in the earth. It grew quickly into an olive tree. The people loved it because it gave them olives for food, the oil for cooking and cleaning, and the wood for fires."

"Game, set and match to Athena then?" said Lea.

"Indeed. Cecrops declared Athena the winner and named his city after her. She became their goddess and protected them and their city."

"And Poseidon took all this like a gent?" Lea said.

"Not at all. He was enraged, and he flooded the Thriasian Plain and drowned half of the Attica Peninsula under seawater with his trident."

"Nice guy."

"And that's the power that Zaugg wants to get his hands on."

"And how do we know all this?"

"It's a famous legend, and one of the places it was recorded was on the Temple of Athena up on the Acropolis in Athens, where it's carved into the stone for all time."

"So what does this have to do with the clue on our vase?"

"Athena's victory was gained by her planting of an olive tree, and the first part of Demetriou's sentence tells us to place our hands into the earth to share her victory. I'd say the key to this is buried under an olive tree somewhere."

"Excellent," Lea said. "There are only a few hundred million of them in Greece."

"This whole thing is like a Cretan Labyrinth!" Ryan said.

"What the hell is the Cretan Labyrinth?" she asked.

Ryan replied: "A seven-circuit maze system designed by Daedalus for King Minos son of Zeus. It was built to contain the Minotaur until Theseus could kill him." He paused for long enough to make Lea turn and ask him if there was a problem.

"Er... well – I'm not sure," was his reply. "Just looking a bit closer into the legend and there's more and more talk of something called the nectar of the gods, but it says something here that I haven't come across before."

"What is it?"

"Something about ambrosia."

"Ambrosia?" Lea asked. "Not the bloody custard?"

Ryan shook his head and sighed. "I used to find your ignorance attractive," he said wearily. "A sort of Pygmalion thing, I suppose, but actually it's really worrying."

"Not the custard then?"

"No, not the sodding custard. Ambrosia was the nectar of the gods which is what many believed made them immortal. Demetriou's research is indicating that it was not merely legendary but actually real."

"This just gets better," said Lea.

"It says here that the vault of Poseidon – and he's citing a passage of Herodotus I don't recognize, which is *odd* – but anyway, it says that the vault is real – which we know now thanks to the Ionian Texts – and that its location was recorded by the Vienna Painter and hidden in two vases, but it also makes these references to the divine nectar."

"You're telling me that Zaugg's not really after the trident at all, but some kind of…"

"Immortality," said Ryan, finishing her sentence.

"But this isn't confirmed, right?"

"I guess not… it just looks like something this Demetriou has dug up on his travels around the internet. It's just to do with the legend of the gods' *ambrosia* and how it mustn't be touched by mortal man or..." he paused again.

"What, Ryan?"

"Sorry – just making sure my translation is good. This Demetriou is very articulate actually, if you look at how he..."

"Ryan!"

"Ah, sorry – anyway, it says here that if mortal man

tries to control the power of the elixir of life the sky will turn to fire and all mankind will burn to death."

"The sky will turn to fire?" Lea said. "And here I was frightened of the freaking trident. What does it mean?"

"Let's hope we don't find out," said Sophie, who had walked over to the desk.

"Ryan, text that to Hawke will, you? If the goddamn sky's going to set on fire I want Hawke to know about it in advance!"

"Sure thing." Ryan tapped out the message.

"And Sophie, get back to that door and keep an eye out for..."

Suddenly the door burst open and they were faced with three armed men holding close-quarter Heckler & Koch MP5 submachine guns. Lea stared at the man in the middle with fear in her heart. It was Heinrich Baumann. She reached for her gun.

"Don't even think about it," he said in heavily accented English.

A voice deep inside her told her to do as she was told, and while she knew Ryan wouldn't do anything stupid, she could only hope Sophie Durand would make the same play. She would be asking her why she never saw Baumann and his crew approaching the house later on, if she lived long enough to pose the question.

Baumann smirked as she handed over her Glock 17, and Sophie followed suit by handing the Beretta over a second later. Was that glance Sophie and Baumann shared a second too long, she wondered?

Baumann stared at Ryan Bale, who was slinking behind Demetriou's Packard Bell.

"He's not armed," Lea said. "Ryan, show them you're not armed. And move slowly, for God's sake."

Ryan did as he was told.

"Now you are all coming for a ride," Baumann said.

"What do you want with us?" Lea asked, hoping with everything she had that Hawke had made it to the museum.

Baumann blinked his one working eye and smirked. She heard the tiny motors whining in his metal hand. "You don't want to know."

CHAPTER SEVENTEEN

The National Archaeological Museum in Athens is acknowledged as keeping one of the greatest collections of antiquities in the world, and is located in the center of the ancient city in the busy Exarcheia district.

A polished expansive floor of white marble tiles stretched away from Hawke and Scarlet as they stood in the main entrance and stared into the vast museum, every wing filled with relics and artifacts carefully divided into special collections for the public to enjoy.

They made their way behind the guide along a quiet corridor lined with offices of various members of staff until they reached the one belonging to Yannis Demetriou.

"Please, wait a moment," the staff member said. "I'll call the professor and tell him you're here."

They knew the professor wasn't there. They had already called both the university and the museum earlier and been told he was nowhere to be found. They were told it was most unlike him to be absent without explanation. They feared the worst, and quickly got into his office where they started work.

The small office was a temporary affair he was using while on sabbatical at the museum, and on his desk, among the clutter and piles of old journals was a single red rose in a glass vase. It needed some more water, Hawke thought.

It took him back to the day he had met Liz. He was standing on a platform at Paddington Station waiting for a train to take him back to his base on the coast, and she had walked up to him holding a single red rose.

"Are you Quentin?" she had asked.

"Sorry, no. My name's Joe."

"Ah…" she looked embarrassed.

"But I've always thought I could pull off the name Quentin if I tried."

She laughed. "You look like a Quentin. That's why I walked up to you and not that guy." She gestured subtly to an old man in a greasy raincoat standing a few yards away.

"Whose name is obviously Marmaduke."

Another laugh.

They talked for a few moments, and then they shared a coffee. Hawke learned her name was Elizabeth Compton, and that she worked as a translator in the Ministry of Defence. He learned her best friend had set her up on a blind date with a colleague named Quentin.

And she learned he was in the navy where he worked as a regular sailor. He couldn't tell her the truth, not until he knew her much better. It was part of the job. He knew they would get married as soon as he realized they had both missed their trains.

"Joe!"

He was startled back in reality. It was Scarlet. "Earth calling Joe!"

"Sorry, I was lost in the past for a second."

"Well, snap out of it and help me look for something that can help us out here, would you?"

He smiled, and began to go through Demetriou's filing cabinet, taking less than ten seconds to tip it backwards and pop open the lock via the little hole on the base. Inside were hundreds of files all written in Greek. Hawke couldn't read a word of it. French and Spanish yes, German maybe, but Greek, no.

"This is no good," he said. "We're not getting anywhere. For all we know Zaugg's already got what he wants and Demetriou's dead."

"We have no choice," Scarlet said sharply. "We have to keep looking. We can't risk another innocent death."

Another innocent death, Hawke thought.

The day after their wedding they flew to Hanoi. Their honeymoon was supposed to be four weeks long, taking in the Imperial City in Vietnam, Angkor Wat in Cambodia and the Grand Palace in Thailand before spending a week on a beach on Ko Samui. It was going to be the start of their lives together.

They had only been in Hanoi one day when it happened.

Liz stepped inside the bar to buy two bottles of beer and returned with one in each hand, smiling. She set them down and took a picture of Hawke. He picked up the camera and took one of the two of them together. The original selfie.

And then they arrived.

Two people on a moped. A driver and an assassin, both wearing helmets.

They turned the corner, no different to any of the other few dozen mopeds flying around, but as they drove past the bar they slowed for a second. The assassin on the back pulled what looked to Hawke like an old Chinese PLA CF05 submachine gun from a satchel slung over the shoulder and fired very deliberately in the direction of Hawke and Liz.

They were fish in a barrel, but his reaction was lightning. He tipped up the metal table to use as a shield, sending beer bottles and peanuts flying into the air as bullets sprayed up the wall behind them, smashing all the windows and blasting holes out of the flimsy door. People screamed and ran for their lives.

And then he saw Liz, on the pavement, blood running through her t-shirt, streaming from her mouth. It was as fast and simple as that to take someone's life, he thought.

Hawke gently shook his head at the memory – his way of trying to rub it out. He had learned to suppress the bad memories that haunt people's lives as a young man. He had joined the marines as a way of getting out into the world and proving himself, of getting away from his mess of a life. But he knew in his heart that you never got rid of a memory like that of Liz dying in his arms. That was here to stay, a permanent ghost.

At first he had tried to console himself with the idea of savage revenge, of tracking down the scumbag that had tried to kill him and instead murdered his wife, but then even that tiny shred of hope was broken when his former CO, Commander Olivia Hart, had told him the hitman was Alfredo Lazaro, a Cuban mercenary hired by an unknown agency to take Hawke out of the game permanently.

Hart claimed to have been given the intel directly by the Secretary of Defence himself. She also told him Lazaro had been killed a few days later in a strip club in the Patpong district of Bangkok in a raid orchestrated by Thai Special Forces. That was the last anyone ever talked about it and his old life went up in smoke.

"For God's sake what is the matter with you?"

Scarlet again. This time her face suggested he should definitely stop daydreaming about the past.

"Sorry. What have you found?" he asked.

"There's someone coming," she whispered. She gently closed the door and stepped back into the office. "He'll be here in just a few seconds."

"Who is it?"

"Funnily enough, Joe, it's Zeus himself, and he wants to know why you're such an arse."

Hawke opened his mouth to reply, but closed it a second later when the door opened.

"What is going on in here?"

A short, dark-haired man with a thick moustache was standing in the door. He looked at them for a short moment and then spoke again: "Who are you people, and why are you in my office?"

CHAPTER EIGHTEEN

"You're Professor Yannis Demetriou?" Hawke asked.

"Of course, and this is my office. Now I ask again – who are you and why are you here?"

Hawke and Scarlet shared a quick glance before returning their eyes to Demetriou. He looked pretty upset that they had broken in to his personal space and were going through his files. Hawke guessed he wouldn't exactly be over the moon about Ryan trawling through his home computer back at his apartment.

"We thought you'd been kidnapped," Scarlet said.

"Kidnapped?" snapped Demetriou. "What are you talking about? There was an emergency at my sister's house. What is going on here?!"

"I think we need to start again," Hawke said.

They explained everything they knew about the vault of Poseidon, Hugo Zaugg and even their encounters with Kaspar Vetsch back in New York and Geneva. Eventually, Demetriou calmed down, and asked a member of the museum staff to bring them coffee.

"It's good finally to meet someone who doesn't think we're crazy," said Scarlet.

Demetriou smiled. "Poseidon's tomb – or as the ancient writers often called it, the Vault of Poseidon – is a crazy concept in most people's eyes, but not in mine. I have always had an open mind, and never stopped believing in the existence of the tomb."

"I still can't get my head around the fact that Poseidon was real," Hawke said. "I thought he was a god."

"But the two terms are not mutually exclusive," Demetriou replied. "How do we know what god is? How do we know he has not walked among us? This is what Christians teach, after all, so why is is not possible to extend such a thought to the ancient gods?"

"It still sounds like a load of tripe to me," Scarlet said. "I'm just here to shoot people."

"No! Our modern Western minds are programmed to see polytheism as an antiquated concept, but the principle is the same. There is no reason why Poseidon, Thor, Mars or any of the other gods could not have been real and walked the earth! Today in Greece we even have the phenomenon of dodekatheism, an attempt to revive the worship of these ancient gods!"

"But gods are immortal," Hawke said flatly, still finding it hard to accept he was really having this conversation. "And if they are immortal, then why are they not alive today?"

"This depends on your understanding of immortality. It could refer simply to the memory of them living on forever, as history shows has happened. Or, it could mean they are immortal in the spirit world. Others would argue that immortality does not mean one cannot be killed, merely that one would live forever if left unharmed."

"And what do you think, professor?"

"For all I know, they could still be alive!"

Hawke laughed. "You can't be serious."

"Why not? They could be walking among us now, out there, on the street. Thousands of years old – maybe millions of years old, endlessly wise, omniscient, omnipotent, and, of course, immortal!"

"And if they were, then their powers would be limitless."

"But gods know how to wield their powers, Mr

Hawke. The same cannot be said for most men." Demetriou stopped and shook his head in wonder once again. "This is all too good to be true. I have spent much of my life trying to find it, but never got anywhere as close as this. It shames me. Are you saying you actually have some kind of real, concrete evidence of the tomb, at last?"

Hawke produced the golden arc from his pocket and slid it across Demetriou's cluttered desk.

"Feast your eyes on that."

His eyes widened like a child's on Christmas morning. "Where did you get this?"

"In New York, at the Met Museum," Hawke said. "It was inside the Poseidon Vase. In the base."

"You mean the irreplacable masterpiece by the Vienna Painter?"

Hawke nodded.

"But how did you get this golden arc out without damaging the vase?"

"That's not important," Hawke said, glancing at Scarlet. "What matters is it's only half the clue – half the information we need. The Vienna Painter broke the location of the tomb into two pieces and hid one in each of a pair of matching vases. The other half of the code is in..."

"In the Amphitrite Vase!" Demetriou said, smiling, turning the gold disc over in his meaty hands. "Which is just up there," he added, pointing to the first floor above his head.

Then Demetriou saw the inscription on the other side of the golden arc. "*Beneath the Highest City, Where The Samian's Sacred Work Shall Guide*. What does it mean?"

"We were kind of hoping you could tell us," said Scarlet.

Demetriou picked up his coffee and sipped it absent-mindedly as he stared at the arc in wonder. "Clearly there is a reference to an acropolis here – probably the one here in Athens, I suppose, but as for the rest..." he shook his head and looked up at them.

"What?"

Demetriou's mind seemed to wander. "I have read that the vault of Poseidon contains not only his sarcophagus, but also what is sometimes referred to by the ancient poets as his ultimate power."

"His trident?"

"Possibly, but more likely they refer to his immortality. I have always presumed the tomb would contain limitless treasure, including his trident of course, but most importantly the source of his immortality. If man were ever to find this..."

"We need to look at the other vase, professor," Hawke said, "and in a hurry. There are other people on this trail – bad people who want the powers hidden in the tomb. Like we already told you – we thought you had been kidnapped by them, and we believe that your life may be in grave danger."

"Then let's have a closer look at the Amphitrite vase!" Demetriou said, rising from his desk and grabbing his jacket from the back of the chair.

Demetriou led them briskly along the corridor from his office and up the stairs, his jacket shuffling as he climbed the marble steps. Moments later they were walking into the section containing all the ancient Greek vases.

Hawke sighed. "I'm getting serious déjà vu."

"The Met, you mean?" asked Scarlet.

He nodded.

"This way!" Demetriou called over his shoulder. "We're almost there."

They arrived at the correct case and Demetriou beamed with pride when he showed them the vase, almost as sincerely as Mitch had done back in the Met.

To Hawke, it looked almost the same as the other one, except this one featured a woman holding a fish.

"Meet Amphitrite, Poseidon's wife," Demetriou said, carefully extracting the vase from the cabinet with a little pear of white cotton gloves. "It is imperative we do not leave grease marks on the pottery."

Hawke winced at the thought of what had to come next. "You asked a moment ago how we got the golden arc without damaging the vase?"

"Yes?"

"The truth is, the Swiss smashed it out of the base, so..."

"Oh no! Absolutely *not*."

"We need the other half of the riddle if we're going to locate the tomb, professor," Scarlet said, trying to back Hawke up. "That's the only way we can prove any of this is real and stop Zaugg, so stop being such a silly little man and hand over the vase."

"It's two and a half thousand years old!" Demetriou said.

Scarlet was unmoved. "Now, professor."

Demetriou looked down at the ancient pottery vase in his hands, up to Scarlet and then back to the vase. "But surely we could x-ray it to make sure it contained the other half of the golden disc first, and then perhaps remove the base with special cutting tools – make as little damage as possible, and then..."

"We're running out of time, professor," Hawke said.

"I'm not going to let anyone damage this vase," he said, adamant. "If there is something within it then it will be found using the correct archaeological procedures. Now you have made me aware of its potential value it's more important than ever that we put it somewhere safer."

Demetriou shuffled away from them with the vase in his right hand.

Scarlet drew her Sig Sauer and with one well-aimed shot she fired before Hawke could even begin to object.

The gunshot rang out in the silent museum, echoing down the corridors and bouncing off the ceiling, deafening. Smoke drifted from the chrome-lined barrel of her gun. As it rose to her face she blew a whisp of it away from her lips.

Demetriou stood perfectly still, frozen in place by the madness of the last second, his hand no longer holding an ancient vase but now purely its shattered rim. At his feet was a pile of tiny pottery pieces and a heap of orange dust.

Scarlet stepped forward and reached into the little pile, pulling out the other half of the golden disc.

"You can't make an omelette without breaking eggs, Professor Demetriou."

"I...I...*you could have killed me you crazy woman!*"

"Aww, that's the nicest thing you've ever said to me, Yannis." She looked at him sternly, the smoking Sig in her smooth white hand. "Now translate this." She handed him the metal.

"Translate this you say! But... you have destroyed an irreplacable, ancient..." the words trailed away as his attention refocussed on the other half of the golden arc in Scarlet's hands.

He stared at the Ancient Greek lettering, taking only a second to translate it. "It says *The Kingdom Of The Eldest Is Where What You Seek Doth Hide*."

Hawke shook his head in disbelief. "Not another one."

"At least we now have both parts of the riddle," said

Scarlet, reholstering her gun.

They put the two halves of the golden arc together and formed a perfect disc.

Beneath the Highest City, Where The Samian's Sacred Work Shall Guide – The Kingdom Of The Eldest Is Where What You Seek Doth Hide.

"What does it mean?" Demetriou muttered.

"It means you have work to do," Hawke said.

"Then we must get back to my apartment," Demetriou said. "All my research and files are there."

CHAPTER NINETEEN

The Ionian Sea

Hugo Zaugg's favorite toy was the Thalassa, his six hundred-foot motor yacht. Designed by the best naval architects in the world and built in Germany under his personal supervision, it was the largest of its kind in the world.

Zaugg often spent his summers on board, enjoying its thirty guest cabins or flying out to private island parties from its helipad. But today was different. Today was business, not pleasure. Today was about fulfilling his fate, and what better place to do it than on board a yacht named after the primordial sea goddess, more ancient than even Poseidon.

He walked along the deck of the Thalassa and into the safety and peace of his private quarters. The cabin was beyond luxurious, taking opulence to an entirely new level – cherry wood floorboards, plasma screen, and walnut-veneer drinks cabinet. As much as he was capable of feeling love, he loved being here.

He slid the door shut and walked casually to his desk, a beautiful piece of Brazilian mahogany empty of clutter except a small platinum statue of Amphitrite and Poseidon in a lovers' embrace, and the more utilitarian presence of a black satellite phone.

He surveyed the coast of an anonymous island outside the window of the yacht, contemplating the sequence of the next few hours, and how it must play out for him to achieve his destiny. Soon the entire world would learn who Hugo Zaugg really was.

It is almost time, he thought.

He took a deep breath. His old, watery eyes wandered from the divine lovers to the phone and back again.

A gentle tap on the door.

"Come."

Heinrich Baumann padded into the room, an Uzi casually hanging from a belt slung around his waist. "They're in the hold."

Zaugg turned away from Baumann and peered out the window as some of his men were hauling an overweight, elderly man through the forehatch. For good measure one of the men kicked him in the ribs and he doubled over in pain, coughing and wheezing.

"Did he admit to it?" Zaugg asked.

"After some persuasion, naturally."

Zaugg raised his eyebrows in appreciation of Baumann's skills. He never thought the old man would confess. Now, lying in a heap on the deck, Grasso would learn his fate. Zaugg enjoyed meting out his own personal justice. It was so much more efficient than the courts, he considered. This he was going to enjoy.

"Bring Donovan and the others to the front deck. It would be a shame if they missed the show."

*

Standing on the deck, his face covered by the shade of a Panama hat, was a man Lea knew without introduction must be Hugo Zaugg. He was shorter than she had expected, and thinner, and there was an aura of power around him she was unfamiliar with. He stared at her with dull, slate-gray eyes and his lips parted for the faintest of smiles.

"Lea Kaitlin Donovan, Ryan Benedict Bale and Sophie Adelia Durand. Welcome to the Thalassa."

Lea moved forward to draw attention away from Ryan, but she was stopped by the muzzle of Baumann's Uzi gently pushing into her breast.

Zaugg frowned and clicked his fingers. The gun was removed.

"Hugo Zaugg," Lea said. "Slime incarnate."

"My reputation precedes me," Zaugg said, pleased with himself.

Zaugg clicked his fingers again and this time two of his men dragged an older man into the sunshine. Lea was shocked at his appalling condition. He had obviously been savagely beaten.

"Meet Matteo Grasso," Zaugg said coolly. "Senor Grasso has worked for me for many years on board the Thalassa."

"Please, Senor Zaugg!" pleaded the elderly man, his hands clasped together in desperate supplication. "I beg of you."

Zaugg ignored him, and continued to address his new guests. "Unfortunately Senor Grasso was caught stealing a great deal of money from the safe in my office here. Sadly, this sort of thing cannot be tolerated."

Zaugg motioned at the men and they obediently began to tie a rope around Grasso's waist.

"In my native tongue, the word we use is *kielholen*, not dissimilar from your own term – keelhaul."

"You can't do this, Zaugg!" Lea said, now restrained by Baumann's bear-like grip.

Ryan and Sophie watched in sober silence as the men finished securing the rope to Grasso.

"This line is looped beneath the Thalassa," continued Zaugg proudly. "And Senor Grasso here will now be keelhauled, which is to say thrown overboard on this side of the yacht and dragged beneath her until he comes out the other side. This will be repeated until he is repentant."

Zaugg gave the order and the yacht began to move forward, its enormous engines gathering speed quickly. Another command saw Grasso hoisted up on the rail and pushed over into the water, where he landed with a terrific splash and disappeared beneath the waves, his bound arms unable to keep him afloat.

"Now, while Senor Grasso is considering his antisocial behavior, perhaps we should talk about the business at hand. Please – have a seat." He gestured at a freshly-laid table – linen cloth, fruit, fresh fish, Champagne. "You really must try the scallops. They were caught fresh this morning and prepared – ah! – how remiss of me, they were prepared by Senor Grasso, naturally."

Lea looked at him with disgust. "You make me sick."

Zaugg smiled, then in a flash he leaned forward and slapped her face hard.

Ryan rose to confront him, but Baumann smashed him in the back of the head with the butt of his Uzi. Sophie took advantage of the moment to hide a bread knife inside the sleeve of her jacket.

"Please, everyone… let us enjoy this delicious meal." Zaugg straightened his tie and buttered a roll. He turned toward Lea once again, but this time instead of hitting her he handed her a glass of Champagne.

"I'll never help you, Zaugg."

"I don't need your complicity, Miss Donovan. Besides, you're not reliable enough. Do think the Irish Army is the only one who knows about what you did in Syria?"

She looked at him sharply, startled. He laughed out loud and broke open a fresh piece of lobster. He was enjoying himself.

"If you know that much about me," she said, glancing at Ryan and Sophie, "then you'll also know I would never help a maniac like you get hold of a weapon like Poseidon's trident."

Zaugg smiled again, cocking his head as he looked into her eyes. It reminded her of the way a falcon looks at a mouse before it swoops for the kill.

"You think so little of me as that, my dear?" he said, stroking her hand. She pulled it away in horror. "You think a man of my means would start an operation of this scale for a golden trident reputed to start earthquakes?"

"Isn't that what you're looking for?" She already knew the answer.

"Thousands of years ago, Miss Donovan, a very ancient power was rediscovered by the ancient Egyptians. It was quickly harnessed by their kings, and we don't know when or how but at some point news of this power travelled to the elite of ancient Greece. I am of course talking about the elixir of life."

Lea shook her head in awe. "You are absolutely insane."

"On the contrary, I can think of no saner thing than the impulse to survive, and in this case the elixir means permanent survival." He chuckled once again, but turned when a commotion on the port side of the front deck interrupted him.

Lea looked to see the men dragging Matteo Grasso over the rail. He collapsed in a puddle of salt water on the deck, struggling for breath. Lacerations on his legs and face from the barnacles on the hull covered the polished teak deck with blood.

Zaugg stared at Grasso for a moment, unblinking, chewing his lobster. "Not repentant enough. Again, but the other way!" he ordered.

The men obeyed, and hauled Grasso up on his feet before dumping him over the other side for a second trip. Grasso gasped for air before going under.

Lea looked at Zaugg, mortified.

"What?" asked Zaugg, confused. He looked over his shoulder again before swivelling in his chair and then sipped his Champagne. "Oh, that? Keelhauling has an ancient and venerable heritage, my dear, going back to ancient Greece itself – in fact if I am not very much mistaken it is even the subject of certain Greek vase art. I don't think anyone will be immortalizing Senor Grasso in the same way."

Lea closed her eyes and prayed Hawke would find them.

Zaugg, apparently invigorated by the keelhauling, continued. "Over the years, there have been many names for this elixir all over the world – the ancients of all the great civilizations knew that it was more than a legend, that it was real."

Behind Zaugg, his men were hanging over the side of the boat, slowly pulling Grasso across the keel of the massive super yacht.

"The Indians called it *amrit ras*, the juice of immortality, and the Vedas described it in their poetry, while the Persians spoke in awe of the water of life, or *aab-e-hayat*. This is because like the ancient Chinese they knew it was real, that what others have called the philosopher's stone really existed. The only problem being, of course, where. And that, of course, is where you come in."

"I told you I will never help you. Besides, I don't even know how I could help you."

"Don't be coy. We have the full translation of Fleetwood's work, you forget. I know you have the first golden arc – and presumably the second one by now, and so what I propose is very simple. I will trade your three lives for both halves of the golden disc. Joe Hawke has an hour to bring them both to me or I will shoot one of you every hour until both halves are in my hands."

Zaugg took a final sip of the wine and patted his mouth dry with a silk napkin. He rose from the table. "If you'll excuse me."

He walked to the back of the yacht with his hands in his pockets and watched as Grasso was hauled out of the water and dumped on the deck a second time, this time dead.

"Cut the ropes and throw him over for good this time." He turned to Lea. "We must recycle, after all."

Then he called out to Baumann. "Take them below and secure them. Kill them if they try to escape."

Zaugg surveyed the sparkling blue water and descended to the lower decks.

CHAPTER TWENTY

Before Hawke and Scarlet could enter Demetriou's apartment his neighbor came running into the street, hysterical and babbling in Greek. She was pointing at the upstairs apartment. Demetriou's apartment.

"What's going on, professor?" Hawke asked.

"She says some men came here today, to my apartment. She said they had guns. I see now you weren't exaggerating when you said my life was in danger. Thank heavens I wasn't at home or they would have me. At least this way no one was hurt."

Hawke and Scarlet shared a glance. "Yeah... about that."

"What?"

"When we arrived in Athens we split into two groups," Scarlet explained. "Joe and I went to the museum, while our friends came here."

"So today you rifle through my office, shoot at me in the museum and now as if that were not all bad enough you have people break into my apartment and go through my personal belongings? You break into my computer!"

The old woman began talking again, this time much calmer, steadied by the professor's reassuring hands on her arms.

Demetriou turned to Hawke and Scarlet, confused. "She says three people were taken away at gunpoint. I'm sorry – these must be your friends."

Hawke sighed. Scarlet surveyed the street for

anything that might offer them a lead.

The woman spoke once more and handed Demetriou a cell phone.

"It's Lea's." Hawke took the phone. "I recognize the cover."

He flipped the screensaver off to see a picture of Lea with a gun to her head. She was trying to look unfazed, but Hawke saw the same look in her eyes that he'd seen that night in New York when she started to talk about her past.

"That picture was taken up there in my study!" Demetriou said, suddenly much more nervous than usual. "I recognize my books..."

Scarlet stepped away to make a phone call, and returned a few moments later: "All right – they traced the origin of the call. They tried to mask it but this is the location."

"Good work, Cairo," Hawke said. "What are the coordinates?"

He typed them into his phone as she read them out, the two of them standing together, working together just like old times. "Well, that's unexpected!" he said.

"What is it? They're not in bloody Antarctica or something are they?"

"No, according to these coordinates, they're in the middle of the Ionian Sea. Must be a boat."

"You think?" Scarlet said. "It could be Zaugg's secret underwater base."

Hawke glanced at her and offered a fake smile. "The cheeky bastard's holding them on a boat."

"I'll get on to Eden and find out if he knows anything else," Scarlet said, putting the phone to her ear.

"So what does it all mean?" Demetriou asked, walking his neighbor to her door and reassuring her it was all over.

"It means we have to get my friends back before those turdwipes hurt them."

"Sorry, but what is a *turdwipe*?"

"Just an expression, professor. I wouldn't use it at an academic conference or anything like that if I were you."

Inside Demetriou's apartment, the professor asked to see the golden arcs again.

"I think there is more to this than the riddle," he said, turning over the two halves in his hand.

"What do you mean?" Hawke asked.

"The riddle is a problem in itself - *Beneath the Highest City, Where The Samian's Sacred Work Shall Guide – The Kingdom Of The Eldest Is Where What You Seek Doth Hide* – I don't know what this means yet, not fully at least – but look at the way the golden arc fits together to form a perfect disc."

Demetriou placed the two pieces together, forming a whole. "If you look closely, the two halves of the sun wheel in the center align to form a kind of circular ridge, and the cross inside it is raised from the base – here, look closely at it – also please note the outer edge is made of polished ivory, elephant's I should imagine."

Hawke took the golden fragments in his hands and Scarlet peered over his shoulder as he pushed them together.

"I see what you mean," he said, "but what's the significance?"

Demetriou shook his head doubtfully, as if he were unsure of his next words. "It's making me think of a particular book in Homer's *The Odyssey*, where Odysseus hides his magnificent treasure from the world in his great storeroom. In that story, Penelope takes a key with an ivory handle and uses it to open the door to Odysseus's storeroom – the place where he stored his gold and iron."

"You think this is some kind of key, don't you?"

"I do."

"You mean not only is it telling us the way to Poseidon's tomb, but it's also the key to gain entry once we get there?" asked Scarlet.

"Exactly!" Demetriou's eyes flashed as he stared at the golden arcs in Hawke's hands. "I think it is not really a simple golden disc, but a key disguised as one. It is a key! A key to the legendary vault of Poseidon."

"And all we have to do is work out where in the entire world it is," Hawke said skeptically.

"This cannot be so hard," said Demetriou dismissively. "It must surely be in Greece, and even then we can narrow it down again – let me look at that riddle once more."

Hawke handed him what they now knew was a key, and took a deep breath as the professor took it in his hands and ran his fingers over the ancient inscription.

"Ah – the kingdom of the eldest!" Demetriou said, rising from his chair and pacing excitedly up and down his study.

"What about it?" asked Scarlet. "You know what it means?"

"Possibly. I've been thinking about this part of the riddle since we left the museum." He reached for a book on one of his shelves and opened it on his desk at a certain page. "Look here – you will see that Poseidon had two immortal brothers, Zeus and Hades."

"And?"

"And each was given control of part of the world by their father, the mighty Kronos, the leader of all the Titans. Zeus was given dominion over the sky, Poseidon, as we all know, power over the oceans, and Hades was made god of the underworld."

"Ryan was talking about this earlier," Hawke said.

"Kronos is the aftershave guy."

"I'm sorry?" Demetriou looked confused.

"Ignore him," Scarlet said. "It's the best way."

"Anyway," Demetriou continued, "Hades was the eldest of the three. I think the kingdom of the eldest refers to the underworld."

Hawke laughed. "Oh, excellent. We're literally going to hell."

"No, well..." Demetriou searched for the English words. "I think we can take it as meaning simply underground – that when it says *The Kingdom Of The Eldest Is Where What You Seek Doth Hide*, it really means that the vault of Poseidon is underground."

Hawke sighed. "I didn't think it would be in the sky, professor."

"No, of course not, but Greece is famous for its tunnels and caves. If you ask me, then this riddle is telling us the vault is in a cave complex somewhere."

"All right, we're getting somewhere," said Scarlet. "What about the rest of the riddle?"

Demetriou returned his eyes to what he now believed was a key. *Beneath the Highest City, Where The Samian's Sacred Work Shall Guide – The Kingdom Of The Eldest Is Where What You Seek Doth Hide*. "Perhaps this reference to the highest city – the acropolis – refers to the acropolis here in Athens – I don't know! But if it does, then maybe the Hades reference means beneath it. There is a tunnel network deep beneath the Parthenon – I know this much."

Hawke looked uneasy. "It's just a stab in the dark, prof."

"I'm sorry?"

Scarlet's eyes flicked from Hawke to the professor. "He means you're inference is tenuous."

"I don't think so! Just look at the words, they speak

for themselves."

"You're not looking at *all* of the words though," Hawke said. "We've worked out the bit about the highest city, and the kingdom of the eldest, but what about the other bit – the section about the Samian's sacred work?"

Demetriou sighed deeply, obviously deflated. "I know, this bit I do not understand."

"And that bit could lead us somewhere totally different. Without understanding the whole riddle we would just be on a wild goose chase."

"So get your thinking cap on, professor," Scarlet said. "Meanwhile, I think we need to talk about Zaugg's yacht and just what we're going to do about getting our friends back."

Hawke agreed, and they both starting making phone calls. Hawke had a powerful new contact in the form of Sir Richard Eden and no doubt Cairo Sloane could trawl her own urban underworld in search of assistance.

As they made their calls, Hawke noticed that once or twice his old SAS rival had caught his eye and kept the contact with him just a second too long than was normal.

He hadn't seen her for so many years it was nice to be around an old friend, but to describe Scarlet Sloane as unpredictable was a gross understatement. Damaged goods was another phrase that sprang to mind. He hoped she wasn't harboring any feelings for him.

Hawke first tried Eden but the line was blocked so he put through a call to his former commanding officer, the resourceful Olivia Hart.

He had worked under her when he was a sergeant and she was a lieutenant in the Royal Marines, but then she had her transfer request cleared and moved across to the Royal Navy. These days Olivia Hart was in the top brass and ran a highly covert sub-unit of the SBS referred to only as V Squadron.

"Not heard from you in a while," Hart said.

"You love me really."

"Seriously, Hawke. It's been too long."

"What can I say?"

"That you only call people up when you need to use them?"

"Don't be like that, Commander."

"It's Commodore now. I got promoted again."

"You were always very good at that, as I recall."

There was a pause. "What do you want, Joe?"

Her use of his first name put him at ease. "An early retirement in the Caribbean with my own private villa and an endless supply of banana daiquiries. How about you?"

"I'm a busy woman, Hawke."

Back to Hawke, but he knew she was smiling.

"Listen, Olivia, I need some help."

As he spoke, he watched Scarlet make her calls and chat into the phone, tracing her finger along the back of the sofa as she paced gently behind it, or twiddling her finger in Demetriou's spider plant. Whoever she was speaking to she knew very well. Knowing her, she'd probably slept with whoever it was. Scarlet Sloane could be like that.

Now she was looking at him again, and then came that smile of hers. For a moment he felt something for her, but then he remembered who he was looking at. Cairo Sloane treated men in roughly the same way cats treat mice.

They ended their phone calls and looked at each other.

"All sorted," they both said in unison, and offered each other a tentative smile.

CHAPTER TWENTY-ONE

Lea and the others watched silently as someone rattled the lock of the hold door. Moments later the door swung open to reveal Baumann and two more thugs standing in the light and holding Uzis.

"It's time," Baumann said.

Lea's eyes widened as she realized what he was talking about. Zaugg was going to hold good to his word and start executing them.

"Untie them!" he ordered. One of the men scuttled forward and cut off the cable-ties which were securing them to the inside of the hull.

"Now get up!" he shouted.

"What are they doing, Lea?" Ryan asked.

"They're going to kill us," Sophie said, her voice soft in the semi-darkness of the hold.

"I can't believe this is happening," said Ryan. "I haven't even finished my *Big Bang* boxset. They can't kill me!"

"Believe it," said Sophie. "It's the only way you have any hope of surviving."

The men chatted casually in Swiss-German as they walked them through the yacht to the front deck, submachine gun muzzles jabbing in the smalls of their backs.

"Ouch!" Sophie said, doubling over.

"What's the matter?" said Lea, concerned.

"My stomach – it's... *ouch!*"

"Was ist das Problem?" hissed Baumann. "Move!"

Sophie fell to her knees clutching tightly at her sides. She began to sob.

Baumann sighed and flicked his cigarette over the side of the yacht. "I count to five and you get up, or I shoot you where you kneel. One."

"I can't – it's the pain, my baby..."

The other man looked at Baumann concerned. He shouldered his submachine gun and reached down to help Sophie.

In a flash she spun around, tiger-punched him the throat and stabbed him in the neck with the knife she had stolen from Zaugg's table.

Without a pause she snatched his HK416 in one fluid movement and as part of the same action she continued spinning around. She fired a savage burst of fire from the submachine gun and struck the third man with a line of bullets from his groin to his shoulder. He dropped his gun and crashed over the side of the boat.

Baumann's commando training kicked in immediately as he instinctively dived for cover behind a lifeboat, but the other man was slower, and Sophie's bullets tore a line of holes in his chest and pummelled him over the rail into the sea below.

Half a second later, Sophie snatched the first man's gun from the deck and tossed it to Lea, who straight away checked it was loaded and raised it ready to fire.

"Lea, behind you!" Sophie gasped as two more men, also armed with submachine guns, appeared at the top of the stairs and began firing bursts in formation as they snaked their way down to the lower deck.

Lea spun around, gun raised. She aimed and fired. Her single shot struck the leading man in the throat and the force of it spun him around in a shower of arterial blood which sprayed up the side of the white yacht. He tottered over the rail and crashed into the top of the foulweather gear locker with a sickening crunch.

Sophie fired at the man above him and hit him in the chest. He fell forwards, head-over-heels down the stairs. She turned and fired a burst above Baumann's head, keeping him pinned down behind the lifeboat.

Lea ran to the dead man and snatched up his submachine gun, a Heckler & Koch 416 and a pistol.

"This should come in handy!" she said, shouldering it and throwing Ryan the pistol. "Safety's on, Ryan. If you're in a corner at least try and look like you know how it works."

Sophie nodded to the rear of the boat. "We should go that way," she said. "We know Zaugg likes to kill his victims on the front deck."

Lea remembered the look on Grasso's face when he finally realized he was going to die, but then she had a better idea.

"No, we need to find the engine room. If we can cripple this boat Zaugg will be a sitting duck."

"*Almost* literally," Ryan said, smiling for the first time since Baumann had dragged him out of the hold.

A rasping, crackling sound followed by a short howl of feedback emanated above their heads. Lea looked up and saw one of the many loudhailers dotted around the superyacht. Seconds later a guttural voice announced something in German to the crew.

"What did it say?" Lea asked Ryan.

He easily translated it and gave them the bad news.

"Just put it this way, *entkommen* means escaped and *Töten Sie* means kill them."

"That's just plain arsing fantastic," Lea said, her mind racing with options. Then a loud siren started honking all over the yacht.

"In here!" Sophie said, opening a door to the lower decks. Inside they found a fire safety notice and a map of the yacht.

"The engine room is on the bottom deck in the center!" Ryan said, speed-reading the German.

"It won't take them long to realize where we are," Lea said. "Let's go."

They sprinted along a plush corridor lined with expensive-looking suites, and reached another staircase, this time leading down below decks.

Shots rang out from the bottom of the staircase, and Lea peered carefully over the banister to see several armed guards making their way up the carpeted steps. Seconds later the deck was crawling with Zaugg's men.

Pinned down in the corridor, with no cover except a heavy oak case full of antique books and manuscripts, Lea unleashed a savage volley of fire from the muzzle of the HK416, spraying polymer-case subsonic bullets across Zaugg's pristine deco murals. Dusty explosions of atomized hardwood blew into the air like volcanic dust.

It had been a while since she had fired a gas system carbine and she was once again struck by the accuracy of it, thanks to a combo of the cold hammer forged 10.4 inch barrel and the tapered bore. *Hell, I like this thing!* she thought.

Ryan screamed and covered his head with an encyclopaedia for protection. He didn't look as fazed as he was when Vetsch was trying to kill them back in New York, so he must be getting used to it, she thought.

Now Ryan was scrambling toward Sophie who was providing cover with her pistol, and then the two of them crawled back along the carpet through the dust and destruction of the firefight, as Lea in turn covered them.

Inside one of the rooms Ryan spotted something that belonged to him. "Hey! That's my sodding MacBook!" He ran inside and snatched it up off the table, wrenching out the wires that had been used to connect it to another computer, now long-gone. "Bastards have been copying my hard disk."

Back in the corridor, the fighting continued. Ryan now had his MacBook case slung over his back, and it took a couple of rounds which ricocheted off and landed with a grim thumping sound into the ceiling above him.

"Get that laptop out of here!" Lea shouted. "We'll need it to find the tomb!"

"Some concern for me might be nice!" shouted Ryan. "And it's a MacBook!"

"Get lost, Ryan," Lea said, "and I mean that literally and in the best possible taste – Sophie, go with him to the engine room and try to stop this bloody boat! Then try and find somewhere to hide until Joe turns up."

"*If* Joe turns up," said Sophie doubtfully.

Lea saw them safely around the corner at the end of the corridor, and turned to see one of the guards struggling with a jammed weapon. A second later she planted a firm double-tap in his forehead and took him out of the equation forever. She was beginning to think they were getting on top of things.

Then, things changed.

Rapidly and for the worse.

She saw four more men appear at the end of the corridor and set up with impressive efficiency what looked from this distance like some kind of updated Browning M2, a heavy machine gun.

Seconds later it was on its tripod and another second after that bursts of fire spat from the muzzle as it propelled its 50 cal tracers along the corridor in a deadly arc.

They struck the walls and book cases with such velocity they acted like a wrecking ball and sent chunks of carbon fiber, aluminum and splinters of wood flying through the air, creating thousands of lethal projectiles. And it was so noisy! She'd forgotten just how noisy the heavy stuff could be.

She returned fire but it was of little use against the M2, and it was only a matter of time before its tracer rounds completely annihilated her cover and took her out of the game permanently.

She had to retreat to a new position and find Sophie and Ryan. This, after all, was the same weapon she had once used to suppress ISIS positions in Syria. Trying to fight it with a submachine gun was the definition of insanity.

Then just when she thought all hope was lost, the moment came that she had been waiting for.

She heard the telltale clunk as the M2 hit the end of its feed, and seconds later one of the soldiers tossed the ammo case aside and slotted a new one into the side of the heavy gun. They were reloading.

She withdrew along the corridor, covering herself with occasional short bursts of fire from the 416 as she retreated back, rolling backwards twice and then crouching on her haunches for the final few steps.

The men fired on her in response but Lea was faster and took out two of them before taking cover behind the corner wall at the end of the corridor.

She made her way to the engine room where she found Ryan and Sophie hiding behind one of the engine housings.

"I took a few of them out but it won't buy us much time," she said. "We need to work fast and really fuck this engine up. It's the only way of making sure Zaugg doesn't get off this boat."

"Er, that's not true," Ryan said.

"What are you talking about?" Lea asked. "He's not likely to swim back to the mainland is he?"

"You're forgetting about the rather splendid helicopter sitting on the rear deck."

"Oh, fuck it!" Lea kicked the side of the engine. "One of us has to go and sabotage that as well."

"Well don't look at me," Ryan said. "I wouldn't know one end of a helicopter from the other. I studied the classics."

Lea steeled herself. "I'll go. You and Sophie stay here and make sure this engine stops working."

CHAPTER TWENTY-TWO

Commodore Hart touched down at Eleusis Airfield in an unmarked Gulfstream IV which Hawke guessed was paid for by some faction inside the British Government. The base was eighteen kilometers from Athens and used by the Hellenic Air Force.

He met her at the aircraft and saw at once that she had aged well and that she was still super fit, as they used to say in the commandos. Her blonde hair was tied back in a no-nonsense style, and she had a determined, honest expression on her face.

The first thing she did was introduce him to two men from V Squadron, code-names Chief and Sparky. As he spoke to Hart the two men unloaded some pretty serious equipment from the cargo door at the side of the plane.

"At least tell me what the 'V' stands for, Olivia!" he asked her.

She ignored him, and ordered the men into a Jeep Cherokee waiting at the side of the plane. "We have a lot of planning to do, Joe, and you've been out of the game for a long time." She glanced at his stomach.

"That's pure muscle," he said, and meant it. "You cheeky cow."

"Same old Joe Hawke."

They drove across the base to an outbuilding she had already arranged with the base commander. As they drove, Hawke watched the Greek air force personnel shuffle about their business and he thought about how it didn't matter where you were in the world, a military base always had the same features.

It reminded him of all those years he'd spent as a commando in the marines and even as an SBS soldier. Life was simpler back then, in the squadron.

"These places never change, do they?" said Scarlet. She too was peering at the base over her sunglasses and presumably recalling her SAS days before she joined the Secret Intelligence Service.

They went ahead of the others and waited in a non-descript military briefing room normally used by the senior officers at the air base.

Moments later Olivia Hart strode into the room with Alexis Pavlopoulos, the base commander. He was a solid-looking military officer with a square, clipped hairstyle and dark brown eyes. After a few brief words of introduction they turned their attention to the attack on the yacht.

"It's been a long time, Olivia," said Pavlopoulos, kissing her on both cheeks and warmly shaking her hand.

"Indeed it has, Alexis. Is your air force still flying paper aeroplanes or have you graduated to real ones yet?"

Pavlopoulos was undeterred by the barb. "I heard a few days ago that the Royal Navy was making yet more cuts," he countered. "Apparently you do not even have one aircraft carrier at sea. A sad end to what was once the world's most powerful naval force, don't you think?"

For a moment there was silence between them, and then they smiled and briefly embraced once again. All was good.

"You know each other?" Scarlet said.

"We go back a long way," Hart said.

"I trained with the commodore here when I was a

junior officer," said Pavlopoulos.

They took their positions at the table and Pavlopoulos suddenly turned to the matter at hand. "Now, I've been briefed by Commodore Hart here about the situation, and of course the Minister of National Defence here in Greece has confirmed everything and given me clearance to assist you in the capture of Hugo Zaugg. I can tell you that our government is very keen to question him about his activities in our territory, particularly the islands."

"Your government will have to get in line," said Hawke. "There are a lot of people who want to get their hands on Zaugg."

"We can argue about that later," Hart said. "We have to catch him first."

"Quite," Pavlopoulos said. "And so on that note, I would appreciate any information you can give me."

Hawke spoke first. "The first thing to say is that those bastards are holding three of our team hostage, and I'm not too keen on them getting killed in the crossfire. The assault team are all in this room, so everyone pay attention."

Hawke described Lea, Ryan and Sophie to the others.

"The basics are that Zaugg has made a push to locate the vault of Poseidon, which we now believe is a real location. He also wants to secure the contents of the tomb."

"The contents?" Pavlopoulos asked, raising an eyebrow.

"They depend on who you ask," Hawke said. "But most people agree it contains pretty much the biggest treasure known to man, especially in the form of gold and precious stones, particularly diamonds, rubies and sapphires. Some of this treasure we think was collected by Poseidon himself, but the rest was probably a tribute to him after his death."

"Or disappearance," Scarlet added quietly. "He was supposed to be immortal, after all."

"And this is what Zaugg wants?" Pavlopoulos said.

"Partly. We know Hugo Zaugg is already rich beyond most people's dreams – worth hundreds of millions of dollars at least. The gold in the tomb would be priceless though and clearly it would increase his wealth beyond measure."

"So what is his motivation?" Pavlopoulos looked at them each in turn, studying their expressions carefully.

Hawke said: "There's some dispute about this, and that depends on how you interpret the phrase 'ultimate power'. Some scholars think it refers to his trident which had the power to cause earthquakes and tsunamis on an unprecedented scale and unlike anything we've seen in our time."

"This is the worst possible news," Pavlopoulos said.

"You'd think so," Hawke said, "but it gets worse. Professor Demetriou here has interpreted the phrase 'ultimate power' to refer to his immortality.

"His *immortality*?"

"Poseidon was a god, and that means he was immortal."

"You cannot say *was* immortal," Scarlet said. "Immortal means he is still alive, doesn't it?"

"Not necessarily, my dear," said Demetriou. "It just means that you will live forever if left alone. If someone cuts the head off an immortal they're hardly going to grow another one, are they?"

Hawke thanked the professor for the image, and started to speak when Scarlet suddenly interrupted him.

"Look, the upshot of it all is we're up to our tits in trouble and we need some help."

"Thanks for that, Cairo."

"Well, let's just get on with it!"

"What are his forces?" Pavlopoulos asked.

"There's a second in command by the name of Dietmar Grobel, but we know next to nothing about him. Under him is a former member of the German Special Forces named Heinrich Baumann, a total psycho by all accounts. He was running another nutcase by the name of Vetsch but we took him out in Geneva."

"So who's on the boat?"

Scarlet spoke next: "It's impossible to know exactly, but Zaugg, Grobel, Baumann and however many men with guns he can accommodate, presumably."

"And Zaugg's the turd at the top," Hawke added.

"There's *that* word again," Demetriou mumbled.

"You're sure?" Hart asked.

"What do you mean?" Hawke asked.

"Maybe someone's pulling Zaugg's strings, is what I mean."

Hawke considered the thought for the first time, but put it out of his mind. "If there's someone higher than Zaugg then we'd be talking political class."

"And your point is?"

"Let's not go there, Olivia."

Pavlopoulous looked considerably more anxious than when he'd walked into the room a few moments ago. "Okay, I can give you one chopper, a new Eurocopter Cougar with two crew."

"Excellent," Hart said. "They seat twenty, don't they?"

"We should be able to take them with twenty," Scarlet said, considering the logistics of it all with undisguised delight.

"You're not getting twenty of my men," Pavlopoulos said sharply. "I've been cleared to give you three."

"Three?" Hawke said, disappointed.

"The Minister wants this kept small and *extremely* quiet. Do I make myself clear?"

"Perfectly clear, Alexis," Hart said, calming the situation. "And we're very grateful for your assistance. Aren't we, Hawke?" Her look told Hawke they were all very grateful, so Hawke nodded reluctantly.

"We can work with your three men," Hart said. "I have two of my men from V Squadron with me, and Hawke and Sloane here are former Special Forces so that makes seven Special Forces soldiers plus me makes eight. You make nine, Alexis. That should be sufficient to take out a boat of mercs."

"Let's hope so," Hawke said. "Or we're all an hour away from a burial at sea. When can we start?"

"It will take another half hour until the transport is ready," Pavlopoulos said.

At that moment the door burst open and a junior aircraftman wheeled a trolley into the room.

"Ah!" said the Greek officer, watching the trolley get closer. "We all must eat before we assault the yacht." On the trolley was a pile of standard Greek combat rations: beef, vegetables, cheese, biscuits and two jugs of coffee. "I'm sorry, but at such short notice..." Pavlopoulos said apologetically.

"Let's get it down us fast, everyone," Hart said, and they all pulled a plate from the trolley and started to eat. "We're not fighting without calories."

As they got stuck into their meals, they spoke more about the mission.

"So tell me more about this Zaugg," Pavlopoulos asked.

Hawke was unsure how much to give away. "We know so little. Our research has turned up a few things – private industrialist turned big-time collector of archaeological relics. He's the son of a former Nazi – an

SS officer by the name of Otto Zaugg. We think that's where all this started, back in the war here in Greece when he killed an Italian archaelogist and stole his research."

Pavlopoulos stopped chewing and a look of serious disgust crossed his lean face. "Don't talk to me about what that *vermin* did to my country in the war." His eyes clouded with hatred. "They executed my grandfather – a brave resistance man."

"I understand," Hart said. "This is your chance for revenge."

"If this is being funded with Nazi money then it will be revenge," he said, returning less enthusiastically to his meal. "We must stop him."

"Or the sky will burn, apparently," Scarlet said cheerfully.

"Sorry?" Pavlopoulos looked up once again, a piece of beef on his fork.

Hawke cleared his throat. "Our other team found a reference to the sky turning to fire if a mortal man tries to control the source of eternal life. We don't know what it means. We didn't get a chance to speak with them before they were taken by Zaugg's men."

"And all mankind burning to death, wasn't it?" Scarlet added, mischievously.

Hawke was dismissive. "It's just an old legend."

They finished the food quickly and packed their weapons as the Jeep returned to drive them to the helipad. Outside Hawke was struck by how warm the winter sun was today. It had been a long time since he had been in the Med at this time of year.

As they climbed into the Jeep, Hawke's cell phone rang. He checked the screen. It was an incoming call from Nightingale.

"I've got to take this," he said. "Just give me a

second."

He stepped off the Jeep and took the call.

"Hi, N."

"Just a quick one, Joe."

"But you haven't even bought me dinner."

Silence, then Hawke said: "Sorry, what is it?"

"Kinda bored a moment ago and decided to go hacking around in your friends' pasts."

"You realize some people watch movies in their spare time?"

"This is something you should know, Joe."

Suddenly Hawke was all business. Nightingale's tone rarely got this sombre, and as his entire relationship with this woman was over the phone he had gotten to know her tone very well.

"What is it?"

"Checked out your girl Scarlet Sloane."

"Cairo? Why?"

"You told me she was in the SAS for a few years and then she joined MI5, right?"

"That's what she told me."

"Then she's lying. I have a close contact in Five and he's never heard of her. Ran some internal checks, and still nothing. I don't know who she's working for but it's not MI5."

"Wait a minute," Hawke said, his mind racing with the information. "First you tell me Sophie Durand is not really with the DGSE, and now you're telling me Cairo Sloane isn't really with MI5. What the hell is going on here?"

"I don't know, but it's something you're going to have to get to the bottom of, Joe, because there's a lot of deceit flying around here and you could could get hurt. It's possible at least one of them is working for Zaugg."

"Which is not a very comforting thought," he

whispered. He knew what had to be done to traitors, but then for the first time he considered if Nightingale was the one feeding him false information. No, never. He shook the thought from his mind and climbed into the Jeep.

CHAPTER TWENTY-THREE

Lea moved long the yacht's corridor quietly and quickly, keeping her head down and her gun ready to fire. It had been many years since her Rangers training – more years than she could remember, but some things you never forgot.

Now, her mind was clear and focused. She had to get to the helipad and sabotage the chopper. Zaugg was probably planning on taking the yacht to wherever he decided the tomb was, but the helicopter was an escape route waiting to happen and it had come down to her to take that option away from him.

As she slipped unnoticed through the enormous superyacht, she thought about the last few hours in her life – meeting Joe Hawke at the British Museum, fighting Vetsch in New York and Geneva and now a final push to thwart Zaugg's insane attempt to secure the treasures of Poseidon.

She wondered if she could ever love a man like Hawke. She'd known enough military goons in her time, but he seemed different. Like her, he had left the service behind him and was trying to fit back into Civvy Street, into the real world.

But then she thought about Syria. She thought about the catastrophic decision she had made when she ordered the soldiers of her covert sub-unit to leave their position in order to rendez-vous with a chopper.

She had made an error on the coordinates and instead sent them into the wrong clearing. They got pinned down under enemy fire and three of them had died.

She knew how Hawke felt about officers, especially incompetent ones, as he had put it so delicately. When he found out she was responsible for the deaths of three of her soldiers it was unlikely he'd want anything to do with her.

The guilt she carried on her shoulders was enough without a jumped-up SBS sergeant adding to it. At least she could get this right – disable the chopper while Ryan and Sophie took the yacht's engines out somehow. That way they were at least giving Hawke and his team a fighting chance when they finally worked out where they were and launched their rescue attempt.

*

Ryan and Sophie stared at the enormous engine in awe. Full-scale marine propulsion engines were bigger than either of them had realized, so big, in fact, that they could walk inside it.

Descending a shining stainless steel staircase into the engine room they were faced with two walls of engine pipes, wires, panels and gauges, all lit by powerful overhead fluorescent lights built into the ceiling.

"It's like a spaceship from a science-fiction movie," Ryan said, amazed.

"Concentrate, Ryan," Sophie said, asserting control. "We're here to disable the engine, not talk about sci-fi movies. *Although*, I do like sci-fi movies..."

Ryan glanced at Sophie's face for as long as he could without looking weird. She was only a few years older, he considered, but her eyes had seen much more of life than his ever had, that much was obvious. The only thing that had ever gone wrong in Ryan Bale's life was the night his wife came home from work and told him she was quitting the army and they were leaving Ireland.

Ryan was shocked, but pleased he could move home to England. When he asked why, Lea had finally told him about what had happened so many weeks ago in Syria, and he had tried to comfort her. She had changed after that tour, but never spoken of it until that moment, and then he understood.

They would be fine. His skills as a freelance computer programmer would keep them afloat. He had just finished a certified ethical hacking course as well, and that could be very lucrative. As for his wife's change in moods, he had no idea of the train wreck their marriage was about to become.

"Ryan – let's get on with it," Sophie said.

"But where the hell do we start?" he said, taking in the massive engine room.

"A good question," said Sophie, her eyes crawling over the wall of pipes and gauges. "So I think we just start wrecking it, no?"

*

Now, Lea was on the upper deck, and she saw an open doorway filled with sunshine. She could smell the sea air blowing on the breeze through the gap, and slipped outside on to the side of the yacht, gun at her side. Covering every angle, she moved towards the rear of the Thalassa in the bright sunlight.

Daytimes she could handle. But sometimes she would wake in the night, covered in sweat. She never saw the faces of her men in the night-terrors, only ever their screaming shadows as the enemy carbines opened up on them in the clearing and they scattered for their lives.

The bodies of those who never made it were captured by the enemy and paraded through the streets. It was all her fault. Even now she could hardly bare to think about the pain she had caused their families. Not even leaving the army had assuaged the crushing guilt she felt when her tortured mind wandered back to that terrible day.

She wanted to tell everyone that it had destroyed her life too, that her mistake that day had ended her career, that it had ruined her relationship with her husband and led to divorce, that she doubted she could ever be happy again, but none of it could weigh up against leading the men in her charge to their premature deaths.

The only slit of light in her life had been offered by Sir Richard Eden, an old family friend of her father's, long ago before he died. He had taken her in after the disaster and given her work, looked after her, become almost another father.

Dedicating her life to Eden's work could be her only salvation, even if it had to be kept from the world. He had offered her a way out and she had taken it. How Hawke could fit into things would not be up to her, but up to Sir Richard.

Ahead of her she spied the chopper. It was a black Bell 429, silent and still on the rear deck, glistening in the sun. She glanced over her shoulder to make sure she wasn't being followed, and when she saw she was still on her own she moved forward to the chopper.

*

"Agreed. I think we just start smashing things," Ryan said.

"C'est une bonne idée, je crois," Sophie muttered.

Ryan lifted one of the spanners and took out a gauge, smashing the glass panel to smithereens. He then hit another, and another. Sophie did the same, and a few moments later they had taken out most of the controls in the engine room.

After a few minutes of total vandalism they forgot their situation and began to enjoy themselves. Ryan made a few jokes and was pleased when Sophie laughed warmly in response.

Then Ryan located the fuel system and shut off the valves. The engines quietened and the yacht began to slow.

*

Lea Donovan had no aviation training at all, but she knew it couldn't be the hardest thing in the world to make sure a helicopter never took to the air again. She glanced around the cockpit for a few seconds and decided that sabotaging the collective was the best option, because without one of those this bird wasn't flying anywhere.

She removed the panel at its base and was faced with a thick bundle of multi-colored wires. She was about to pull them out when she heard his voice.

"Come out with your hands up, Miss Donovan."

It was Zaugg, and he sounded pleased and in control.

Lea climbed out of the helicopter with her hands raised.

"Give Herr Baumann the weapon, please."

She tossed the submachine gun on the deck, cursing herself for screwing things up yet again.

"I want you to know I already have men searching the ship for your two friends. There's nowhere to hide on the Thalassa and they will be caught in good time."

"It's too late, Zaugg. They've already taken out your engines."

"We shall see about that... I'm very disappointed in you, Lea," Zaugg drawled. "And I think we both know what happens to people who disappoint me."

As he spoke, Baumann unfurled a length of rope from a mounted holder on the side of the yacht. For you, it is time to join Senor Grasso."

CHAPTER TWENTY-FOUR

The silhouette of the Thalassa appeared on the horizon, and Hawke and the others prepared to go to war. He'd done enough fast rope drills in his time to know what was coming, and for that reason Yannis Demetriou would be staying on board the chopper with the crew until the yacht was secured.

Hart's V Squadron men readied the abseiling equipment at the doors while Pavlopoulos and his men were calmly talking in Greek and pointing out the window at the water below. Scarlet checked her weapons and tied her hair back.

Hawke watched her and smiled.

"I want to look my best for when I kill Zaugg," she said.

Then the chopper veered heavily to the right, causing everyone to hold on to the grab handles and steady themselves. "They know we're here!" shouted the pilot. "We're coming under heavy fire."

The pilot took more evasive action before swinging around to a parallel position along the portside. Chief swung open the door and unleashed a terrific burst of fire from the M60 clamped inside the chopper. It spat fire all over the boat, splitting the wooden deck and taking out two rows of cabin windows on the superyacht's upper deck.

"Damn that's fun!" he shouted, spinning the gun around to take out an offensive position on the rear deck. Down on the boat, the surviving men scattered to take cover.

"We can't get near the rear deck and the helipad," the pilot told them over the radio. "Too heavily defended. We'll go to the front as per Plan B and you fight your way back."

The pilot brought the chopper down to a hovering position over the broader front deck and Hawke led the way down the ropes while Chief provided cover with the M60. Then with Chief on the deck, the chopper banked hard to the right and flew to safety.

It was time to fight.

*

As soon as they were on the deck, they fanned out in a standard position and began their assault. Hawke staked out his territory by firing into the bridge and taking out two men in a hail of hot lead and smashed glass. Maybe he would get back in the saddle faster than he thought.

He approached the lower deck, submachine gun raised, butt in his shoulder and eye firmly down the sights. A man appeared at the top of a flight of metal steps on the starboard side of the yacht. He was holding a pistol, but a cool double-tap from Hawke and he was over the side of the boat, gun and all.

Between Hawke, Scarlet, Pavlopoulos and one of his men, they made the classic four-man SAS patrol, with Sparky set up behind them on the bow with the M60, pinning down Zaugg's men inside the boat. On the other side of the boat Hart led Chief and the other two Greek men.

Hawke's unit arrived at a door on the starboard side which he smashed open with a solid kick from his boot. Behind them they heard more blood-curdling screams as Sparky took out another man on the bridge.

Hawke was beginning to wonder if their small military unit was more than a match for Zaugg's crew of sloppy part-timers and unpredictable mercs. But now, as they moved closer to the heart of the yacht, the fighting got more intense. Zaugg's men fought hard to protect not only their boss's life but their own.

Hawke charged the next door and burst inside, his bullets taking two men with Uzis totally out of the game and redecorating Zaugg's plush interior with unsettling amounts of their blood. Nothing he hadn't seen before, he thought, but this time he questioned the morality of the thing. Was he losing it? He shook the thought from his mind and stormed forwards.

"We have to find Lea and the others!" he shouted, ducking behind a well-stocked bar. As he spoke, a volley of submachine gun fire from two directions raced over his head and slammed into the wall behind him, splintering the oak veneer and sending shards of smashed vodka bottles into the air like chiselled ice.

This was going to get nasty.

He made a swift double-roll across the glass-encrusted carpet and slid into the main corridor on the starboard side of the yacht. Somewhere to his left he heard Hart's team hard at work fighting what sounded like a heavy general purpose machine gun. Zaugg had this place armed like his own private military base, he thought.

The others joined him, with Pavlopoulos at the rear covering them with his M4 carbine and making a serious mess of the yacht as he did so. He looked like he was enjoying himself.

Hawke saw a staircase ahead, and knew it must lead to the rear deck and the helipad. He had noticed that they were now meeting less resistance. Either Hart and her team had too many of them tied down on the port side or Zaugg was planning a retreat to somewhere he could gather more forces for his main attack on Poseidon's final resting place.

Then, he heard a familar voice. “Joe!” It was Ryan and Sophie.

“Bloody hell!” he said, relieved to have secured two of the hostages. “You’re alive, Rupert.”

This time, Ryan was too relieved to comment. “We’re alive, but only just.”

“All good?” Hawke asked.

“They keelhauled someone, Joe!” Sophie said. “A man named Matteo Grasso – a worker here on the boat. He was under the water for several minutes and when they dragged him back on the deck he was cut to ribbons.”

“She’s telling the truth,” Ryan said. “These guys are total maniacs.”

“Where’s Lea?” Hawke asked.

“We disabled the engine and she went to sabotage the helicopter.”

Hawke smiled. “Smart girl. Let’s get to the helipad. That’s Zaugg’s only way out now.”

They ascended the carpeted stairs, and Scarlet went into the lead. She turned the corner at the top of the steps and was out of sight for a few seconds.

“If this is as good as it gets, I’m disappointed,” Pavlopoulos said, smiling. He had a flesh wound on his left temple. He wiped the sweat from his eyes and reloaded the M4. Somewhere on the deck was another burst of machine gun fire followed by hoarse screams. “Hopefully not one of ours,” he added, breathing hard.

“Nope,” Scarlet said, returning with a smoking gun. “Turns out he wasn't my type.”

They hit the landing and went through a door leading to the rear deck. Pavlopoulos’s man took the lead. He moved too fast, and then Hawke saw it but it was too late.

"No!" he shouted, but the soldier had already tripped the wire, and was blown to pieces by a booby-trapped grenade.

Pavlopoulos could do nothing to save him, and watched with uncontained horror as the smoke cleared and the devastation appeared before him. He gritted his teeth. "For this, they will pay a thousand times over."

Before Hawke could stop him Pavlopoulos sprinted onto the deck with his carbine spitting fire.

Hawke and Scarlet followed him out, taking secure positions and covering him, but he was like a man possessed, wiping out three more of Zaugg's men without fear of being struck. He had clearly been away from combat situations for too long and was making a serious misjudgment.

His bravado was misplaced, and seconds later he was peppered through from the rear by a man hiding behind a circular staircase winding up to the helipad. Blood exploded through his chest like an over-the-top Hollywood special effect. His eyes widened in terror before he slammed face down into the deck with a sickening crunch as his face hit the hard teak.

Now, renewed chaos reigned. Hawke and Scarlet had no time to grieve for Pavlopoulos, He had reacted unprofessionally to the loss of his man, possibly haunted by memories of his grandfather, and his wreckless act had cost him his life. Hawke wouldn't make the same mistake.

On the deck they met up with Olivia Hart and Chief. The other soldiers Pavlopoulos had given them were also dead, a stunning testament to the abilities of ordinary soldiers in a Special Forces environment, Hawke thought.

Now all of the Greeks were dead and they were down to a handful of specialists at the stern of the boat, Sparky at the front with the GPMG and Ryan and Sophie. He had to find Lea.

More machine gun fire was pouring down on them from somewhere up on the top deck where the helipad was situated. They returned fire, and a man fell over the rail and sailed past them on his way into the drink. He landed with a tremendous splash and disappeared beneath the waves.

Hawke sprinted up the circular staircase leading to the helipad, followed closely by Scarlet and the commodore. All three of them firing in formation to keep the last of Zaugg's men pinned down.

A tall man with a flesh wound on his head fired a submachine gun at them but scrambled for cover when Hawke returned fire. His shots tore a line of holes in the mesh support struts of the helipad. Hawke rolled across an exposed section of the deck and rose up to fire on the men guarding the chopper.

"We need to take that chopper out of the equation," he shouted. "Without that they're not going anywhere."

But then Zaugg appeared from the top of the other staircase, with Lea in his arms and a silver pearl-handled revolver at her head, flashing in the bright Mediterranean sun.

"Mr Hawke, I presume," he shouted across the windy deck. "We meet at last, but sadly, I am sure, only for the briefest of moments."

"Let her go, Zaugg!" Hawke shouted back.

"Drop your weapons, or I will put a bullet in her head." Zaugg was no longer grinning, but instead looked mildly rattled. He slowly paced backwards, nearing the helicopter, and shouted some orders at Baumann who then climbed into the Bell.

"Do as he says!" Hawke told the others. He lowered the submachine gun to the deck, never once taking his eyes off Lea's terrified face.

Everyone put down their weapons and then Zaugg relaxed. "You come at a very opportune moment, Mr Hawke," Zaugg said. "For just a few seconds ago we were preparing to keelhaul Miss Donovan here."

Lea struggled in Zaugg's icy grip.

"You bastard, Zaugg!" Hawke shouted.

"Ah! The English gentleman... You need have no fear. Miss Donovan is saved, because you are the one I want to see keelhauled."

Before Hawke could react, Zaugg barked some orders in German and some men grabbed him and dragged him across the helipad.

"I do prefer to perform this operation at the bow of the Thalassa so I can enjoy it over my breakfast, but as it is, we shall be forced to do it here, because I have much business to attend to and so little time."

The men began to bind the ropes tightly around Hawke, pinning his arms at his sides and permanently ending any chance he had of either escaping or being able to swim. Lea and the others held their breath in horror.

"It will bring me great pleasure to watch this," Zaugg said, and clicked his fingers. Upon that command the men raised Hawke up over the side of the yacht and dropped him into the water below.

He smashed into the waves feet first, which was a small mercy in the circumstances. Training for the Special Boat Service is among the hardest and most gruelling in the world, being largely SAS training and then on top of that additional specialist underwater training.

Hawke had completed his commando training with ease and was soon a respected NCO in the Royal Marines, easily catching the attention of SBS recruiters.

He had sailed through the endurance training, including the notorious 'long drag', a forty kilometer trek with a crushingly heavy bergen on his back, to be completed in less than twenty hours.

He had skipped easily over the special weapons training, the anti-terror training and the covert demolition courses. Combat survival techniques, jungle training, white noise torture training, food and water deprivation, piloting a boat from the ocean at full speed into the back of a hovering Chinook, interrogation resistance training that would break the hardest of men – all passed with flying colors.

But the worst was what made the men of the SBS so formidable: the underwater training. Being dropped from a helicopter into the sea in the middle of the night and having to make his own way on board a ship posing as an enemy vessel was as tough as it got, but proved to be useful because he'd had to do it for real since then on numerous occasions.

But as hard as SBS training was, no one ever tied him in ten meters of yacht rope and keelhauled him underneath a superyacht.

He knew what he was going to find down there – he had dived down beneath keels to fix mines on them enough times – and he wasn't disappointed. Despite the yacht's pristine appearance from the surface, the bottom of the hull was peppered in razor-sharp barnacles, each one a savagely sharp blade. The lacerated body of Matteo Grasso that Sophie and Ryan told him about would have been an illustrated testament to their lethality.

Under the water the temperature dropped fast, and the light faded as he went deeper. He felt the tugs on the rope as Zaugg's men dragged him deeper beneath the keel. Luckily, Ryan and Sophie had sabotaged the engine and this meant the ship was stationary in the water.

Thanks to that, his weight would ensure he would likely miss most of the devastating barnacle plates, and all he had to do was avoid drowning. His SBS training had taught him to hold his lungs for longer than Grasso had presumably been left underwater, and he clung to that hope as the ropes tugged him roughly under the yacht.

CHAPTER TWENTY-FIVE

Lea struggled against Zaugg's grip as she watched several of his men run to their leader and inform him that the SAS man at the front of the Thalassa was dead.

Lea and the others knew they meant Sparky, a man with whom Hart had shared work and life for two decades. With Alexis also dead she had lost two close friends to Zaugg's insanity. Lea saw the rage rise in her, but she fought it away out of a sense of self-preservation.

With Sparky dead, that left only the four of them, plus Chief, who was now being dragged up from below decks, badly beaten in the face and body.

"Sorry, boss," he croaked up to Hart. "Overwhelming numbers. Twelve to one. I could have taken ten, I reckon, but not twelve."

"Silence!" screamed Zaugg. He kicked Chief hard in the face and knocked him unconscious. "Even your SAS is no match for me."

"You'll pay for this, Zaugg," Hart said, her voice cold and clipped.

"I think not. With your man Hawke currently drowning beneath the boat, all that remains is to execute the five of you and dump your bodies overboard."

Zaugg walked toward the chopper which Baumann had fired up a few moments ago. The blades began slowly to whir and pick up speed until they were at full operating velocity, the rotors invisible now and pushing a powerful downdraft in Lea's face.

Zaugg spoke with another person whom Lea

presumed was Dietmar Grobel, a short, fat man who waddled away from the chopper and returned a few moments later with what unnervingly looked to her like a pack of C4 explosives. He secured them to the side of the yacht and the men climbed into the Bell.

"I bid you all farewell!" Zaugg shouted.

"I guess he changed his mind about shooting us then," Ryan said.

Lea turned to him. "Don't count your chickens yet."

The chopper rose gently from the deck. It was blown to the side a little by the wind but Baumann corrected it before ascending fast into the bright blue sky and veering away from the yacht.

Lea pointed up. "We have to get off this boat. Look!"

The chopper turned in the sky and the side door swung open to reveal Grobel at the handles of an M60. Flames flashed from its muzzle as he strafed the side of the yacht.

"But we have to get Hawke!" said Ryan. As he spoke Chief began to regain consciousness. He rubbed his temple and spat some blood on the deck.

Ryan began heaving at Hawke's rope, helped by Lea and Chief.

"It's jammed!" Ryan shouted. Without saying another word he took a knife from one of Zaugg's dead guards and jumped into the water, diving beneath the surface. Moments later he emerged, dragging Hawke behind him. The SBS man was slipping in and out of consciousness.

Behind them the M60 chattered away, peppering the deck.

"They're aiming for the C4!" Hart shouted. "Everyone off the boat!"

Down in the water, Ryan cut at the nylon yachting rope which secured Hawke's hands behind his back as everyone else leaped off the yacht and joined them.

Ryan hacked at the rope and released Hawke. As he did so, Hawke smiled for half a second but slipped into unconsciousness again. With seconds to spare the others hit the water and dived for cover as Ryan hauled Hawke back under the surface again, this time to protect him from the blast.

Lea went into the water the second the yacht went up in flames. The shockwave felt like a punch, but being underwater had protected them from the worst of the explosion as the yacht turned into a giant fireball. Through the distorted surface and the burning wreckage she watched as Zaugg's chopper spun one-eighty and headed for the mainland.

*

When Hawke came back up for air, the bright blue Mediterranean sky was now black with the burning oil and wreckage of the Thalassa.

He knew he'd been unconscious, but for how long he wasn't sure. He could smell the fuel on the surface of the sea, rank and nauseating. Then, he heard the cries of his friends as they scrambled in the water, trying to find anything to cling to. None of them except Hawke and Scarlet had the benefit of serious underwater training. Luckily, they had located the box of emergency equipment and flares.

He swam over to Ryan, pulling a piece of smashed door along under his arm. Ryan slipped under, but Hawke dived down and pulled him back up again. He hoisted him over the door fragment.

"Thanks, Joe," he said, coughing sea water from his lungs.

"It's me who should be thanking you," Hawke said.

"What for?"

"You saved my arse back there, so thanks Ryan."

Ryan was speechless for a few seconds, half-drowned, and dazed with concussion as he bobbed up and down in the Ionian Sea. "Really, there's no need to – hang on – you called me Ryan."

"All right, calm down. We're not getting a room or anything. I just said thanks."

"Sorry."

"Seriously though – thank you, Ryan. There's more in there than I thought," he said, tapping Ryan's chest. "I owe you, mate."

"So what do we do now, He-Man?" Lea shouted.

Scarlet laughed. "Yes he does look a bit like He-Man. We'd need to dress him in those silly little shorts for the full effect."

Hawke sighed and rolled his eyes. "Even now, here, in the middle of the sea..."

"Where's Chief?" Hart said, looking frantically around in the water.

After a short search, Sophie saw him, bobbing about in the water, face down. "I'm sorry," she said.

There was silence for a few moments as they considered the destruction Zaugg had wrought since all this began, and all those who had died trying to stop him. Then Scarlet saw Ryan's MacBook give up the ghost and sink slowly to the sea floor. "Hey boy – there goes your IQ."

"At least mine's heavy enough to sink," Ryan said.

A long period passed when even Hawke began to get nervous about their chances of survival when Ryan perked up and craned his neck, protecting his eyes from the sun's glare with his hands. "Look over there!" he shouted, clinging to the door for his life.

"It's another boat!" Sophie said. "Thank God!" She lit a flare and fired it into the air.

"The sun shines on the righteous." Hawke lit the second flare.

A few moments later a high-powered catamaran pulled smoothly alongside them.

"You need some help?"

The accent was French, southern by the sound of it, and the man who had spoken looked as close to a professional wrestler as you could get without the ring, the umpire and the popcorn. He had the thickest neck Hawke had ever seen, and that was saying something. The full effect was finished off with a shaved head and an enormous no-nonsense handlebar moustache.

"You took your bloody time," Scarlet said, laughing.

The man offered a nonchalant Gallic shrug but made no reply.

"Everyone," Scarlet said. "Meet Reaper. Reaper, meet everyone."

"Ça va?" the man said, and roared with laughter as he lowered the boarding ladder into the water.

*

On board, they ate a meal of freshly caught sardines with a grilled avocado and tomato salad, all courtesy of the mysterious owner of the catamaran, before taking a few minutes to relax and regain their strength.

Hart made use of the communication system on board to organize a conference call between several concerned agencies, including Sir Richard Eden, and a senior officer at the CIA. They were informed that Zaugg had gotten away with the full golden disc and had now dropped off the radar. Demetriou was back on shore and would meet them there where air transport was being arranged.

"Where the hell did you get a luxury catamaran from,

Reap?" Scarlet asked.

"I am a resourceful guy," he said, smiling. But that was all he said.

The others looked at her, shocked. Hawke was awaiting an explanation.

"When we were in Athens and we realized you'd been stupid enough to get yourselves caught," Scarlet said, looking casually at Lea, who rolled her eyes in response, "we decided we needed some back-up. So Joe called the commodore in there," she jabbed her thumb at the comms room, "while I thought about who I knew in this part of the world."

"And the answer... c'est moi," Reaper said with a broad smile.

"We go way back to some dark days that would put you off your lunch if I were to describe them, but I knew he was down here so I gave him a call. I told him about the boat and its location but that we would meet him on the mainland."

"Luckily for you guys I anticipated your incompetence and decided to borrow this catamaran, or you would all be dead and your man Zaugg would have the tomb and its treasures all to himself, no?"

They finished their meal, and Hawke and Scarlet joined Reaper who was steering the boat towards the mainland as fast as he could go. Thanks to the commodore's phone call someone was arranging a chopper for them, but where they were going they had no idea.

"So what's your real name?" Hawke asked.

Reaper clicked his tongue dismissively. "You can call me Reaper."

"Reaper?"

"Oui. That is my name as far as you are concerned."

Reaper checked the navigation system and looked

back to the horizon. He lit up a cigarette.

Scarlet said: "Reaper is his codename. Please forgive him. He can be *brusque* sometimes."

"What are we talking about here?" Hawke asked. "Former French Foreign Legion, now a merc?"

Scarlet arched an eyebrow in surprise. "Exactly. How did you know that?"

"Let's just say I recognize the attitude."

Reaper laughed. "Fine. I'm a former Foreign Legion man. 2REP section."

"The infamous paratrooper section," Hawke added with respect. "No doubt you're none too fussy about your mission briefs since becoming a merc, either."

"You think you're better than me because..."

Then Ryan was shouting.

"Oh my God, I've got it!" He came running into the room holding a triangular serving dish full of green olives.

"Well stay away from me then," purred Scarlet.

"No – the second clue – I think I have the answer. Look!"

He held the dish up in front of them.

"Have you been smoking coffee again, Ryan?" Scarlet said.

"No, look!" He set down the dish and swivelled an old laptop belonging to the catamaran's owner so the others could see.

"When we were trapped in the hold on Zaugg's yacht something kept on bothering me."

"Me too," said Lea. "They're called cable-ties."

"Not the cable-ties," Ryan said. "What was bothering me was that weird cryptic reference to the Samian's sacred place in the second clue – you remember?"

Hawke sat opposite him and bit into an apple. "Sure – *Beneath the Highest City, Where The Samian's Sacred*

Work Shall Guide – The Kingdom Of The Eldest Is Where What You Seek Doth Hide. What about it?"

"We all presumed that the highest city – the acropolis reference – was pointing us in the direction of the famous Acropolis in Athens, the one with the Parthenon where all the tourists go every year, right?"

The others listened as Ryan's moment in the sun dawned. Sophie spoke to Reaper in rapid French before bumming one of his cigarettes and lighting up. She kicked back next to Ryan on the soft chair around the low table.

Ryan looked at her and they shared a glance before he continued with a smile on his face. "But there was that part about the Samian. It just didn't make sense. Then, thanks to Zaugg I had time to think about it without access to the MacBook, and so I *really* thought about it, if you know what I mean."

"Go on, *boy.*"

"Clearly the Samian is a reference to Pythagoras – I'm sure you all got that much, right?"

The others shared a glance, thought about it, but then Hawke said: "No, Ryan. Only you got that much. Please carry on, mate."

"Pythagoras was also known as Pythagoras the Samian, for the simple reason that he came from the island of Samos, but that's not important. What's important is the reference about his sacred work."

Reaper turned from the helm and spoke over his shoulder. "Triangles, no?"

Ryan was impressed. "Yes, exactly! Pythagoras is most famous for discovering and demonstrating the proof of what we now call the Pythagorean theorem – the mathematical law that states that the square of the hypotenuse is equal to the sum of the squares of the other two sides."

"This is like being back in school, Ryan," Scarlet said. "Only without the bikesheds. Do speed things up."

"Sorry – anyway. That takes care of the reference about his *work* – clearly it is directing us to look at a triangle of some sort."

"Like a monument?" Sophie asked, leaning into him.

"No, I don't think so. Just listen for a second." As he spoke, he typed something into Google Earth and the Mediterranean Sea spun into view. He zoomed in on Greece.

"So I had the triangle part kind of sorted, but that left the bit about *sacred* and it was driving me crazy. Seeing that dish just now brought it altogether – the triangle and so on, and that is when the reference to the *sacred* finally made sense."

"Still not following you, mate." Hawke grabbed a second apple from the bowl. The catamaran bobbed gently up and down as it cut effortlessly through the waves.

"The ancient Greeks were famous for their love of geometry, and they achieved amazing things that we don't even think about today. One of these things is called the Sacred Triangle and it's right here - look."

He used the path facility on Google Earth to draw out a perfect isosceles triangle over the Greek islands and mainland.

"I'm connecting three points on this map. If you look closely you'll see they are the Acropolis in Athens, the Temple of Aphaea on the island of Aigina to the southwest and the Temple of Poseidon at Sounion at the southernmost tip of the Attica peninsula. These three places were built to form a perfect isosceles triangle across the earth."

"So not a monument," Sophie whispered, "but a shape on the earth itself."

"Exactly!"

Hawke peered into the screen, his apple-munching gradually taking second place to the revelation before him. "That's actually amazing."

"I'll say it is," said Lea, subconsciously taking hold of Hawke's harm, causing Scarlet to raise an eyebrow.

"So next I started thinking what was the relevance of the triangle. It couldn't be a coincidence or a mistake – it was just too perfect. So I gave it some more thought and realized that perhaps the lines of the triangle were pointing to something. I drew lines from the Temple of Poseidon to the Acropolis but found nothing that made any sense, and again from Aphaea's temple to the Acropolis but again couldn't find anything that stood out."

"But then?"

"But then I drew a line from Poseidon's temple to Aphaea's temple and found two things straight away – the line connects both temples with the Temple of Isis in the east on Delos..."

"So we need to go to Delos?" Hart said, staring wide-eyed at the screen.

"No – I don't think so. The line also connects perfectly with another location – pointing very clearly and perfectly to Sami, on Kefalonia, the biggest island in the Ionian Sea. I think *The Samian's Sacred Work Shall Guide* means follow the southern line of the triangle to Kefalonia – to Sami."

"Does Sami have anything to do with the Samian?" Hawke asked.

Ryan shook his head. "Coincidence."

"That's confusing."

"To you maybe..." Ryan stopped and apologized. Hawke laughed, his admiration for Ryan Bale growing by the minute.

Hawke replied: "But how can you be sure it's pointing us there and not to the Temple of Isis on Delos?"

"Because of the reference to the acropolis in the first clue."

"Still not with you."

"Just outside Sami, on Kefalonia, is a famous acropolis."

For a few seconds there was only the sound of waves as the catamaran moved through the water, and everyone considered Ryan's logic.

"If you break it down - *Beneath the Highest City, Where The Samian's Sacred Work Shall Guide – The Kingdom Of The Eldest Is Where What You Seek Doth Hide* – it's actually rather simple. It means "Under the acropolis at Sami, on Kefalonia, there's some kind of underground complex – Hades, the eldest brother – and that is where we're going to find the vault of Poseidon."

More silence, and then Hawke spoke: "Somebody get this lad a beer. We're going to Kefalonia."

"First," Reaper said. "I suggest you get some sleep. It's going to take a couple of hours to get to the mainland, and we know Zaugg has a head start on us, but there's no way he'll attempt to access the tomb without more men. When he left the Thalassa he was down to a handful."

"What happens when we get to the mainland?" Lea asked.

Hart spoke: "I've made some calls and organized the chopper that brought us to the Thalassa. Demetriou is waiting for us there with more men. Now we know we're going to Kefalonia it's just a matter of getting there as fast as possible."

Ryan and Sophie disappeared below decks while Lea sat next to Hawke on the front deck. It was a long sail, and the sun was bright.

"I think Ryan might be over you, Lea."

"Eh?"

"Have you not seen the way he and Sophie are looking at each other?"

"Oh... no. Good for him."

"So you're not going to thank me for rescuing you?" Hawke said.

"You didn't rescue me!"

"Of course I did!"

"Hardly. You landed on a yacht, got captured, keelhauled and then Ryan saved you. How is that you rescuing me?"

"Well..."

"And who the hell gets *keelhauled* in this day and age?"

"Keelhauled in the act of rescuing you, yes. You could be a bit more grateful if you ask me."

"But I didn't ask you," she said, smiling gently in the warm sun.

"You're welcome, all the same..."

Lea pursed her lips. "You've got a real nerve, Joe Hawke, did you know that?"

"Yes, as a matter of fact I did know, and why do you always call me by both my names? It sounds weird."

"I didn't know I did."

"Well, you do."

"And so what if I do?"

"Just saying it's weird, that's all."

But there was no reply. Lea had fallen asleep, her head rolling down onto Hawke's shoulder.

Hawke stayed awake, and began to plan the assault on Zaugg at Kefalonia.

CHAPTER TWENTY-SIX

Kefalonia

Thirty miles west of the Greek mainland, Kefalonia is the largest of all the islands in the Ionian Sea. Its coastline is punctuated with a blend of rugged cliffs, pebble-covered coves and golden beaches glistening in the Mediterranean sun. Tourists amble along the waterfront and the tavernas, oblivious to what is buried deep beneath their feet.

Now, the island's mountainous east coast slipped beneath the helicopter as it swung around into the bay and began to descend to the peninsula to the east of Sami.

Hawke and the others weren't taking in the view. Their minds were too focussed on the dangers that lay ahead in whatever subterranean hell Zaugg and his men were opening up on the island below them in their insane quest to become immortal.

Hawke was uneasy. He was finding the whole idea of living gods and armageddon weapons hard to handle, and as for the concept of immortality actually being real – that really blew his mind.

On top of that were the usual fears when going into a combat situation, only this time he wasn't backed by one of the best Special Forces units in the world – the SBS, but a loose collection of misfits, most of whom he'd only just met.

He knew from experience that Lea, Cairo and Olivia

could look after themselves, and he was pretty sure that Sophie knew how to handle things as well. The less said about Reaper the better, he thought, but when he looked at Ryan Bale and Professor Demetriou he knew they were at great risk entering into a situation like this.

Now, as he looked at their apprehensive faces, he wished he'd asked Hart for some back-up instead of telling her to focus on Zaugg's headquarters.

She'd made a joke about how if anyone could save the world single-handedly then it was him, but now he was getting closer to the action it really did feel like he was going into war again. And yet... it wasn't Zaugg and his thugs that made him uneasy, but whatever the hell was lurking in that vault.

The Vault of Poseidon. Lost to mankind for thousands of years, and holding the greatest and most terrifying secrets in history. Now it was within Zaugg's grasp, and only Hawke could stop him from seizing its guarded treasures.

The pilot decreased the power and lowered the collective. As they approached the ground, the trail of Zaugg's destruction was clearer to see. A column of black smoke twisted into the bright blue Greek sky, emanating from half a dozen police cars, now burning wrecks at the side of the road which lead up from Sami to the acropolis.

"Looks like they were hit with a rocket launcher," said Scarlet as she loaded her MP5.

Hawke nodded gravely. He wondered what other nasty surprises Zaugg had in store for them.

"That's probably all the local law enforcement taken care of." As he spoke, the chopper made its final descent and touched down just below the acropolis, as near as the pilot could get without putting the helicopter at risk.

They jumped from the helicopter and ran out from under the whirring blades.

"We don't have much time!" he shouted at the others. "Let's get on with it!"

He saw Ryan and Sophie exchange a warm glance as they left the chopper, and their hands brushed together for just a moment. Great, he thought. Now he finds love.

They hiked the half mile to the acropolis, where they were saved the effort of finding the entrance to Hades's underworld courtesy of Hugo Zaugg who had beaten them to it. A great slab of stone that once formed the floor of the acropolis had been hauled away from the ruins, presumably by the Bell which was now long gone.

The sun beat down, hot for winter even this far south. Hawke squinted in the sunlight as he peered down into the hole. He saw a pile of rubble created by Zaugg's descent maybe fifty feet beneath the surface. A warm breeze blew the scent of sea-salt across them as they stood on the cliff top. To his right, a single olive tree bent gently in the wind.

"So this is it." Hart and Hawke set up the abseil line while the others kept a lookout for any approaching dangers.

Hawke scrambled onto his stomach and craned his head down into the hole, lighting his way with the flashlight.

"This is it, all right," he said, his voice echoing strangely in the cavity below. "I hope none of you is afraid of small spaces."

He crawled out again and sat up to look at the others.

"How small is small?" Ryan asked.

"It's a good job none of you is a serious beer drinker, let's put it that way."

Lea smiled. "One thing I love about you is your honesty, Joe Hawke."

"Then you'll love it when I tell you Zaugg has a real head-start on us because all his glow-sticks are burned out."

Hawke held the flashlight in his mouth and rappelled down into the void. It widened slightly as it got deeper, and the walls were roughly hewn out of the bedrock. It must have taken months of hard labor, he thought.

At around fifty feet down, he reached the floor – mostly sand with a few small rocks strewn about the place, untouched since the time of the ancient gods. He called up to the others and told them to come down, and moments later they were all standing in the small dugout at the base of the tunnel.

Ahead of them was another tunnel. Hawke led the way, shining his flashlight into the darkness ahead. The bright yellow light dissipated in the black distance of the tunnel, so he kept its beam fixed to the floor as they walked.

"It's cold." Lea shivered.

"As cold as a tomb," Ryan added.

"There's a turn-off here," Hawke said. He swung the flashlight into another tunnel on their right.

"And one up there on the left as well," said Sophie. Their voices echoed strangely in the tunnels.

Hawke moved the flashlight back around to the tunnel Sophie had found. There were steps in this one, and it descended even deeper into the earth.

"I don't like the look of that," Ryan said.

"Where's your spirit of adventure?" joked Hawke.

"We're not actually going in there, are we?"

"What do you think?"

They moved through the darkness for several more minutes before they reached what looked like a small room, carved painstakingly out of the bedrock. Hawke was finally beginning to enjoy himself.

Back in the SBS he had done all the usual Special Forces training – parachuting techniques, desert warfare, but after that they sent him down to Poole, in Dorset, where they gave him the specialist training in diving and just about anything else to do with maritime warfare.

He had also trained in pot-holing and caving, and had been part of the SBS commando team engaged in the fierce firefights in the Tora Bora cave complex where Osama Bin Laden was hiding. Not that he had ever told anyone that – no one except Liz.

Caves for him meant fun.

"It looks like an antechamber of some kind," Lea ran her hands over the walls, amazed by their smoothness. "This place is the find of the century."

Hawke looked concerned. "No, I think Poseidon's tomb is the find of the century. This is just one more step on the way there."

In the dust at their feet they noticed another burned-out glow-stick.

Hawke stared at it. "Zaugg again."

They turned a corner and saw one of Zaugg's men pinned to the cave wall with a spear through his heart.

"What the hell?" Ryan said.

"Did Zaugg do this?" Sophie asked.

"No," replied Hawke, studying the path of the spear. "This looks like some kind of ancient booby-trap – look there on the wall and you can see where the spear came from, and if you look on the floor you can see where he stepped on a pressure pad of some kind built into the path."

"Zaugg's obviously the kind of guy to lead from behind," Hart said.

Demetriou suddenly looked very nervous as they silently moved past the dead man and left him in his final resting place, where his bones would hang for the rest of eternity.

"Everyone be very careful where you step," Hawke shouted. "This place is rigged!"

They kept going deeper into the complex and a few paces later they emerged into an enormous cavern.

"A place this size must have been an aquifer once," said Lea. "No one could have carved something like this."

"Unless they were a god," Ryan said.

Moments later they found another hole in the ground.

Hawke began to lower himself down, negotiating the rough, crumbling edges of the ancient tunnel with care as he went. He reached the bottom and shone the flashlight around to find a tunnel stretching into darkness on the western edge.

Lea was next, then Ryan who was followed closely by Sophie and then Demetriou and Reaper. Hart lowered herself down last.

They pushed into the tunnel, Hawke staring up at the tiny aperture fifty feet above them and wondering if they would ever see daylight again.

They walked for several minutes, holding their silence and proceeding with a kind of anxious diligence, guns and glow-sticks raised and eyes adjusting to an even greater darkness.

"What are these marks in the ground?" Lea asked.

Hawke shone his flashlight to reveal gouge marks in the dirt. "Looks like Zaugg's dragging a lot of gear down here. He obviously doesn't want to leave empty-handed. And he's taken a lot of care to take his abseil lines with him as well. Obviously doesn't want anyone following him."

Then Hart spoke, her authoritative voice shattering the silence. "Watch out, everyone! There's another hole here – it looks like we're going further down."

They dropped a glow-stick down to reveal another descent of around fifty feet. Hart set up another abseil line, and a few moments later they were all together again on the lower level where a second tunnel now stretched further away to the west.

"Sooner or later we're going to end up under the bloody bay!" Hawke said.

With the thought of going under the sea in their minds, they pushed on into the tunnel, taking care not to stumble and injure themselves. This was not the time or place to get a broken ankle.

Then, without any warning, one side of the tunnel was gone – receding away into the darkness. "What the hell?" Hawke shone the flashlight at the wall and saw the tunnel had now turned into a ledge. To their right the safety of the carved tunnel wall had given way to a drop hundreds of feet down.

"Everyone get back!" he shouted. "We're on a ledge!"

Ryan peered down over the edge where a ravine formed and rows of razor-sharp stalagmites twisted up like needles. "I'm surprised this isn't on the tourist trail – and look!" He shone his flashlight at the far wall and illuminated a series of giant carvings of figures in the rock.

"And who might they be?" Scarlet said. She almost sounded impressed.

"Those are Hades and Zeus, and that must be Poseidon himself," Ryan said. "I'm not sure about that fella there though." His flashlight settled on the ghostly stone lines of the biggest face of all.

"He looks pretty angry, whoever he is," Sophie said.

"That is Kronos, the father of all time," Demetriou whispered in awe. His eyes were glazing over as he stared at the ancient god's face. "It can mean only one thing – we really are in the right place and must be getting closer to the tomb."

They moved on, and after a short walk they emerged at the top of more steps which led into yet another tunnel.

Lea looked up. "This place is like a labyrinth."

"It actually *is* a labyrinth," said Ryan.

Ahead, they saw Zaugg's team. They had caught them up. From their position further back they watched Zaugg and his men working their way forward deeper into the complex.

"He's been a busy boy," Scarlet said, frowning. "Where the hell did he get all those men from?"

Hawke looked at her. "A man like Zaugg is very resourceful, and very rich. Put those two qualities together and you get what you want, when you want it."

"Either way," Lea said, "we've got our work cut out for us now, Joe."

Hawke agreed, and nodded in appreciation of the fact.

"So what do we do?" Sophie asked.

Then Ryan sneezed.

Lea tutted. "Good work, genius."

Zaugg's men turned and opened fire with a ferocity Hawke had rarely seen outside of full military combat. The bullets traced over their heads and peppered the cavern wall behind them, blasting chunks of the ancient walls into smithereens and forcing them to take cover behind a handful of inadequate boulders at the mouth of the tunnel.

"Return fire!" Hawke screamed.

But it was too late. Already Zaugg's men were upon them, and he saw they were massively outnumbered. Seconds later it was close quarter combat as Zaugg's men were ordered forward to capture them.

Hawke met them head-on, punching one in the face and knocking him out, and then spinning around and grabbing another by the back of his head. He slammed him face-first into the rock wall and he fell into the dirt.

Another man fronted up to him. Hawke had been in more fights than he could remember, and knew how to assess his opponent quickly. This one looked like he was up for it. Hawke saw the tension in his fists and shoulders, and the hateful gleam in his eye.

The man pulled a knife from his belt and lunged toward Hawke. It was some kind of hunting knife in a black-matte finish with a very nasty serrated blade.

Hawke stepped aside and avoided the blade. As it sailed past him he spun around and leaned into the man, holding his knife-wielding hand at arm's length while he brought his hand down hard on the man's wrist and knocked the knife from his hand. It fell with a thud into the sand.

The man struggled to free himself but Hawke brought his right elbow up into his face and broke his nose, turning on his heel to land a solid inside power punch on the man's jaw and send him flying out of consciousness into the dirt.

Hawke turned to take stock of the situation.

Demetriou and Ryan were at the back, out of sight, and ahead of them was Scarlet Sloane, teaching some of the Swiss mercs about the pleasure of underestimating a woman with an intimate knowledge of Krav Maga. Hawke thought he could have been watching a Bruce Lee movie as she used Zaugg's men for her daily workout.

Lea and Reaper were fighting together, back to back, but slowly they were overwhelmed by the sheer force of numbers as a mix of Zaugg's Swiss mercs and local hired thugs piled forward into them.

Ahead, Zaugg, Grobel, Baumann and a dozen men moved forwards toward the tomb, their precious goal almost in sight.

One man turned to see his great leader deserting him, and Hawke took advantage of the moment, seizing the muzzle of his Uzi, and snatching it from the dazed man's grasp. He mercilessly smashed the butt into the center of his face. The man fell like a sack of potatoes into the dust.

"What's the plan now?" Lea screamed.

"You and Hart lead the others towards Zaugg while we finish up here, then Cairo and I'll bring up the rear."

"You were always good at that," Scarlet muttered.

"Oh, for *fuck's* sake!" Lea rolled her eyes. "Don't you ever give it a rest?"

"Take it easy, darling," Scarlet said coolly. "You'll not impress Joe here with foul language."

"Why, I ought to smack you in…"

"Not now chaps," Hart said. "We have arses to kick."

Slowly they turned the tables on them, and after taking out the last of the enemy, they moved forwards to attack Zaugg.

They gradually made their way deeper into the underground complex, closing in on the Swiss team, who were now in what looked like a dead end.

Zaugg screamed a string of curses in German and kicked the cave wall. The others moved forward to see what had enraged him so much. Hawke watched as he and Grobel discussed something at the end of the tunnel. There was nothing down there except a simple rock pool.

"He's saying that Grobel has led him the wrong way," Ryan said. "He's not very happy."

"I think that's obvious in *any* language." Hawke

watched Zaugg smack Grobel over the back of the head with his gloved hand and knock him to the ground.

Grobel tumbled forward and fell into the pool, and to the great surprise of everyone watching, completely disappeared.

"What the hell?" Ryan said.

Hawke sighed. "It's another buggering tunnel, only this time it's filled with water."

"The seventh tunnel in between us and the tomb, Ryan said. "Just like you wrote about professor."

"I always believed there would be seven levels," Demetriou said.

"If I were going to hide something like the tomb of a god," Lea said, "then I reckon at the end of an underwater tunnel might be a good place to start."

"Exactly my thinking," said Hawke, and smiled at her. Her face looked younger in the gentle light of the glow-sticks, and for the first time he saw her more as a woman and less just another ex-soldier.

Ahead of them, Grobel emerged from the pool and spat some water out of his mouth as he crawled out into the cave. He looked like a drowned rat.

"If I could just get a closer look," Ryan said, clambering up on the boulder.

"Get down!" said Hawke, as urgently as he could in a whisper.

Ryan whispered almost to himself: "I wonder how deep…" but then he lost his footing and slipped over, bringing a pile of stones and dust tumbling down on top of him.

Zaugg spun around and pointed toward them. He screamed more orders and Baumann and some men lunged forward with guns blazing.

Before they could even work out their position, Hawke was on his feet, grabbing the gun from Baumann, and forcing the barrel to point down into the dirt as he raised the back of his hand into the Bavarian's face at the same time. Baumann screamed as his nose smashed into pulp and then he staggered back into the wall.

Then pandemonium as Zaugg's forces scattered to defensive positions and Grobel ducked back down into the water to save himself. Zaugg turned his gun on Hawke but it jammed.

In the chaos, Hawke grabbed Zaugg around the neck and held him at gunpoint, slowly pacing backwards away from the Swiss and toward the relative safety of his own people behind him.

"Put your guns down or I'll kill him!" Hawke shouted, pushing the Uzi into Zaugg's neck. He watched as Zaugg's men looked to their leader for their next command. Hawke felt Zaugg tense with rage, and then reluctantly order his men to lower their weapons.

They began to put them on the dirt when everything changed.

"Not so fast!" a voice shouted behind him. The men stopped what they were doing and picked their guns back up. Before Hawke could react, he felt the muzzle of a gun pushing into the base of his skull. "All of you are to stay armed! It is you, Mr Hawke, who will be lowering his gun, or I will blow your head off."

Only now did he recognize the voice.

Demetriou.

Hawke's mind raced with possible plays, but he knew it was over.

"Release Herr Zaugg, please," Demetriou said.

Hawke released Zaugg, who turned around slowly and took the Uzi out of his hands, grinning as he did so, and never taking his eyes from Hawke.

"Thank you, Yannis," Zaugg said. "I knew I could rely on you."

CHAPTER TWENTY-SEVEN

Demetriou stepped swiftly away from Hawke, covering him with the Uzi at all times, and moved over to where Zaugg was rejoining Grobel. Baumann was nursing his broken nose.

"You filthy traitor!" Lea said.

Demetriou shrugged his shoulders. "I have been working with Zaugg for many weeks. He promises me all the funding I need for my researches. When your team arrived at my office I knew all I had to do was play along and I could deliver you to him as easy as *one, two, three*."

"Are you insane, professor?" Hawke said. "You can't trust a man like Hugo Zaugg."

"Well, I…" Demetriou began. Hawke wondered if he was thinking about the dead man on the spear further back in the complex – Zaugg's canary in the coalmine. "I…"

Zaugg's hoarse cackle filled the cavern. "This is actually most fortuitous," he said, cutting off Demetriou's reply. "I find myself wondering what terrors might lurk in this watery hole and then you turn up, the perennial bad penny."

He pointed at the pool with the Uzi. "And I also wonder who among us has demonstrated an amusingly entertaining capacity to hold his breath for extended periods of time."

Hawke knew where this was going.

"Mr Hawke – I desire of you that you climb into that

pool and swim to wherever it leads and return with the news of your discovery. If you do not return, I will kill your friends. If you try and double-cross me, I will kill your friends. If you are not climbing into the hole in ten seconds I will kill your friends."

For added effect, Zaugg cocked the Uzi and pointed it at Lea's face. "I will start with this one."

Hawke knew he had no choice, and watching the smug realization of his victory dawn on Zaugg's face was almost more than he could bear. He moved forward slowly, silently mouthing the words "I'm sorry" to Lea as he passed her, and climbed down into the rock pool.

"Grobel!" snapped Zaugg. "You will go with him, and take this." He handed Grobel the golden key. "If we have the right place then you will need it. If you too think about double-crossing me, simply remember that I know where your family lives."

Zaugg tossed Hawke a dive-light from the pile of equipment at the side of the pool, and Grobel climbed down beside him, clutching the tiny golden disc in his hand. Before he went under the surface Zaugg handed him one of the harpoons from the equipment box.

Hawke dived into the black water, shining the light ahead of him. Behind him, Grobel tried to keep up, harpoon in one hand and disc in the other. The tunnel stretched ahead, narrow at first but gradually turning into a much wider space. After swimming for a minute or two it twisted upwards and Hawke realized they were at a dead end.

He turned in the tunnel and made a signal with his hands to indicate to Grobel that there was nowhere else to go, but then he noticed a small carving in the rock, lit for just a second as his light passed over it in the cold, watery darkness. He returned the light to it and saw it was the same shape and size as the disc.

Grobel swam forward and pushed the disc into the slot, twisting it to the left and then to the right. There was a judder almost like an earthquake and the end of the tunnel began to shift to the side.

It was a door fashioned from a massive boulder. They swam through the new aperture and Hawke saw a strange kind of mechanism was built into the rock. It looked like it was using gravity to slide the boulder downwards and to the side when the key released a metal bar from behind it.

Inside, Hawke saw the familiar sight of surface water above him. He swam up toward it and surfaced to see he was in another huge underground cave. He shone the torch into the blackness and was almost blinded by the flash of gold reflecting back at him.

It was an enormous pile of gold bigger then he could possibly have imagined before setting his eyes upon such a thing. In the distance was a heavy-looking stone monument covered in ornate carvings and the same strange, ancient inscriptions he recognized from the golden key – something told him it could only be the sarcophagus.

He had found the Vault of Poseidon.

*

Swimming back through the underwater tunnel, Hawke considered taking Grobel out and snatching the harpoon. It would be easy enough, he considered, but where would it get him?

He would have to emerge in the rock pool surrounded by Zaugg's men. He would do anything to protect the others now, even Ryan who had saved his life back in the sea. He couldn't risk their lives in some crazy attempt to play the hero.

He ruled out attacking Grobel and emerged in the other cave, crawling out of the rock pool soaking wet.

Zaugg was overcome with excitement when Hawke and Grobel gave their report. He had his team set up a pump connected to a generator and began to suck the water from the underground tunnel. His destiny was almost upon him.

Hawke joined the others while Zaugg oversaw his men as they put down a line of pipes and connected them to the generator set up in the bigger cave behind them. Its tinny engine roared in the enclosed space and started to fill it with fumes. They watched as the water was slowly removed from the tunnel and pumped into the larger cave. It spilled out and began to form an enormous pool.

Lea sidled up to Hawke in the semi-darkness. "If this is your idea of a date, Joe Hawke," she said, "You're not even getting to first base, never mind second."

"Are you warming to me, Miss Donovan?"

"I could get a guy like you if I clicked my fingers," she said, smiling, embarrassed by her words the moment they left her lips.

"Oh, you think so, do you?"

"Listen, Joe," her words were quiet now, and vaguely hesitant. She looked at Scarlet who was standing closer to Zaugg's team, and then to Sophie. "There's something I have to tell you."

"I know, you could have me anytime you please."

"No, it's important. I shouldn't be telling you this but..."

"If it's about what you started to tell me in New York, you don't have to justify anything to me. You don't have to explain yourself, expecially if it's about something that happened in the army."

Lea moved closer to him, but then moved away again,

as if frightened of getting too close, physically and emotionally. "No, it's not that. It's something else, something about Eden."

Hawke turned to look into her eyes. He had known all along she and Eden were keeping something back from him. "What is it, Lea?"

Ahead of them, the operation to pump out the water was coming to an end. All that remained in the previously underwater tunnel was a few inches of water. Zaugg ordered his men to remove the pumping equipment and shut down the generator.

Seconds later Baumann threw the switch and the engine sputtered for a few seconds before quitting completely, leaving a new, deafening silence in the cavern complex.

Hawke turned to Lea and held her gently by the shoulders. "What is it?" he asked. "What do you want to tell me about Eden?"

Lea looked up at him, her eyes filled with uncertainty. She glanced at the others and then back to Hawke. "I... I can't tell you now. I'm sorry."

She moved out of his grasp and stepped away.

Zaugg began barking orders at Baumann, who in turn shouted at the men, who then scurried about with boxes of equipment, flashlights and glow-sticks. Slowly, they slipped into the tunnel.

"You!" Zaugg shouted, aiming his gun at Hawke and the others. "I hope you will accept my invitation to die in the vault of Poseidon. Get moving!"

Hawke moved forward first, and Lea and the others followed his lead. He knew there would be few chances of survival deep inside the tomb, but they were covered by at least half a dozen submachine guns and Zaugg wasn't about to take any chances after the disaster on the Thalassa. He didn't look like the kind of man to underestimate the same enemy twice.

As they approached the tunnel entrance, Zaugg stepped up to Hawke, muzzle of the Uzi aimed at his stomach.

"You thought you could save the world," Zaugg said. "But instead, you have helped me to bring about its total destruction. A glorious new dawn is about to rise over mankind, Mr Hawke, and you are here to witness it!"

Hawke's heart sank. All he could do was hope to heaven that Hugo Zaugg had badly misjudged the power of whatever he thought was inside the tomb.

Slowly, with guns at their backs, they entered the darkness of the final tunnel and moved towards the vault.

CHAPTER TWENTY-EIGHT

With the water gone they were able to walk through the tunnel to the vault of Poseidon. Once inside the giant cave they turned the corner by the boulder-door and were instantly speechless when they saw the treasure before them.

It was mostly gold in the form of coins, jugs, flasks and goblets, but there were vast piles of glittering diamonds forming a strange, warm amber in the light of the glow-sticks. Other heaps of gems – rubies, sapphires, emeralds and even opals littered the vault's floor and left Hawke stunned with awe.

It didn't seem possible, Hawke considered, that so much wealth had been hidden down here for so many countless centuries, lost to history, lost to mankind. But however awe-inspiring he thought the treasure was, he knew Zaugg was here for another reason.

And Ryan saw it first. "It's Poseidon's sarcophagus!"

With his exclamation still echoing in the cavernous space, everyone turned to see the ancient stone sarcophagus in the center of the tomb. It was partially obscured by another great pile of gold coins pushed up against its carved stone sides like a golden snowdrift, but there it stood, formidable, undeniable. The legend turned real.

Hawke found himself moved in a way he hadn't thought possible until this moment. For the briefest of seconds he thought he knew how Zaugg felt, the obsession with power and immortality coursing through his veins like adrenalin and taking over his rational mind. Was Poseidon really inside that sarcophagus? Where was the trident? And, most intoxicating of all, where was the source of eternal life?

Zaugg was even more captivated by it all, and was now wandering among the heaps of diamonds and golden goblets muttering to himself like a madman. He picked up a simple coin and tossed it casually back down again when he saw something that pleased him even more.

"Finally my destiny will be fulfilled!" Zaugg said. "I will raise the greatest army known to man."

Hawke smirked. "I'd be surprised if he could raise an erection."

Baumann struck him hard in between the shoulder blades with the butt of his gun. "Enough!"

The Englishman staggered back to his feet and his mind turned slowly away from the treasure and back to the tactical situation. He noticed that on the wall behind the sarcophagus there was a small trickle of water running through a split in the rock. Baumann saw it too.

Zaugg saw nothing but the glistening gold before him and his eyes crawled over the treasure. He was beginning to look nervous. "Open the sarcophagus!" he screeched.

"Be careful, Zaugg!" Lea shouted. "You have no idea what you're doing. You're playing with fire!"

"Silence!" said Zaugg, reddening with rage. "No one tells me what to do! This is a great moment in history. I have waited all my life for this! What my father tried and failed to do, his only son has succeeded in achieving. Inside that sarcophagus Poseidon keeps the greatest secret of all time and now it is rightfully mine to use as I wish."

Hawke turned to Lea and whispered in her ear. "Now

there's your guy who was smacked too hard as a child."

Zaugg ran his hands over the smooth, carved edges of Poseidon's tomb as if he were caressing a lover. His eyes sparkled with a crazed, obsessive look. "With the power of immortality my victory over the world will be final. I will rule in the way that even Hitler was too weak to do."

"You can't say he lacks ambition," Hawke muttered.

Then Zaugg ordered Demetriou to approach the sarcophagus.

The Greek scholar looked anxious, but did as he was told, picking up a crowbar and walking through the piles of gold coins to the sarcophagus. Zaugg barked another command in German and seconds later two more men joined Demetriou.

Demetriou muttered a series of inaudible words – prayers, maybe – and began to jam his crowbar into the gap running around the lid of the ancient sarcophagus. A cloud of dust billowed up into his face and he coughed and wiped his eyes. He seemed to be having trouble getting any further.

"What's the problem?" Zaugg said.

"It's not moving," Demetriou said, his voice wobbling. "Perhaps we should remove the sarcophagus to another location before…"

"Open the sarcophagus!"

"I can't," Demetriou said. "I won't!" He stepped back in fear. He looked like he had seen a ghost.

"Very well," Zaugg said. He raised his gun and filled Professor Demetriou full of holes, exploding his chest with the impact of the bullets and knocking him down with a heavy thud in the dust at the base of the sarcophagus.

"You!" Zaugg screamed at the two men. "Remove the lid!"

With startled terror on their faces, the two men tried their best, but they too found the lid unmovable.

"It weighs more than lead!" one said, desperately trying to avoid the same fate as Yannis Demetriou.

A few garbled sentences in German and Zaugg stalked over to them, knocking one out of the way and trying with all his might to force the bar under the stone lid of the sarcophagus.

"The real treasure will be in here," he said. "It must be opened!"

On the wall behind the sarcophagus the trickle of water had grown larger. Hawke realized it was some kind of booby-trap, activated if anyone tried to tamper with Poseidon's sarcophagus.

Several minutes of puffing and panting later, Zaugg cursed and kicked the side of it with his boot. "*Verdammt!*"

"That's not very respectful," Lea whispered.

"I wonder if this place puts a curse on everyone who enters it, like Tutankhamen's tomb did?" Ryan asked casually.

'Silence!" Zaugg shouted. "Baumann, place a charge on the sarcophagus and get that lid off, now!"

Hawke watched the former German Special Forces man place a couple of modest charges around the lid of the sarcophagus before ordering everyone back behind the safety of some boulders.

Zaugg watched with zeal as Baumann blew the charges and the tomb filled with a fine gray dust and the smell of burned explosives.

"Grobel! To the tomb, now. Tell me what is inside."

Grobel was hesitant, but Zaugg's Uzi helped him make the decision to go. He walked slowly over to the shattered tomb and held his glow-stick over the lid as he peered inside.

Hawke and the others watched him in the settling dust, their flashlights illuminating him from a safe distance as he craned his neck over the giant sarcophagus.

"It's safe!" he called back. "There's a lot of rubble inside, and dust, but…"

Zaugg clambered to his feet and pushed Baumann roughly out of his way as he moved forward to the sarcophagus. Hawke watched him closely as he too leaned over the edge beside Grobel. He lowered his hands inside and began to rummage around inside, muttering to himself incoherently.

For a moment he simply stared into the dusty sarcophagus, then turned away, wide-eyed with either fear or amazement.

Then the split in the far wall began to grow in size, and small pieces of rock started to crumble out of it. The trickle of water doubled in size and began to flow out into the tomb like a small river.

"It's a trap!" Baumann said. "The whole bay is above us – we'll all be drowned."

Zaugg looked coolly at the rushing water and then back to the sarcophagus. For a moment, a sort of desolation shadowed his face, but then his eyes were lit with a new idea, and an evil, frozen smile began to dance on his lips.

"Baumann, get the men to start loading everything in this cave back to the trucks. We cannot risk being here any longer. Everything goes back to the mountain in Switzerland. I do not want a single penny left in here, not one single gem or coin! And start with the contents of the sarcophagus, is that understood?"

Baumann understood, and moments later the men loaded the contents of the tomb into smaller boxes and walked them through the drained tunnel and back along the complex to Zaugg's fleet of trucks. Slowly the water began to pour down the wall and collect on the tomb's floor.

"I have a bad feeling about this," Reaper said. "I need a cigarette."

As the men emptied the tomb, Zaugg began to grow more and more anxious, peering into other chests and boxes littered around the sarcophagus's base with increased concern. "Wo ist die Karte?" he said, quietly at first, and then screaming at the top of his lungs with his arms outstretched in supplication. "Poseidon, wo ist Ihre Karte?!"

Hawke leaned closer to Ryan. "I'm guessing that means 'map', am I right?"

"You are indeed. He's asking Poseidon where his map is."

"A bloody map?" Hawke muttered. "It took me long enough to accept he was guarding the secret of eternal life in his tomb, and now you're telling me Zaugg was just looking for a map all along?"

Ryan nodded his head. "Looks that way."

"That means it could be anywhere in the world."

"Not that you will ever find it," Baumann said. He smacked Hawke in the back with the butt of his rifle and knocked him into the dirt on the floor. "Because you're all going to be dead in a few minutes. Now get up."

As Hawke clambered to his feet, Baumann's men walked over with more rope and cable-ties.

CHAPTER TWENTY-NINE

Hawke watched the last of the treasure disappear down the tunnel, followed by a soaking wet Dietmar Grobel, his terrifying reputation diminished somewhat by his new sodden demeanor. It was hard to look intimidating when you were dripping with sea water and cave slime.

Zaugg wasted no time in ordering his men to tie them up and start blocking them into the tomb by placing boulders in the entrance tunnel. Having failed to deal with the problem on board the Thalassa he seemed much more determined to end their challenge to his quest this time around.

Several men, led by Heinrich Baumann, roughly bound their arms behind their backs, cutting into their flesh with the careless application of plastic cable-ties, and then tying them back to back in pairs with short lengths of rope.

Hawke watched uneasily as Baumann fitted the C4 explosives to the wall a few inches above where the water from the bay above their heads was pouring through the slit. He went about his work methodically, enjoying every step of the process as he secured the explosives and set the radio antennae up.

Zaugg proudly explained to them what was about to unfold in the last few moments of their lives. "When that tomb wall blows, thousands of tons of seawater will explode through the hole and fill this cave in a few short minutes," Zaugg said with undisguised pleasure. "And that will end all evidence of this tomb, as well as bringing your irritating existence to a swift and permanent conclusion."

"Why don't you untie me so we can sort this out man to man, Zaugg?' Hawke was baiting him, trying to make him lose his cool. "Or are you not man enough for that?"

"My dear fellow, men of my social rank do not brawl in public with men like you."

"I'll let you throw the first punch, Zaugg. I'll even let you tie one hand behind my back."

Zaugg frowned, his cold eyes sparkling with a menace Hawke had never seen before. "You seem remarkably composed for a man so close to death," he said calmly. "Was it Plato who once said, *No one knows whether death, which people fear to be the greatest evil, may not be the greatest good*? I shall never know, because I will be immortal soon enough. On this one matter you will beat me to the answer!"

"Cheerfulness in the face of adversity, Zaugg! That's the commando's way."

"Really? *That's* the commando's way?" Scarlet said. "This is why I joined the army."

"Pfft, the *army*," Hart said.

Zaugg ordered the last of his men from the flooding tomb. "Besides, I will take an insurance policy in the form of the wonderful Miss Donovan."

Baumann dragged Lea to her feet and held the muzzle of his submachine gun in her ribs.

"I never felt we really got to know each other on the Thalassa – may I call you *Lea*?" Zaugg said, gently stroking the side of her face with his bony fingers. "Perhaps, with a little encouragement you will learn to be more *accommodating*?"

With her hands restrained by the cable-ties, Lea's only way of reacting to Zaugg's repulsive touch was to spit in his face, which she did with violent accuracy.

Zaugg wiped the spit from his eye and stared at in his hand. "In that case," he said slowly, "perhaps your personality is better suited to Baumann here."

Baumann grabbed Lea and dragged her through the tunnel entrance as the last boulders were pushed into place.

Zaugg laughed and stepped jauntily from the tomb, the last of the light receding into the tunnel with him as he took the glow-stick to light his own way to safety. Then the final boulder was pushed in the entrance, blocking their way and sealing them in the tomb.

"Your girl makes a bit of a habit of getting kidnapped, doesn't she?" Scarlet said.

"She's not my girl, Cairo, so pack it in. He's taken her so we can't attack him on the way to the bloody airfield, or even shoot the bastard down in midair. When he's used her for that he'll just hand her over to that freaking maniac Baumann, and God knows what that psycho will do to her."

He desperately looked on the wall where the C4 was stuck a few inches above the cracked rock.

"When that thing goes off, we're all dead, right?" Ryan asked.

"No," said Hawke. "It's too far away to kill us with the blast."

"Thank heaven for small mercies," Ryan said.

"Instead we'll drown like rats when the Bay of Sami bursts through that wall and fills this tomb with sea water in about three minutes."

"Great, and we're trapped in here."

"Maybe not," Hawke said. "I'm hoping the force of the water will knock out those boulders they put in the door."

Ryan looked at Hawke, to the C4 and then back to Hawke. "You know, I'm really beginning to enjoy this."

And then the C4 exploded with a terrific detonation that was almost deafening in the cavernous tomb. Before the smoke and rubble had cleared they heard the water rushing into the vault.

Seconds later it was deep enough to give them buoyancy, and then they were able to slip out from beneath the ropes but their hands were still tied behind their backs. As Hawke had thought, the pressure of the water building against the boulders was beginning to push them clear of the entrance.

"We have to work fast!" he shouted. "In a few minutes the water will be over our heads and at the roof of this cave."

He turned and rubbed the cable-ties that bound his hands up against a piece of serrated boulder, and seconds later the plastic split into two and he was free.

Now the water was up to their waists as he struggled to slash the cable-ties from everyone else's wrists.

When he had done this, they waded through the tunnel as fast as they could go in the darkness until they reached the other cave along. Zaugg's generator and other pieces of now unnecessary equipment were just left scattered on the floor.

The water began to rush up though the rock pool behind them and suddenly the ground beneath their feet began to tremble and shake. Chunks of rock fell from the ceiling of the cave and landed with a heavy, crunching thud into the stone floor of the underground tunnel system.

"The flood has destabilized the entire complex!" Hart said.

Hawke watched in horror as part of the cave wall beside the rock pool began to sink into the floor, bulging forward and crumbling as it went down.

"The whole place is about to implode!" he shouted.

"This is not good," Reaper said. "In fact, I wish I was at home right now, maybe with some wine..."

"We have to get out the way we came but we need to run right now or the water will overtake us."

They all ran back along the tunnels, but their escape was cut short when they realized Zaugg had taken their abseiling lines.

"What now?"

Hawke stared up at the vertical shaft – fifty feet up and impossible to climb before the rushing water reached them.

"We have to let the water take us up," he said. "We have no other choice."

'But the shaft's not wide enough for all of us. Some will have to stay at the back and swim up afterwards."

Hawke stepped forward. "No problem for me."

"Or me," added Scarlet.

"Pour moi, c'est pas de problem," said Reaper.

"Ryan and Sophie go first, then the commodore and Reaper," Hawke said. "Then Cairo and I will swim up."

"Water's coming!" Ryan shrieked.

The ice-cold water rushed over them and bubbled up around them as it pushed them into the shaft. Ryan looked terrified but he and Sophie quickly disappeared from view when the water pushed them upwards. Then Hart followed them up, her head a few inches below the water line, Reaper not far behind. Finally, Scarlet and Hawke swam up beneath the others, straining their eyes in the darkness, aware only of the kicking heels of their friends above them.

Moments later the water spat them out into the next level and left them gasping for air as it began to fill up around them yet again. This time it filled at a slower rate because of the bigger size of the recess, but it was still too fast for comfort.

"There won't be a sodding bay left at this rate," Ryan said. "It'll all be down here."

They repeated the process for the other vertical shafts and then made their way up the stone steps, twisting in a spiral as they climbed, their flashlights bobbing about erratically as they ran to escape the chaos behind them.

They could feel the cave complex collapsing behind them with the power of an earthquake and the terrible noise of the destruction chased them up the circular steps like a monster with a taste for their blood.

Towards the top, they began to slow a little. Hawke and Reaper were now at the front, with Scarlet directly behind them. Ryan and Sophie were in the middle and Hart at the back.

Finally they reached the exit, following the tiny slit of sunlight until it grew large enough to reveal itself as the entrance to the dugout at the bottom of the initial vertical shaft.

Again Zaugg had taken the abseiling lines with him, so they repeated the process once again and allowed the water to push them to the top of the shaft.

When they were all clear, and panting on the side of the hill, the water rose up just high enough in the shaft to spill a little over the edge, and then slide back down again to around halfway up.

"So *that's* how wells are made," Scarlet said, deadpan. A moment later, they all started to laugh.

CHAPTER THIRTY

Their moment of humor was cut short when they heard the sound of diesel engines laboring somewhere in the distance.

"What's that?" Sophie asked.

"Sounds like trucks to me, darling," said Scarlet.

Hawke cocked his head. "She's right – I can hear vehicles to the south." He scrambled up a low rise and took up a covered position behind the trunk of an umbrella pine. "It must be Zaugg making his escape back to the airfield."

Hawke watched as three black Jeep Cherokees drove slowly down the hill to the south of Sami. They kicked up a trail of orange dust from the unsealed road. He turned to Hart. "Olivia, listen – Reaper and I will go after them – make sure everyone's all right here and organize an aircraft. Something tells me we're going to need a flight back to Switzerland as soon as possible."

Reaper was still watching Zaugg's getaway through his monocular.

"He's getting away!" said Ryan, who looked like a drowned ferret coming in at ninety pounds max.

"This man is a genius," Reaper added, bringing his heavy hand down on Ryan's shoulder in a gesture of feigned admiration.

"We need a vehicle," Hawke said. "Any suggestions?"

"Try that," Reaper replied. He pointed at the last of Zaugg's Jeeps, now caught in a rut at the top of the hill and separated from the others.

"Idiots. Must be one of the locals Zaugg hired out of desperation."

Hawke and Reaper picked up some weapons and split up to approach the stranded Jeep from different directions. An overweight man dressed in brand-new military fatigues and a cowboy hat, obviously bought online for the purpose of the treasure hunt, jumped from the Jeep and aimed his rifle at Hawke.

Hawke raised his hands while Reaper approached stealthily from behind and knocked the rifle from the man's hands before landing a bear-like punch square on his jaw and sending him flying to the ground.

"Please – please don't kill me!" The man was in his late sixties, and overweight. He spoke poor English in a heavy Greek accent, and when Reaper kicked his cowboy hat off it revealed a thin gray comb-over now out of place and hanging forlornly to the side of his chubby face.

"Don't kill you?" Reaper said, stony-faced. The bear-like Frenchman flicked a small stone over the cliff with the steel toecap of his combat boot and watched it fly out into the air above the ocean.

"I have money now! Look – gold! Look in the Jeep. More gold than you can imagine! I'll pay you anything you ask. Anything! Look at the diamonds!"

Reaper offered the panic-stricken man a broad, generous smile. "But some things are too expensive to buy," he said. "Including your life, it turns out."

A short burst from the machine pistol induced a second of terrible convulsions in the man, who then slumped to a lifeless heap, his chest peppered with bullet holes.

"Turns out, mon ami, you can dish it out," Reaper said, with satisfaction, "but you cannot take it. This is the right expression, no?"

Hawke nodded. "Yes, that's the right expression."

From their position on the cliff they watched Zaugg's Jeep leading the others down the road. They got out of the rut in seconds and began their pursuit of the Swiss. A battle between saving Lea, punishing Zaugg and saving the world from this madness fought for supremacy in Hawke's frantic mind.

"Do you think he knows it's us in here?" Hawke asked as they drew closer to the convoy.

"The answer is yes because we've got company," Reaper said, looking in the rear-view. It was a second Jeep from the front which had looped around and come in behind them.

Reaper stamped down on the throttle and the Jeep jolted forward in the scrub in a roar of revs and dust. The Jeep had a serious 4x4 capability and no trouble climbing the rocky slope ahead of them and regaining the higher ground where they joined another track and turned south in the search for the other vehicles.

Zaugg's men in the other Jeep behind them drove over the body of the hired Greek lackey and swung around in the gravel. Moments later it was behind Hawke and Reaper and gaining on them.

Reaper floored the throttle while Hawke climbed over to the back seats and cleared a space among the loot-laden boxes.

"Let the dog see the rabbit!" Hawke blasted out the rear window with the Heckler and Koch MP7 machine pistol, showering the track behind with shards of the reinforced safety glass.

"I think we are the rabbit right now, my friend."

"Where's your optimism?"

Reaper laughed. "I lost it along with everything else when Monique divorced me. The *bitch*."

The Jeep raced along the east coast path, a sheer drop of at least a hundred feet just a few yards to its right, and a thick row of impenetrable scrub and olive trees on their left.

Through the newly opened window to the rear, Hawke could see their pursuers more clearly now, especially now they were closing on them with such speed. There was a driver, and another man, presumably one of Zaugg's Greek facilitators. This second man leaned out his window and aimed his gun at them. From where Hawke was sitting it looked like a Strasser hunting rifle.

"A shame we got such a crappy Jeep," Reaper said, glancing in the rear-view mirror at the 6 litre bearing down on them.

"You can only play with the hand you're dealt," Hawke said. He fired the MP7 through the rear window and watched with pleasure as a line of bullets struck the Jeep's grille and peppered across the hood and windshield.

The noise of the machine pistol in the enclosed cab of the Cherokee was deafening, but not unexpected to the two former soldiers. The other Jeep swerved violently for a few moments, causing the passenger to fire off a shot aimlessly into the air.

After he had composed himself, the passenger used his rifle butt to smash the windshield glass out and the driver was able to get back on track in his lethal pursuit of them.

"That bought us five seconds," Reaper said. "Thanks, Joe."

They followed the track down a steep incline, at one point striking a deep pothole and nearly veering off the cliff to the right.

The Jeep behind them accelerated, the driver clearly

more familiar with the intricacies of the track than Reaper. "He must be another local."

Hawke watched with horror as the passenger disappeared back inside the Jeep and fumbled around for a moment before emerging again with an RPG-7D, a portable, handheld anti-tank rocket-propelled grenade launcher. Developed by the Soviets in the early nineteen-sixties, it was cheap and readily available, used by armies, terrorists and guerrilla forces all over the world.

"Yeah, maybe we have a slight problem," he called over to Reaper.

They were still hemmed in by the olives on their left, and the cliff-edge immediately to their right. Neither offered a realistic escape from their pursuers.

The passenger took a few moments to aim the RPG. He was clearly having trouble getting a fix on them because of the roughness of the terrain, and his reluctance to fire it made Hawke conclude he didn't have an abundant supply of warheads with him in the Jeep.

Reaper called back to tell Hawke that a low, dry-stone wall had replaced the olives to their left, but before Hawke could reply there was a cloud of gray smoke from the rear of the RPG, and a bigger flash of white smoke from the front – the signature calling card of the RPG-7.

Hawke flinched as the lethal munition left the launcher, a second flash as the rocket inside the warhead fired up to propel it into their Jeep, screeching through the warm Greek day like one of the Trojan dragons sent by Poseidon to kill Laocoön.

"Then go left!" he screamed at Reaper, who instinctively swung the heavy 4x4 over to the left, sliding down a shallow embankment and striking the wall in a shower of white sparks. A terrific grinding sound filled the cab as the front wing of the Jeep scraped along the stones and slowed them down, flinging rubble behind them like gravel chips.

Reaper struggled to steer the vehicle away from the wall but keep out of the way of the warhead, which flashed past them and disappeared into the distance. A few seconds later they saw another puff of smoke and the crack of an explosion in the side of a hill a few hundred yards ahead of them.

With the danger past, for now, Reaper swung to the left and their Jeep scrambled up the rocky slope away from the wall, but in his zeal to escape he drastically oversteered and seconds later their Jeep almost drove straight off the coast path, forcing another correction on the part of Reaper to bring the vehicle under control.

Their hunter had gained on them significantly in the chaos of the RPG warhead, and Hawke saw they were preparing a second RPG.

He thought fast. Ahead of them the road was running out – they were now approaching the descent into Sami.

Another puff of gray and white smoke from the RPG.

"Go right!" screamed Hawke.

"Right! That's the cliff."

"Then get ready for a swim."

Reaper swung the Jeep to the right, but more cautiously this time, as an error wouldn't mean swimming, but certain death.

The Jeep skidded over to the right in a cloud of dust and gas fumes before running up on to the scraggy grass verge that precipitated the cliff edge. Reaper was on the left, so Hawke shot out the rear right passenger window and shifted across to get a better look.

"You have about an inch and we're over," he shouted, ducking instinctively as the second warhead raced past them, this time to the left, and ending its days in the same way as the first.

"Close," Reaper said.

"Not as close as this," said Hawke. He aimed the MP7 and fired another long burst of bullets at the Jeep. Closer now, their pursuers were an easier target, and the second volley tore across their Jeep from the top to the bottom, striking the driver several times in the head and chest.

He slumped forward and the Jeep spun out of control. Hawke saw the passenger trying to push the driver away from the wheel but it was too late. They flew off the side of the road, dust, grit and grass spraying in a wild arc behind them as they plunged behind the line of the cliff.

Seconds later Hawke heard a metallic crunching sound as the Jeep thudded into the rocks at the base of the cliff, and then an enormous explosion.

"Where did they go?" Reaper said, straining to see in the rear-view mirror while keeping the Jeep from sharing the same fate.

"They had to fly." Hawke reloaded the MP7 with the ammo from the back of the Jeep and climbed into the front passenger seat.

"What about Zaugg?"

Hawke watched as Zaugg's convoy trundled to the south of Sami on its way to the airfield. "We keep following them. I'll call Hart and have her join us at the airport. I don't want him leaving our sight."

Hawke and Reaper kept their distance as they tailed Zaugg's convoy to Kefalonia International Airport, and weren't surprised to see them pull up alongside a white Boeing 767 idling on the apron. It had the words ZAUGG INDUSTRIES painted on the side in black letters.

"He doesn't do things by half, I'll give him that," Hawke said.

"You think we can stop him?" Reaper asked.

"No. He's obviously bought his way out of here – the customs guys aren't even looking in those boxes. A pay-off, I guess. We just have to hope Hart and the others get here fast."

*

Hart and the others arrived in an old Land Rover, courtesy of Sophie's hotwiring skills, but it was too late to stop Zaugg.

"He flew out a quarter of an hour ago," Reaper said, casually sucking on a cigarette.

"Did you manage to organize a plane?" Hawke asked Hart.

She shook her head. "Not enough time, sorry. Not even *I* am that amazing."

"Then we'll have to make other arrangements."

After customs and security, it didn't take Hawke long to persuade a cleaner to part with his clearance card and then they were airside and walking across to a line of private jets parked outside a hangar on the east side of the airport. Moments later they were inside one of the jets.

"Who the hell are you?" said an obese businessman. He spoke in a Central Russian dialect. He was surrounded by women.

"We're your new flight crew." Hawke powered a fist into the man's face and knocked him unconscious to the floor in less than a second.

One of the women screamed hysterically. "Do you know who that was?"

"I couldn't care less. Now sit down and shut up."

"That was Yevgeny Gorokhov! Greatest glamour photographer in Russia."

"Glamour photographer!" Scarlet said. "They're porn models for God's sake."

"You've got to be kidding," said Reaper, arching an oddly appreciative eyebrow.

"They're porn stars?!" Ryan said, a grin spreading across his face.

"We're models," said one of the women haughtily but not particularly convincingly. "Not porn stars. How *dare* you?!"

"Only you could hijack a plane full of porn stars, Joe," said Hart.

"Hey! How could I have known what they were? We needed a plane and I got us one. You could be a little more grateful."

"They're not porn stars," Ryan said. "They're models. She just said so."

"He's right," Reaper said. "She did just say that."

"Please, guys," said Ryan, never lifting his eyes from the women. "I think we need to get in the air. I feel a warm front coming on."

"Oh, do shut up, Ryan," Scarlet said. "And stop being so bloody sexist and pathetic, you little nerd. I cannot believe a woman like Lea married you. I guess she was young. That's what it must have been, am I right? Young and stupid."

Hawke laughed. "Ouch."

"And you can shut up too." Scarlet folded her arms and pursed her lips.

"Where are you flying tonight?" Hawke asked the women.

"We go back to Moscow. We had a photoshoot here."

"A *photoshoot*," Ryan said. "I love it. Where's the camera?"

"We go to Moscow!"

"Not any more you're not. We're going to

Switzerland and we need to get going right now, so everyone shut up and buckle up, in that order."

In the air, Ryan busied himself serving the women drinks, and then brought Hawke and Scarlet some beers.

"Having fun, Ryan?" Hawke asked, smiling. He was starting to feel like his older brother.

"That one's Tatjana," Ryan said. "And the one in the boa is Liliya."

"You can't keep them, all right Ryan?" Scarlet said.

Hawke resisted the temptation that had so easily devoured Ryan, and spent the flight considering tactical options and discussing the next phase of the attack with Hart. No matter how hard he tried to focus on the matter professionally, his mind kept wandering to Lea. He couldn't let her die the way he had let Liz die back in Hanoi.

On the approach to Sion the Citation banked gracefully to the port side to reveal a stunning vista of the Swiss Alps, snow-capped and glistening a pink-white in the late afternoon sun.

The aircraft then swung back with a heavy forty degree turn to starboard to line up with Runway 07. Hawke watched the lights of Sion grow larger as the plane extended flaps and he heard the gear go down.

A few moments later they were racing along the runway, speed brakes activated and the powerful reverse thrusters deployed bringing the jet to taxi speed in seconds.

It was only a matter of time before he got his revenge on Hugo Zaugg.

CHAPTER THIRTY-ONE

Swiss Alps

The powerful Sikorsky swooped over the town of Sion and thundered through a narrow valley, flanked on either side by steep tree-lined mountainsides and rocky precipices.

Less than thirty minutes ago they had touched down at Sion International Airport in the 767, and they were now racing toward Zaugg's stronghold in the mountain peaks to the south of the town.

Zaugg himself had been out of sight in his private cabin for the duration of the flight from Kefalonia, but now he was sitting opposite Lea Donovan in the luxury cabin of the helicopter, along with Dietmar Grobel and Heinrich Baumann.

After what he had done to her, she hated the sight of him, sitting there so close to her in the confined space of the helicopter. She wished she could push him out of the door and watch him fall to his death in the rocky valley below.

"How long until the men get the hoard to the mountain?" Zaugg asked.

"No more than an hour," Grobel replied.

"Good."

Lea saw the silhouette of Zaugg's compound on the horizon. They drew nearer, and now she saw more detail below the helicopter – his private ski lodge was nearby, a stark postmodern black against the smooth white snow all around them. Elevated above the other buildings was a large building, constructed in glass and chrome in another modern architectural style – Zaugg's mansion.

"We are here," he said, peering through the window as the chopper descended to the helipad outside the enormous house.

Baumann pushed her out of the Sikorsky, but there was something about the way he touched her that made her flinch with revulsion. He had *stroked* her shoulder before nudging her forward at gunpoint.

Ahead of her, a short distance from the mansion and down a shallow snow-covered slope she saw what looked like some kind of cargo bay carved into the mountainside. A forklift was moving large metal containers from the back of a Mil Mi-26 transport helicopter into the gaping hole in the mountain, while a group of men carrying clipboards were issuing others with directions. They looked like they were waiting for something important to happen.

"Who are they?" she asked anxiously.

"Loyal employees," Zaugg said.

Before she could ask anything else, someone grabbed her from behind and she felt a warm cloth over her mouth. Then she was out cold.

*

It didn't take Lea long to realize where she was – she was slumped against a cold wall in a wine cellar. She rubbed her eyes and winced in pain at the headache – the chloroform had been given to her sloppily and in too strong a dose.

She was probably lucky to be alive. She tried to get up, but she was still dizzy, and she had to fight back a wave of nausea as she struggled to her feet and regained her balance.

The cellar was vast – smooth polished marble floors, and labyrinthine in its construction. She walked along a corridor – flanked on either side from floor to ceiling with wine bottles, carefully stored inside stone alcoves. A series of narrow striplights cast a ghostly silver light on everything.

She stopped at a crossroads to see just more wine-filled corridors stretching away into the distance, the far wall at the end of the corridor was perhaps over one hundred feet away. The sound of her shoes clicked loudly in the cool silence as she walked. Even her breathing seemed to echo off the walls.

"Now this is a wine collection," she said, her voice unexpectedly loud in the enclosed space.

Before she had time to investigate her surroundings properly, or look for a way out, she heard the sound of heavy footsteps coming from behind her – somewhere outside the cellar she heard the unmistakable sound of Zaugg's voice, only he was speaking in his native Schweizerdeutsch. It was followed moments later by the sound of Heinrich Baumann's hideous chuckle.

The talking stopped. A moment of eerie silence was followed by the sound of heavy keys clunking on a metal hoop, and then one of the men was unlocking the door.

Only as the two men stepped into the cellar and confronted her did her fate begin to dawn on her. She wondered if Joe and Ryan and the others had survived the flooding of the tomb, knowing that if they hadn't she had no options left, and that her time had almost run out.

"Guten abend," Zaugg said.

"What the hell is this, Zaugg?" She knew what the hell it was, but she was asking in an effort to buy herself more time to think. She peered behind them to see what was outside the cellar but all she saw was a flight of stone steps receding out of view to the right.

"As you will recall, I have promised you to Baumann here, Miss Donovan, to calm one of his many mutinous rages. He is a loyal employee after all, and it would be churlish of me not to indulge his... *fantasies* from time to time. He is not exactly a gentle man, but what he lacks in tenderness he makes up for with creativity. My advice is not to struggle."

Baumann chuckled again, almost uncontrollably, as he looked Lea up and down like a piece of meat in a market.

"I'm sorry I cannot stay but as you will appreciate, I have important work to do, and a very important map to locate which was not where it should have been. A real mystery, to be sure, but one I will certainly solve. As for you, your friends are all dead – their bodies trapped in the tomb, somewhat ironically, and you will soon wish you had died with them. Auf wiedersehen."

Zaugg turned on his heel and closed the door behind him.

Baumann shuffled toward her, at first looking as though he were on an awkward first date. Then he grinned, and his good eye blinked. She looked at the long scar running down the other side of his face, the one that had cost him his eyesight and left his eye an opaque, milky egg staring at nothing.

Lea held her breath in fear and slowly stepped back from Baumann, never once taking her eyes off him. Up close he was even bigger than she had realized, his enormous bulk towering over her like a bear. His metal hand made a terrible scraping noise as he flexed its fingers, his one eye blinking in the half-light of the damp cellar.

Then he lunged at her.

Lea ran back from him, wrenching the arm of her

sweater out of his meaty hand. She stumbled back a few paces and turned on her heel, running away for her life.

Baumann laughed loudly and pulled a long hunting knife from a holster on his belt. "This is going to be beautiful." he said, in a grim, hoarse whisper. Then he started after her.

Her mind raced with fear. She knew Joe Hawke would know what to do, but she was out of her depth. She needed him, but she didn't even know if he was dead or alive. The last time she saw him was back in the caves of Kefalonia when Zaugg had ordered Baumann to blow the wall of the tomb and drown them all.

Baumann smiled. He knew what she was thinking.

"If you're waiting for your action-hero, he's dead," he said. "All of your friends are dead. They drowned like sewer rats. No one's going to save you."

Without warning, Baumann leapt forward and lunged at her again with the metal hand, catching one of the pockets of her jeans and tearing it off. The shred fell to the floor and Baumann giggled insanely.

Lea screamed and jumped back, hitting a wall of wine bottles. Panicking, she quickly searched for the fastest way out and decided to make a run for it along the corridor to her right. As she sprinted down the corridor into the darkness, she heard Baumann whooping with joy behind her and banging his hand on the steel frame of a wine rack with excitement.

"You can make this last all night, bitch!" he screamed.

Then he sprinted after her.

Lea was breathing hard, and terrified to stop, but an instant later she ran into a dead-end. Before she could back out of it Baumann rounded the corner. He smirked at her and made a fake sad face in mockery of her.

"Shall we have merlot or cabernet sauvignon?" he asked.

Without taking his eyes off her, he reached out and pulled a bottle of red wine from the wall, snapping its neck off with his metal hand. The shattered glass splinters fell to the concrete floor and he took a large gulp of the wine before wiping his wide mouth with the sleeve of his jacket.

"It's time for our date," he said, and padded toward her.

Lea struggled to concentrate, but she knew now was no time to lose her mind to panic and fear. He approached her, placing the wine on a shelf. Before she could think, Baumann was upon her, grabbing her shoulder with his metal hand.

She heard it contract and then something in her shoulder cracked. She screamed in pain, but he laughed loudly and powered his other hand, his human hand, hard into her stomach.

She doubled over in agony, gasping like a fish out of water and she strained to heave the air back into her winded lungs.

"As first dates go, bitch, I have been on worse."

On her knees now, and struggling to breathe, she could sense the hideous man above her, and watched in horror as his steel toecapped boots shuffled closer toward her, now almost touching her thighs.

She heard him take up the wine bottle, drink heavily, and after belching loudly in the semi-darkness he smashed the bottle into the floor with extreme force. A great puddle of wine seeped out like blood all around his boots.

Lea flinched and felt her face – some of the glass had cut her cheek. Out of pure instinct, she cried out, and Baumann laughed again, even more heartily. He really was enjoying this.

"You remind me of the waitress I killed in Salzburg,"

he said, suddenly very serious, and his voice a cold whisper. "Some of them struggle, but others, like you and the Salzburg girl – they just go without a fight. Very disappointing."

She felt his human hand caress the back of her neck, and then heard him humming with sordid pleasure as he moved closer. Lea had seconds to think, seconds to react. This was her life to live, not his to take, and she wasn't going out of this world on his terms, not in this way. And then the answer came to her – sparkling on the floor like a ruby ring was a long splinter of glass from the wine bottle.

Baumann moved closer, purring with a depraved kind of satisfaction at the misery he was inflicting on her, and then she took her chance, thrusting the glass splinter hard into his thigh and yanking it down as if she were trying to saw through wood.

He screamed in agony and kicked her in the face out of pure reflex action. She flew backwards but stopped herself from banging her head on the wall. She looked up to see Baumann hunched over in agony and blood pouring down from the wound.

She had obviously hit the artery in his leg. Baumann looked at her, a terrifying mix of rage, fear and revenge crossing his face like a dark shadow, and he stalked towards her, dragging his wounded leg behind him in a trail of blood and wine.

*

Hugo Zaugg stared at the small statue on his desk. It was a small, smooth sculpture in bronze, over two thousand years old – a perfectly water-preserved rendering of Poseidon. The god was looking meaningfully out across the expansive room, and across time itself, with pensive eyes and a firm grip on the trident.

A few inches to the left of the statue and in a commanding position in the exact center of his desk was a shiny black Bakelite telephone. Zaugg's eyes moved from Poseidon to the phone.

He had been waiting anxiously for it to ring for some time. Yes, he had located the tomb. Yes, he had found the trident wrapped in furs inside the otherwise empty sarcophagus.

But no, he had not found the map.

And so he waited nervously to explain the news.

And yet the gods made him wait.

He drummed his fingers along the edge of the smooth mahogany desk and closed his eyes. His mind wandered immediately to what could be such a glorious future, if only he held the map in his hands. The torment of delay could only be soothed by the concomitant sweetness of victory.

How many times had he cradled that dream in his mind – seeing the smooth, golden water running through his dreams, staring at his ageing face in its rippled bronze surface? How many times had he read those Ancient Greek texts with their tantalizing references to eternal life? And how much he needed the missing map to solve this most glorious and divine of puzzles.

But he knew he had to remain calm, and proceed in a tactical, measured way. The map must surely exist – it was inconceivable that the tomb and the trident could be real but not the map. He would simply have to redouble his efforts if he wanted to drink of the divine nectar.

He would search harder for the map – there would be other clues in the tomb and with them would come the location of where to find the source of the water of life.

And then the telephone rang harshly in the soft silence of the climate-controlled study.

Zaugg fumbled for the receiver, almost dropping it on his way.

"You have good news for me?"

As usual, the voice was distorted behind a series of morphing applications. It sounded ghostly, and distant. The only man in the world Hugo Zaugg genuinely feared.

"Yes. We have secured the tomb and we have the trident.

"Good. This pleases me."

"I am honored." Zaugg was sweating.

"And what of the map?"

Zaugg waited a few seconds before giving his rehearsed reply. "We have not found the map yet, but my men are searching through the contents of the tomb."

"Don't fail me, Zaugg."

"No, sir. It is just a matter of time."

"Everything is just a matter of time."

And the phone line went dead.

CHAPTER THIRTY-TWO

Hart and the others were directed to a private stand and met by Sir Richard Eden himself, and they were quickly shown to an idling Eurocopter Super Cougar, a five-bladed beast of a chopper that was going to take them up the mountain to Zaugg's compound.

"How did you get all this sorted?" Hawke asked Eden.

"Let's just say we have the blessing of certain sympathetic elements in the Swiss Government."

As they loaded their kit and weapons into the back of the Cougar, Eden once again stressed the necessity of keeping the operation as quiet as possible. It was nearing nightfall now and the temperature was slipping below zero. A light snow blew in the air from the east and promised to make the night harder than it had to be.

Hawke took the moment to write a text to Nightingale. He told her was going in to rescue Lea and take Zaugg out. He hoped Lea was still alive and asked Nightingale for any help she could offer. He sent the message. He hoped she'd received it, and slipped the phone back in his pocket.

With a handful of soldiers from the Swiss Army and a couple of men Reaper had organized in the back of the helicopter, it was seriously less cosy than Gorokhov's Flying Circus, and the earlier atmosphere of contemplation and quiet conversation he had shared with the others was replaced with the usual one found on covert ops – a weird blend of tense anticipation, nerves and crude humor.

Hawke was also feeling jittery, but the sight of Ryan squashed in between two former Foreign Legion mercs, trying – and failing miserably – to make them laugh with his unique blend of wit and observational humor was enough to bring a smile to anyone's face.

As they flew up the mountain, Eden was still furiously trying to make contact with Matheson to update him on the operation and receive any new information. Hawke wondered just how far up all of this went.

But he refocussed his mind on the task at hand: "This is one hell of a mission," he said.

A peal of grim laughter rippled through the small group. Reaper lit another Gauloise and leaned against the side of the chopper to smoke his cigarette. Hart and Scarlet were arguing about the relative merits of their branches of the military.

Then a voice spoke next to Hawke.

"She doesn't love me, you know."

It was Ryan. He had joined him at the back of the Cougar.

"What?"

"Lea. She doesn't love me anymore. I know that – I'm not stupid."

"What are you telling me for?"

Ryan simply looked at him.

"Ah. Is it that obvious?"

"Not to Lea, no. She's pretty focused on her career right now."

"I had noticed."

"She's not the sort of woman to take a hint, Joe. I've known her a long time, so trust me on this one. She's the kind of woman you just have to grab hold of and tell her how you feel."

The Cougar flew low along an elevated valley before

ascending into the snow clouds on its way up to Zaugg's compound and their final approach with destiny.

They emerged through the clouds to see the last few rays of sunlight on the western horizon as they streaked across the tops of the alps. Ahead of them a razorback ridge of mountain peaks loomed silent in the frozen dusk. Concealed into the crevices of one was the sprawling compound of Hugo Zaugg.

They flew closer and then Hawke saw it for the first time.

From his vantage point of twelve thousand feet altitude, Hawke examined the compound which now nestled below the chopper in the western crags of one of the mountain peaks.

Zaugg's lair.

It was to this place that he had brought Lea Donovan, not to mention the looted contents of Poseidon's tomb.

"So," Ryan asked more perkily than the situation would have suggested was appropriate, "where's the helicopter going to land?"

Hawke glanced at Reaper and both men burst out laughing.

"The helicopter is going to turn around now and land in Sion," Reaper said.

"Yes, sure, but where is it going to drop us off first?"

"Drop us is the right word..." Reaper said, his words trailing as he swung open the side door and flicked his cigarette out. Moments later he hoisted a parachute on his back and tightened the harness's adjuster straps.

Ryan turned to ask Hawke what was happening, but Hawke was also putting a parachute on, securing the leg straps and clipping the v-rings into their snap fasteners.

"Joe, you're not seriously expecting me to jump out of this thing?"

"You can if you want." Hawke put on his helmet and

tightened the chin-strap. "Or you can go back to Sion and wait with Eden. I thought I'd let you make the decision, mate. You saved my arse back in Greece and now I've got your back. I think you can do it, but if you want to go back I'll understand."

"Storming a mountain stronghold? What do you think this is, *For Your Eyes Only*?"

Hawke smiled. "I'm impressed you've seen the film. I was thinking more of *Where Eagles Dare* though, to be honest. Me being Burton, of course."

"Yeah, right."

"So, are you coming or not?"

He looked at Ryan. Ryan looked back, then peered over Hawke's shoulder as he watched Hart, Scarlet, Sophie and the handful of soldiers and mercs hoisting their parachutes on, checking weapons and preparing to jump. The freezing wind from the dark night outside scratched at his face and whipped his hair around as his mind raced.

"Ten seconds to make up your mind, Ryan."

"I'm just not that sort of person, Joe!" Ryan said.

"This isn't about what sort of person you are now, Ryan. This is about what kind of person you're going to be from now on."

Ryan looked outside the chopper into the winter night. It was now hovering a few thousand feet above the peaks of the alps, and somewhere below he could see the faint twinkling of Zaugg's compound lights in the frozen darkness.

*

Joe Hawke steered the parachute strongly to the right and made landfall in a flat snowfield a few hundred meters below Zaugg's compound. He released his chute and counted the others down one by one.

Reaper was next to land, then Sophie followed by Scarlet. After that came the mercs and Swiss soldiers. Hawke watched with pride as he saw the figure of Olivia Hart emerge from the clouds and brake as she steered towards the landing ground.

She had executed a perfect tandem jump, and Ryan Bale, secured to her front, was smiling like the cat that got the cream as they came to a stop in the snowy field, even if there was a light green hue to his face as he took off his helmet.

The others freed themselves from their chutes and readied their weapons. Above the clouds they heard the sound of the Cougar's rotors recede into the night as it flew back to Sion with Eden. Now they were truly alone.

"Okay, are we all ready?" Hawke said.

"As ready as we'll ever be," Sophie said.

"You sound nervous," said Hawke. "Don't be. Whatever they've got up there, down here we've got more."

"How could we fail?" Scarlet said. "We have *him*." She turned to Ryan who grinned sheepishly in return.

"But I'm a genius, don't forget!" he said, his voice barely audible in the laughter. "We're generally too sensitive for this sort of thing."

"I understand," Reaper said, half-seriously. "By being too sensitive I have wasted my life."

"Seriously?" Ryan said,

Reaper arched an eyebrow and then burst into more laughter. "Of course not – what do you take me for? I was quoting Rimbaud. A great French poet! You'd think a genius like yourself would have recognized it, no?"

More laughter, and Ryan blushed heavily.

Reaper brought a heavy hand down on Ryan's shoulder, almost knocking him over into the snow.

"Come on, kid... I only make the jokes. I know we're all different, and we must all accept those differences."

"Thanks, Reaper," Ryan said.

Reaper gave a gallic shrug. "Hey, no problem. If we didn't accept those different from us, people like you would be truly fucked."

Yet more laughter and Ryan stomped off into the snow.

"Ryan – forget about it!" Hawke flicked a disapproving glance at Reaper. "He's just French – forget about it, mate."

Hawke had started to feel protective towards Ryan now – he had saved his life on the Thalassa after all, but it was more than that. There was the way he had tried to tell him that he wouldn't get in the way if he wanted to pursue Lea, and then the tremendous effort it took to jump out the chopper. As far as Hawke was concerned Ryan Bale was all right.

They hiked the last few hundred meters until they were at the compound's perimeter fence which they cut through with bolt-cutters in seconds and marched on the main building. Ahead of them, the Swiss Special Forces guys and Foreign Legion mercs had already taken out a large bay window and fought their way inside on the ground level. Hawke's job was to secure the upper level.

They stopped against the back wall of a garage block to regroup, and he looked at his watch – time was getting short. He heard a crackling through his headset. It was Reaper. "Okay everyone this is it. Any man here kills less than five he buys the beer afterwards."

"Less than five?" Scarlet said "Why are you making it so easy for us?"

Hawke heard Hart laugh through the headset.

"We go in through the top as usual," Scarlet said. "Let's do our thing."

Reaper ran to the back of the house and placed charges on the rear doors. This would make another distraction when they entered on the upper level.

Hawke readied the Heckler & Koch HK416, a gas-operated submachine gun designed and built with startling German efficiency, and waited for the signal to go, which came a second later from Hart.

They skirted around the back of the garage block and along the low line of the stables until reaching the west wing of the house. Here they fired rifle-launched grapnels from their crossbows and rappelled up the side of the mansion. Moments later they were on the roof, an enormous maze of gray slate slopes and turrets.

Hawke could see out across the valley from here. It formed an enormous v-shape leading away from the mansion, with snow-capped mountains on either side, illuminated by a bright, full moon which shone intermittently through breaks in the clouds. They found the correct locations for their abseil down the back of the house to the third floor windows, where they positioned small explosive charges on the panes of glass.

Below they could hear a terrific gunfight as the other team fought its way inside on the lower levels of the house.

“Okay, everyone,” Hart said, her tone as calm as if she were giving someone directions to the local church. “We go in twenty seconds.”

“Roger.”

“Reaper, fire your door charges in three, two, one…”

Hawke heard two massive explosions emanating from the rear of the house. Reaper had successfully blown the doors in and caused the mother of all explosions. They fired their charges and the four windows on the third floor exploded inwards in balls of hot white flame. Seconds later they were inside the mansion and cutting their lines.

Hawke and the others entered the upper level, covering all angles with their submachine guns.

Inside, they fought their way through a hail of bullets to a locked door.

"Stand back!" Hawke said, and took a few steps away from the door. He ran back toward it and shoulder-barged it with all his might, smashing it away from its hinges and spraying splinters of wood into the room. A bullet fired from inside the room and whistled past Scarlet's head, almost killing her.

"Now, that's just not cricket!" she said.

"And that cat's on her ninth life," Hawke muttered to himself as they entered and cleared the room. They exited the room at the far end and found themselves in the main hall. An enormous sweeping staircase twisted away to the next floor below them. Faced with the enormity of searching a compound of this size, he knew it was time for help.

Moments later he was talking to Nightingale through his headset.

"Which way to Zaugg's private quarters?" he asked her. "Use my cell phone signal to place me in the schematic."

Her voice was distant, and emotionless. "Like I need you to tell me that. This is how I saved your ass in Serbia all those years ago, remember?"

He did remember. "Sorry."

"You need to go straight ahead for around twenty yards and then there should be a staircase. You need to go up that staircase and then hang a left."

Hawke followed her instructions, trusting her implicitly. Behind him, the others followed with the same unquestioning degree of trust.

At the top of the stairs they turned left and found

themselves in another large room.

"You should be in another reception room right now."

"Looks like it."

"According to these schematics, his private section of the compound is up on the next level. Can you see a mezzanine or balcony?"

"Sure."

"So go up to it. His quarters are up there."

An instant after her last words several waves of Zaugg's men launched an attack at them from concealed defensive positions on the upper level. Machine gun muzzles flashed orange and white as they spat their lethal fire at them.

One of the mercs ran forward halfway up the stairs. He screamed in pain and Hawke turned to see his chest exploding with the terrible force of dozens of bullets as they tore into him and blasted him off his feet. He fell to the lower level and landed with a sickening smash on the parquet tiles below.

Then, before they could regroup, another wave of soldiers approached them – but this time on foot and running directly toward them from a door beneath the mezzanine.

Hawke spun his HK around and struck one of the men in the face with the butt of the weapon. A terrible crunching sound came from inside the guy's mouth, but before he could react Hawke punched him on the nose, breaking it and knocking the man into instant unconsciousness. He reached for the man's weapons, leaving the submachine gun but taking a Sig Sauer and some ammo.

Hawke looked up just in time to see another man aiming an assault rifle at him. He dived to the floor and rolled to his left where he reached the cover of an antique chest at the side of the hall.

He raised the Sig Sauer and squeezed off a few rounds in the man's direction, planting a line of hollow-points across his chest and exploding his throat. The man slumped dead to the floor.

Then, Zaugg's forces decided the battle had turned against them and began a tactical retreat.

"I have to get to Zaugg!" Hawke screamed in the roar of gunfire. "He still has Lea."

Reaper and Hart made an effort to run after the fleeing soldiers, going deeper into the compound and diverting their attention away from Hawke's assault on the private quarters.

Hawke charged up the stairs and prepared for the end game.

CHAPTER THIRTY-THREE

The wounded man grunted like an animal and heaved himself over to her with every last bit of energy he could muster.

"I will make you suffer for this," he said, spitting with rage.

Baumann grabbed Lea by her shoulders and lifted her off her feet as if she were a rag doll. He smashed her back into the wine rack behind her, and she howled in pain as the corks rammed into her spine. He growled and smashed her into the bottles a second time. Then a short giggle.

Lea's spirits were raised when somewhere above her head she heard the unmistakable sound of machine gun fire – Hawke must have survived and was launching a rescue attempt at this very minute.

But how long could she hold out against Baumann?

She saw her torturer was pale now – he had lost a lot of blood since she'd stabbed his leg, but was it enough to take him down? She kicked out against him, but this only made things worse because Baumann simply grabbed her around her neck with his metal hand so he could use his free hand to hold her legs down. She felt the icy cold steel as it gripped her soft throat.

Her tormentor grinned like a maniac as he closed the steel claw around her throat and she felt her windpipe constrict. She gasped for air, instinctively expecting the cold air of the cellar to flood into her lungs, but none came. She began to panic in response, flailing her arms out wildly trying to strike her attacker, but his arm was too long, and he held her at a distance long enough to avoid any reprisals from her much smaller body. He nodded his head in appreciation of some unvoiced thought and increased the grip on her throat.

"Because you tried to kill me," said Baumann, his breath in her face, "I'm going to make this last a very long time."

Up closer than ever now, less than half a meter from her face, Lea looked at the face of Heinrich Baumann – his repellent milky eye and scarred face, the stench of some kind of lubricant on the mechanism of the steel claw, the gentle whirring of the humidifier on the wall beside her aching head. This, she thought, was going to be her last minute on earth – her last sight, her last sound, her last smell – all Baumann, for now and forever.

She began to lose consciousness.

With the blackness encroaching all around her, Lea Donovan had only a few seconds to think before her processing faculties left her forever. Her world was tiny now – Baumann and his claw, the feel of his breath, the sound of the humidifier…

The humidifier. Just a few inches to her left was a humidifier gently whirring away, and she saw now that it was plugged into the wall right beside her. Without stopping to think anything through, she reached with the last of her strength behind her head and searched with her hand until she felt a wine bottle, which she pulled from the rack and brought crashing down on Baumann's head.

The giant man screamed in pain and released Lea, who now, finally free of his devilish grasp, collapsed in a heap on the floor. Both were now on the ground on their hands and knees – Lea heaving the breath back into her body and Baumann in a puddle of wine woozily trying to regain his balance and hang onto consciousness.

Lea acted fast, and out of pure instinct. She tore the cable from the humidifier, and then climbed out of the spilled wine and onto the wooden crate.

"Go to hell you fucking freak!" she screamed, and dropped the cable into the wine, causing a massive electric shock to course through Baumann's body. She was pretty sure that wine was an excellent conductor of electricity, and was only too glad to put her theory to the test.

Now, Baumann writhed on the floor in a fiendish shower of sparks, convulsing like a dying fish, his blood-curdling screams bouncing off the cellar walls.

He groped and slipped about in a vain effort to free himself of the terrific electric current now frying him alive. His metal hand sparked and scraped on the concrete floor in his final death throes, and then there was nothing left except a damp, smoking heap, reeking of wine.

Lea pulled the cable from his corpse and pushed the end into the straw bedding around one of Zaugg's most expensive bottles of wine. She watched the fire grow for a few moments before running to the cellar door.

She made it up the twisting stone steps and to the door leading back from the cellar into Zaugg's compound. Gently craning her neck around the door to see if the coast was clear, Lea Donovan decided to make a run for it, but before she could even get into the room she heard a familiar voice behind her.

"I'm impressed."

She spun around to see Dietmar Grobel standing in the corridor.

"You!"

"The very same," he said. He pulled out a Sig Sauer and pointed it at Lea. "I was sent down to get Baumann, but instead I find you as free as a kite. How did you get away from him?"

"I burned him alive, and I'd do the same to you given half a chance."

"Unfortunately I have at least double the IQ of poor Heinrich, and I don't give out chances, half or full. Get moving." Grobel waved the gun at the end of the corridor. "Herr Zaugg doesn't like loose ends."

*

Lea Donovan watched in horror as the elevator doors slid open to reveal a vast complex deep inside the mountain. Dozens of men and women were hurrying about, completing tasks in preparation for something big. Some were checking inventories and loading crates onto a monorail whose rail twisted way into a darkened tunnel. Others were examining what looked like an air-conditioning system on the rock wall at the back. They all wore black boiler suits with a white Z on the back.

"Bring the girl with us," Zaugg said. He was holding in his hands Poseidon's trident – heavy, gold, but smaller than she had imagined it would be.

Grobel acknowledged the command by pushing Lea out of the elevator with a hefty nudge in the small of her back, almost causing her to fall over. Lea turned and gave him a look that would freeze mercury, but she knew there was nothing she could do to help herself – yet.

At Grobel's gunpoint, Lea followed Zaugg down the galvanized steel staircase which connected the elevators to the main loading bays. It was like any other industrial space, and reminded Lea of Victoria Bus Station with its smells of oil and machinery and the sound of heavy vehicles turning on the polished concrete floors.

"What the hell is this place?" she asked, simultaneously amazed and terrified.

"This is the future, Miss Donovan," said Zaugg, proudly assessing his work and presenting it to Lea with a generous sweep of his hand. "This is the Ark. Built two thousand feet under the mountain and able to withstand a fifty megaton nuclear blast. This is the safest place on earth in the event of a *catastrophe*... Now, if you please..."

Zaugg pushed a button on the door of the monorail carriage and it swooshed silently open. "Ladies first."

He tipped his head to one side and smirked grimly as Grobel pushed Lea into the carriage, keeping the muzzle of his Sig Sauer firmly aimed in her direction.

When Zaugg was safely inside, the monorail began to slide gently forward and a few moments later the bright lights of the loading bay were gone, replaced with the subdued underlighting of the freshly carved transit tunnel. Lea felt the temperature drop once again, and was sure they were traveling deeper down in to the mountain, as well as towards the center of it.

"You impressed me a great deal with the way you dealt with Baumann," Zaugg said. "By the way, what happened to him?"

Grobel replied: "She electrocuted him in a puddle of Coche-Dury les Perrieres."

Zaugg was unperturbed. "And what's the damage?"

"He's dead."

"I meant to my wine."

"Oh..."

"Anyway, Miss Donovan – where was I?" Ah yes! Of course – the future. You see, the trident has yet undiscovered powers, but our reading of the ancient texts is that it is a weapon of such awesome power it would have been quite remiss of me not to make preparations for its use, as I am sure you will agree."

Lea was horrified. "You can't possibly know the extent of its power, Zaugg. You would be insane to try and use it."

Zaugg was placid. "As ancient megaweapons go, Poseidon's trident is the mother of them all. It is true we are not aware of its true power – not yet – but I cannot risk my life's work, or my destiny. This is why we built the Ark – to keep us safe while the trident – how shall I put it – cleans up the world. After that, the way is clear for me to enjoy my immortality."

"But without the map, you have no idea where the source of eternal life is."

"Touché once again, Miss Donovan, but I fail to see how using the trident could make the search for the map anything but far easier. Once your puny rescue force has been eradicated, I will show you the first use of the trident in centuries – perhaps millions of years!"

They stepped off the carriage and walked to Zaugg's private office in the Ark, but no sooner had they arrived when a man rushed into the plush room.

"Sir, our forces are being overwhelmed! It's time to evacuate!"

"What are you talking about?" Zaugg said contemptuously.

"The enemy forces have taken control of the main compound. Your men are deserting you."

Zaugg's face collapsed into a mask of rage and bitterness.

"Just give up, Zaugg!" Lea pleaded.

"Never!"

"There's no escape now."

Zaugg laughed. "You think I would leave myself vulnerable to that possiblity?" He grabbed Lea by the arm and pulled her roughly across the room. On a bookshelf was a single statue of Poseidon. Zaugg pulled it forward and the entire shelf began to slide to the right.

"We're going for a ride."

He turned to Grobel, nervously waiting in the office and yelled more orders at him: "Initiate the self-destruct sequence."

CHAPTER THIRTY-FOUR

The entire compound had now ceased to be Hugo Zaugg's peaceful refuge in the mountains and instead an atmosphere of total pandemonium pervaded every corner of the place.

Previously loyal servants to Zaugg were now stealing anything they could get their hands on as Hawke and his forces swept through the rooms and corridors, the gym and the swimming pool, clearing them with their guns and grenades.

Only his most committed followers kept up the fight, firing back with machine guns and leaving booby-traps where they could in order to slow Hawke as he expedited the assault and closed in on Zaugg and Lea.

Now, in Zaugg's private quarters, the resistance was even fiercer. Hawke ducked low and sprinted down a corridor lined with plush carpet and black and white pictures of Nazi rallies.

"Who the hell is this guy?" he said to himself as he ducked to dodge a hail of bullets fired over his head from a room at the side. He spun around and threw in a grenade, diving for cover as it exploded and fired shards of splintered desk and door and pieces of burned carpet back out in the hall.

"You talking to me?" said a voice in his ear. It was Nightingale.

"Sorry, no, N. Just enjoying Zaugg's taste in interior décor. He has quite a nifty style of neo-Nazi gothic combined with postmodern whimsy."

“Well, if you want to talk to him about it his office is a right turn then dead ahead.”

“Thanks.”

Hawke turned into the corridor to see two men with shaved heads standing outside a large oak door. They were armed with Heckler & Kochs and Hawke guessed they weren’t guarding the drinks cabinet.

“Got it, N – thanks for your help.”

The men began firing at him, tearing up the wall over his head and shattering a giant Chinese vase into a thousand pieces.

“Always a pleasure, she replied. “Don’t get your head blown off, please.”

She disconnected as Hawke launched his final assault, dropping to his stomach and firing the machine gun at the men who were, for all their firepower, sitting ducks at the end of a corridor. They returned fire but he made short work of them, and then headed towards Zaugg’s study.

*

In his panic and rage, Zaugg pulled a Luger from his desk and dragged Lea from his office in the Ark into the hidden passageway behind the bookcase. They stepped into another elevator and moments later the shiny steel doors opened to reveal they were standing on a windy platform jutting out of the mountainside. Lea watched the snow race past them as Zaugg pushed her out into the cold. She saw a single cable-car blowing gently in the wind.

“None of this will exist in ten minutes. You are coming with me as my insurance.”

“What are you talking about?”

“Another insurance policy, my dear. Recently

scientists induced an avalanche in the Vallée de la Sionne, which is what you see below you. They used explosives to trigger the avalanche so they could study the results and learn more about these terrible acts of nature."

"Why are you telling me this, Zaugg? If this is your way of charming women I think you need to rethink your strategy."

Zaugg smiled coldly. "They wanted to study what they call avalanche motion, and the snow they exploded off the side of the mountain crashed down the slopes at a terrifying three hundred kilometers per hour. Do you realize how utterly futile it would be, trying to out-run millions of tons of snow moving at that speed?"

"And?"

"And I am about to detonate a similar series of explosives, but this time considerably more. They will cause avalanches ten times greater than those of the experiment and send millions of tons of snow crashing down in the valley below, killing tens of thousands of people."

"You're insane."

"Not at all. The explosives are designed to ensure this entire compound is buried beneath half the mountain that now looms above us, crushing everything here, including anyone still in it when it happens. It will take months for the authorities to work out what happened here and go through whatever isn't totally destroyed. It will also kill all of your friends. It is the ultimate home defense!"

"Please don't do this!" she pleaded, looking over the rail at the town's lights twinkling in the valley below.

Zaugg smirked. "I can't let Hawke destroy my life's work. Do you have any idea of the sort of effort and patience required to put a plan like this together – to wait until everything aligns? You think I would let anyone else have these treasures? Do you think I would let any other man control the trident or locate the source of eternal life?!" He waved the trident in his hand and held it aloft insanely, as if he were a god. For a moment Lea thought she saw it flash, but it was merely the reflection of one of the lights.

"You can't kill all those innocent people, Zaugg!"

"No one is innocent! Any one of those people would kill their mothers for the chance of eternal life!"

"Don't judge everyone else by your own disgusting standards."

"I will not let anyone else have these riches. This entire compound will be destroyed and the whole valley below will be swallowed by millions of tons of snow and ice."

Lea was horrified. "I've never heard anything so crazy in all my life."

"Like all the ants, you have no imagination."

"You'll kill everyone!"

"Not everyone, my dear. You think I am as stupid as that? Oh, no! I will survive and so will you, for now!"

"Let me go!"

"Silence! You're coming with me!"

Zaugg grabbed Lea by the arm and dragged her from the platform towards the cable car.

*

Hawke found the study empty, but saw the elevator, which he rushed inside and ordered down to the lowest level. When the doors opened he was met by the same warehouse Lea had seen, but instead of a hive of activity it was now all but deserted.

Whatever Zaugg had been planning had obviously

been big – this place looked like it could survive a nuclear winter. Stacked up along the walls was everything anyone could possibly need – food, water, weapons, generators, snow-plows, skis – the list went on.

"You!" he screamed at a man in a boiler suit. "Where's Zaugg?"

The terrified man pointed down the corridor, and Hawke was at his office seconds later, bursting into the room to find Dietmar Grobel hurriedly stuffing gold coins into a suitcase. The German stared at Hawke with terror in his eyes.

"Where's Lea?" he screamed.

"You're too late, Hawke. Zaugg's already gone, and he took her with him." Grobel continued to stuff the gold into the case. "Listen, Zaugg is going insane! Get away while you can."

"I think that ship sailed a few years ago," replied Hawke.

"You can't catch him now. He had a secret escape route built into the wall here. It takes him to a cable car which goes straight down into the town. He's heading for the airport – I heard him ordering the pilots to ready his private plane for a long-haul flight."

"You've been very helpful," Hawke said, and knocked Grobel unconscious. He disappeared into the secret passageway and took the elevator up to the platform where he too was met by a blast of icy, snowy wind.

He turned and saw the cable car, and watched in horror as Zaugg dragged Lea roughly into the gondola.

Zaugg raised his gun to Lea's temple.

"So we meet again, Mr Hawke," Zaugg stroked his goatee beard and examined Hawke as if he was an insect. "Under any other circumstances perhaps I would describe it as a pleasure to make the acquaintance of someone like you, but as it is I'm sure you will forgive me if I tell you I am quite sick of the sight of you and wish you dead. As it happens, I always get my wish."

Hawke took a step forward.

"Get back! I will shoot her, I swear it! Lower your gun."

Hawke stopped and did as he was told.

"Admit it!" screamed Zaugg. "You lost! Like so many before you, you tried to beat me, but once again I have won! Ich habe gewonnen!"

*

Lea felt Zaugg's slate-gray eyes burning into her as the cable car began to descend out of the compound's housing and into the howling snowstorm outside.

Now safely away from the imminent explosion of the compound, Zaugg stood motionless and stared at her. She saw him up-close for the first time. He was skeletal-thin, with a few days' stubble covering his horribly sunken cheeks like thin gray moss.

Horror crossed Lea's face as she watched him pull a radio control device from his pocket and slide out an aerial on the top of it.

"Please don't do this!" she shouted.

"Silence! The last thing I will do before we take to the air is push this button. That will explode a series of charges carefully located in the compound and along the snowline of these mountains. The entire valley will be crushed and the compound annihilated. I will survive, however, and so will this."

Zaugg caressed the golden trident resting in his arms as the cable-car jolted downwards towards the valley, buffeted by the growing power of the snowstorm.

CHAPTER THIRTY-FIVE

Hawke watched the cable-car descend into the snowy night and knew he had only one play left. He raced back to the Ark's warehouse and grabbed a pair of skis and ski poles. A quick search in the weapons section revealed a sniper's rifle which he loaded in double-quick time before making his way back to the slopes outside.

There was only one way he could beat Zaugg to the valley below.

*

"You can't get away, Zaugg, you freaking maniac!" Lea said.

"Why ever not? I have my own plane, and no one knows I'm responsible for any of this. I will simply fly away into the night and bide my time. And you're coming with me. Pushing you out the back of my jet at ten thousand feet will bring an indescribable satisfaction to me. I may even film it and keep it for posterity."

Zaugg pulled a cell phone from his pocket and tapped a number.

"Is the plane ready? Good."

He slammed the phone shut and weighed the Luger in his hands. "Or then again, perhaps I should just shoot you now? I know what my father would do... I know what he would tell me to do, if he were here..."

He closed one eye slightly and raised the gun at her in a mock execution.

"Bang!" he shouted, and laughed violently.

Lea screamed and scrambled back on the floor, fear in her eyes.

"You really are insane!" she shouted, her voice hoarse with terror.

"No. I am a realist and will live forever!"

"You will die a failure just like your father!" Lea screamed, trying to make him lose his composure. It was her only chance.

"No! Silence!" Zaugg was spitting with rage now, barely able to control himself.

"The only immortal thing about you will be your reputation as a genocidal maniac!"

"You will die for this, and I will be your executioner."

Zaugg raised the gun a second time, with murder in his eye, but a strong gust of wind rocked the gondola and knocked him off his feet.

Lea snatched her chance, and pulled herself up through the maintenance hatch in the top of the gondola as fast as she could. But before she was safely through she felt Zaugg's hands swiping at her ankles.

He grabbed one and tried to pull her back inside the gondola, but she lashed out with her foot and kicked him hard in the face, sending him flying back inside the car.

She was breathing hard, adrenalin coursing through her system. She thought fast and slammed the hatch down, but now she was out of ideas. She was standing on the roof of a cable car five thousand feet above a rocky valley, swaying wildly in the freezing wind, blackness all around her.

The hatch slammed open.

Zaugg began to crawl out of the hole in the roof. He reminded her of a kind of black insect, crawling out of a hole on its way to a kill.

She had nowhere to run, but instinct made her look around for an escape route all the same. Nothing but mountain ridges thousands of feet away, their distant peaks dimly lit by a fleeting flash of moonlight through a thin break in the snowclouds. The grim howling of the snowy wind highlighted her terrible isolation in the middle of nowhere.

Zaugg was now on the roof of the gondola, grinning insanely. He wiped the blood from his face on his sleeve and spat a tooth over the side of the car.

It fell into the oblivion. "I told you not to defy me, Donovan."

Again from instinct, Lea stepped back away from the horror of Zaugg, each step taking her closer to the smooth, cambered edge of the gondola. She felt herself begin to fall backwards, and wildly flailed her arms to grab anything to stop her slipping over the edge.

Her fingers made contact with a support beam holding the car to the steel cable and she grabbed hold of it with a second to spare before her legs slipped over the back of the gondola.

She screamed in terror, her legs kicking out in an attempt to clamber back on to the roof. One of her shoes fell off and tumbled out of sight into the swirling void below her.

Zaugg laughed and closed in on her like a cougar ready to pounce on a wounded deer.

Lea knew it was fight or die, and there was no Joe Hawke to save her now. She was as alone as she could be, and facing a cold-blooded killer with nothing to lose.

Zaugg was upon her, and reached out with his hands to grab her jacket. For a second she thought he was trying to save her, but then she realized he merely wanted to prolong her suffering. He took hold of her and roughly spun her around and flung her down hard on the gondola roof.

She hit the aluminum alloy roof with a metallic crunch and cried out in pain as her head struck the hatch handle. She rolled over onto her stomach and reached out to open the hatch in a desperate bid to get back inside and lock Zaugg out. It was her only chance now. She gripped the metal handle and tried to heave it up.

Zaugg padded over to her and stamped on her hand. The movement of the cable car as it trundled slowly down to the gound station and the wind cutting across from the west almost knocked him off his balance once again, but the look of determination on his face told Lea that this time he wasn't go to stop until she was dead.

He stamped on her hand a second time.

She screamed again – it felt like he'd broken her fingers.

She flipped herself back over onto her back and scrambled away from him like a crab.

He followed her to the other end of the gondola roof, his eyes narrowing now. He held his hands out, rigid like claws, and leaned forward to grab her throat. He was going to strangle her.

*

Hawke sprayed a great arc of snow into the air as he skidded to a halt. Without waisting a second, the sniper rifle was off his back. He kicked off the skis and ran over to a low rock which he used to steady the weapon.

He looked through the sights to see the tiny cable car suspended in the darkness, lit only by the greenish striplight inside the gondola.

"Oh my God!" he said. Zaugg and Lea were fighting on top of the cable car. For a while it looked like she was going to get the better of him, but after a few seconds the tables definitely turned, and Zaugg was on top.

He watched Zaugg pointing at her, and ranting. From this distance he could see everything but hear nothing – but what did it matter? He knew what the deal was up there.

He remembered his training, now nearly twenty years' old, and slowed his breathing. He aimed the weapon. Zaugg's head was in the center of his sights. Hawke knew there was a precision formula used by professional snipers, but it required time and a better knowledge of the distance. He had neither of those things, and could only make a rough correction based on a simple and quick guess of the wind speed, which he judged by watching how Lea's hair was blowing around.

This was his moment to right the balance. This was his only chance to save her life. This is what he failed to do back in Hanoi all those years ago. This was as close to redemption as Joe Hawke was ever going to get.

He slowed his breathing again.

Then he squeezed the trigger so gently he barely touched it.

It took the 50 cal just over one and half seconds to cross the one thousand yards between the muzzle of the rifle and Hugo Zaugg, hitting him in the throat, which blew out in a spray of red mist.

Hawke watched the reaction through the sights.

Zaugg flailed around like a marionette with its strings cut, grabbing at his throat and staggering backwards at the same time. Incredibly, he made one final lunge at Lea with blood pouring from his throat. Hawke wondered how long before he passed out from the inevitable drop in blood pressure, but didn't want to wait to find out.

He readied a second shot and fired again, this time

hitting his target in the chest, causing another burst of red to spray out into the snowy air, and blasting Zaugg off the roof of the gondola into oblivion.

He spiralled down to the rocks, screaming for every single one of the seventeen seconds it took before his body smashed into the frozen granite with a distant thud. Hawke considered if he should have made it a head shot, giving him the mercy of being unconscious as he fell, but shrugged his shoulders and put the rifle back in the sling on his back.

Without sparing another thought for Hugo Zaugg, Hawke fitted his skis back on and started to ski down the mountain to be at the cable car when it arrived at the ground station.

*

"Joe!" Lea said, and wrapped her arms around his neck. "Thank God. I thought he was going to kill me."

Hawke held her. "No bloody chance. I'd never let a tosser like that get the better of..."

Before he could finish his sentence, Lea stood on tiptoes, held his face in both hands and kissed him hard on the mouth. It seemed to last forever.

"Wow!" Hawke said. "That was longer than Zaugg's death spiral."

Lea sighed. "You are just so damned romantic, Joe."

"Hey, did you notice that?"

"No, what?"

"You called me Joe, and not Joe Hawke."

""That's because Joseph is such a good Irish name."

"Sorry to disappoint you, but my name's not Joseph."

"It's not Joseph? So what's it short for?"

"You have more chance of being reincarnated as Amphitrite than ever finding that out."

Lea sighed again. "It just goes to show no one's perfect, Joe *Hawke*."

She kissed him again.

"But my kissing *is* perfect, right?" Hawke shot a quick glance at Lea to see that she was smiling at him. He brushed her cheek with his hand.

"You are so arrogant!" she said.

"I'm far too amazing to be arrogant."

"If this is your idea of a date, Joe Hawke," Lea said, "I think maybe you could be looking at second base after all."

"Are you warming to me, Lea Donovan?"

They walked to the tourist viewing platform to see a team of search and rescue police already making their way to Zaugg's corpse.

"Can't say the Swiss aren't efficient," Lea said.

"True, but it's sad really." Hawke looked at Zaugg's broken body on the rocks below, the snow around him red with blood. "In the end, it looks like he really fell for you."

Lea ignored him. She was starting to fall in love with Joe Hawke.

CHAPTER THIRTY-SIX

After the battle was over, they secured the trident from the gondola and flew back up to the compound where they began to disassemble the charges that were supposed to cause Zaugg's mega-avalanche. Grobel had decided stealing the gold was more important than setting them off, and when Hawke knocked him out cold back in Zaugg's office that permanently ended the threat.

Now, it was dawn, and the sky filled with more helicopters. The first to arrive was a white Sikorsky S-76C, a powerful twin-engined chopper which swooped over the compound a couple of times before touching down on Zaugg's tennis courts. Moments later James Matheson, the British Foreign Secretary appeared. He was met by Sir Richard Eden who shook his hand and began the debrief immediately.

A second wave of choppers came in behind that, led by a black Sikorsky Sea King. They landed on the lawns behind the tennis courts and as the rotor blades slowed the doors swung open to reveal the American Secretary of Defense George Chambers, flanked by his Secret Service detail and followed by a familar face which Hawke took less than ten seconds to identify: Eddie Kosinski, the CIA officer from New York.

Kosinski recognized Hawke at the same time, and gave him a sarcastic salute as he walked past, flanked with men in military fatigues.

"What's going on, Richard?" Lea asked.

Sir Richard Eden began to speak when James

Matheson interrupted him.

"Seems like our American friends here caught on that something was up and joined the chase. They're rather keen to get their hands on the contents of the tomb, I'm afraid."

"But we found it!" Hawke protested. "The gold, the jewels, the trident... the whole bloody lot is ours!"

"But not the map," Scarlet said, smirking.

James Matheson and Richard Eden shared a glance.

"You found a map?" Matheson said bluntly.

Hawke shook his head. "Nope. Poor old matey-lad Zaugg was under the impression that there was a map in the tomb somewhere, but he couldn't find one. He was most upset about it."

"Did he search the sarcophagus itself?" Matheson said.

"Yup – nada."

"Could mean anything," the Foreign Secretary said.

Hawke looked at Eden and Matheson. "Listen gents, I've been shot at on the streets of London, New York and Geneva, nearly drowned in a speedboat chase on the Thames and in a Greek cave, and almost crushed to death in an avalanche."

"And your point is what?" Eden said, the thin trace of a smile appearing on his lips.

"My point is, I think I've earned the right for someone to tell me just what the fuck is going on."

Matheson's eyes narrowed, but Eden laughed.

Eden spoke first: "All I can say is that it looks like Zaugg may have been working on the orders from an unknown agency, and we're already looking in to who it could be, but we can't rule out an inside man."

"But what is this damned map about?"

"The map is reputed to lead the bearer of it to the source of eternal life," Matheson said flatly. "It's probably nothing more than a legend. The real treasure is the trident – archaeological treasure, I mean, naturally."

"And that's going back to the States," a loud voice said. Hawke turned to see Chambers and Kosinski approach Matheson and shake his hand. "Along with everything else here. Your government was most obliging when we reminded you about who controls the nuclear codes."

"Quite," Matheson said bitterly.

Hawke watched in disbelief as the Americans walked all over the top of Matheson and Eden, removing the trident and everything else they had ultimately rescued from Zaugg.

Hawke and Lea left Hart with the dignitaries and walked over to the others who were now sitting on a low wall beside the tennis courts. A light snow began to fall and the high mountain air was crisp and cool. They watched the teams of American soldiers dragging the final contents of Poseidon's tomb from Zaugg's compound into the back of a US Army Chinook, blades whirring above the hurried activity of the military personnel.

"So that's the last evidence on earth of Poseidon," said Lea.

Hawke sighed. "I still can't believe that Poseidon was real."

As he spoke these words, they watched the Americans leading a bruised Dietmar Grobel out of the compound and throw him in the back of a Huey.

"This one's an extraordinary rendition," Kosinski shouted to Eden.

Over on the tennis courts, Sophie asked: "But what about the source of his ultimate power – it was the trident, no?"

"No I don't think so," Hawke said. "I'm more convined than ever that's a reference to his immortality, and that Zaugg knew that too, which is why he wasn't bothered about the gold and gems – or even the trident – and just searched for this mysterious map."

"Which could just be a legend," Lea said, shrugging her shoulders.

"The whole thing is probably just a legend," Scarlet said. "Tombs full of bones and gold is one thing, but the idea of immortality is quite another. Oh, look! They're off." She gestured casually at the Chinook as its rotors sped up and the giant helicopter slowly lifted off the tennis courts and powered up into the air. It flew up and away from the compound and dipped below the horizon as it descended into the valley below, taking the contents of the vault of Poseidon with it.

"A successful mission," Reaper said.

"How'd you figure that?" Sophie asked.

"Zaugg and Baumann are dead, Grobel will be taken into custody, and the vault of Poseidon was located and secured."

Hawke frowned. "Yeah – by the wrong people."

"Too bad – I beat you in the end though, right?"

It was Kosinski. He had walked over with a big, smug smile on his face.

"Just wanted to say goodbye, guys."

Hawke stood up. "Maybe you won the battle but you didn't win the war, Eddie."

"What's that supposed to mean?"

"That's for me to know and you to worry about."

Kosinski looked confused and walked back over to a smaller Bell helicopter. Moments later it was airborne.

The other helicopters followed behind him until only Eden and Matheson and his security were left. Swiss police pulled up the main drive and began to turn the place into a crime scene.

"Time for us to go," Eden said. Shall we?" He indicated his helicopter.

Ryan, Sophie, Hart and Reaper climbed on board and the chopper made its way down the mountain toward the town below.

Hawke and Lea decided to spend the afternoon walking back down the mountain, and it was then that she told him about what had happened to her men in Syria fighting the insurgents.

Hawke listened carefully as she spoke, but made no judgments just as he had promised her back in New York. There were stories – terrible stories – he could tell her from his own past, and maybe one day he would. He could only hope she would be as understanding.

"Terrible things happen in wars, Lea. You can't live with guilt forever," was all he said, and then he took her by the arms and kissed her.

CHAPTER THIRTY-SEVEN

Zermatt

The next afternoon, Hawke and Lea managed to slip away from the international press which had gathered in the snow outside the Hotel Grand Kempinski in Geneva. They drove a hired car into the Swiss mountains, passing through Sion on the way – the small town was still oblivious to the threat that had so nearly destroyed it.

Hawke had booked a small ski lodge in Zermatt under a false name. The last few days had drained both of them and they both needed the kind of break from reality that only a place like this could offer.

Hawke was stoking the fire when he heard the door click open. He turned to see Lea standing in the door. She was smiling, her cheeks red with the cold. In her arms she carried a basket of logs which she placed beside the fire.

"How are you feeling now?" he asked. He knew the recent struggles with Baumann and Zaugg, as well as the crushing guilt over the death of her unit in Syria would take many years to heal.

"I'll be fine," she said. "Thanks to you."

Hawke put more wood on the fire. "I was thinking about what you said back in Kefalonia."

"What was that?"

"You said you had to tell me something about Eden."

"You want to talk about Richard Eden now, really?" She removed her jacket and let it fall to the floor. A devious smile played on her lips as she drew closer to him.

"When you put it like that, I guess not…" he said, looking at her in the firelight. "You know when they find out we're missing they're going to send a search party out to get us?" he said.

Lea smiled again. "I'm not afraid of anything anymore. This is the week I found out who I really am. This is the week I found out the truth about the world."

Hawke stood up and faced her. "Fun, wasn't it?"

"I wouldn't go *that* far."

"But how far would you go?" he said, smirking.

"At least it's over now," she said, ignoring him.

Hawke looked at her. "I wouldn't say that, exactly."

"Oh, crap! What does *that* mean?"

"I didn't tell you yesterday because things were so crazy, but I found this in our hotel room back in Geneva."

Hawke reached into his pocket and handed Lea a tiny paper insect.

"What the hell is this?"

"It's an origami dragonfly – a clue, really."

"And it's a clue… *why*?"

"It just is. Call it a calling card. I found it on the end of the bed when I woke up this morning. Let's not spoil today with it."

"Someone broke into the hotel room?"

"Easy as pie for the person concerned. Forget about it. It's not important. Besides, I'm more worried about Ryan." Hawke pulled a bottle of chilled Champagne from a bucket of ice and popped the cork.

"How so?" Lea said, dropping the dragonfly into the soft white carpet.

"I don't think it's very fair to let someone like that out in a big city without his carers."

"He's not that bad, Joe," Lea said, playfully slapping Hawke's shoulder.

The fire crackled and outside the sun began to sink behind a mountain on the other side of the valley leaving a pink glow on the snow outside their cabin. Hawke poured the Champagne into two glass flutes.

"Maybe he doesn't like Sophie at all," said Hawke. "Maybe he still loves you."

"He does not! And even if he did it would be too bad."

Hawke looked into her eyes and stepped closer. "Why's that?"

"Because I don't love him. In fact, I think I might be falling in love with another man, anyway."

"Really? I'm pleased for you but I'm not sure Reaper's looking for a serious relationship right now."

Lea shook her head and sighed. "*Men.*"

She kicked off her snow-covered boots and unwound the scarf from her neck.

"Hello!" Hawke said. "What's all this then?"

"You could call it a thawing in Anglo-Irish relations," Lea said, and began to unbutton his shirt.

Hawke moved his hands to her waist. "I'm so glad our two nations have decided to come together at last."

They slid down onto the carpet in front of the fire. Outside, the first stars of the night had appeared in the sky above the snow-capped range to the east.

*

The woman known only as Nightingale turned off her phone and clicked it into the recharger. It was breakfast time in New York, but it had been a long night, and she was tired. She sighed and gently rubbed her temples for a few seconds. The chance of another one of her migraines was high.

She fired her remote at the blinds and watched as they closed around the room one by one, reducing the light in the spacious loft apartment. She wondered what Joe Hawke was doing right now in Switzerland. Was he really going to take it easy for a few days, or simply play around with yet another woman?

She thought the latter was more likely. She had never met him, and she was sad at the thought. She liked the sound of his voice, and even though it would be the easiest thing in the world to bring up a picture of him, she had resisted. She didn't want to change the image of him that she held in her mind, shaped by the tone of his voice and his personality, the way a chisel rendered a face from a block of marble.

She pushed her wheelchair from her desk over to her bed, locked the brakes and pulled herself up into the cold sheets, an act that always took a great deal more effort than many would think likely. She sighed heavily. How could a man like Joe Hawke share his life with someone like her? She closed her eyes and imagined him in Switzerland. The rain and bustle of Manhattan was slowly replaced by the sunshine of the Swiss mountains, and the smooth clean snow of the ski slopes. Moments later she was asleep.

THE END

AUTHOR'S NOTE

The Vault of Poseidon is the first book in the Joe Hawke series. I intend each of the Joe Hawke novels to be a standalone work, but like all series there will be some overarching storylines, particularly in the first three. The second book in the series is scheduled for release later in 2015 and follows Hawke to many exciting new locations on an even faster-paced action-adventure mystery to save the world all over again from new and old menaces alike…

For more information and the latest news and updates please see my website – www.robjonesnovels.com and I'm always happy to reply to emails at robjonesnovels@gmail.com.

Finally, many thanks for reading my novel. Writing a book is only half the story – the reader provides the other half, and no writer's work is ever really finished until the reader turns the last page. Every author depends on good reviews to keep going forward, and if you enjoyed this story I would appreciate it if you might think about writing a brief review on Amazon.

Many thanks – Joe and I will be seeing you soon!

Rob

The Joe Hawke Series

The Vault of Poseidon (Joe Hawke #1)
Thunder God (Joe Hawke #2)
The Tomb of Eternity (Joe Hawke #3)
The Curse of Medusa (Joe Hawke #4)
Valhalla Gold (Joe Hawke #5)
The Aztec Prophecy (Joe Hawke #6)
The Secret of Atlantis (Joe Hawke #7)
The Lost City (Joe Hawke #8)

The Sword of Fire (Joe Hawke #9) is scheduled for release in the spring of 2017

For free stories, regular news and updates, please join my Facebook page

https://www.facebook.com/RobJonesNovels/

Or Twitter

@AuthorRobJones

Made in the USA
Lexington, KY
16 March 2017